WINE & FAITH

19 Days in Napa

A Novel by

NADIA CRANE

Cover Design: Alex Levich
Publisher: The Paisley Frog
Copyright © 2024. All rights reserved.
ISBN: 979-8-9889278-0-8 eBook
ISBN: 979-8-9889278-1-5

PRAISE FOR WINE & FAITH

That Wine & Faith is a deep dive into a pool of raw emotion is, at best, an understatement. The author masterfully correlates scripture with said emotion so as to paint a picture of Jill's inner struggle with historical roadblocks and future decision-making. A highly recommended read for anyone - women in particular - seeking to strike a balance between God, self and the external world. Beautifully crafted.

— Ronald J. Glassman, PhD, MPH
Former Visiting Scholar — The Neuroscience Institute, Columbia University College of Physicians and Surgeons, New York, New York.

DEDICATION

To all humans who strive to live by faith yet struggle to apply ethical and moral principles to marriage and relationship issues.

A special thank you to the six sensational soul sisters who know who they are.

My heartfelt gratitude to Carolyn, Miriam, Deb, Cat, Arlene S., and Meg who each read and provided edits and invaluable insights.

And two special guys who drop everything to hear my scatterbrained ideas.

TABLE OF CONTENTS

AUTHOR'S NOTE

Have you ever felt trapped in a relationship where you are losing yourself? Or worn a mask to hide the pain on your face that manifests in your soul? Have you struggled with your faith trying to do the "right thing?"

If yes, you will relate to Jill, the protagonist of *Wine & Faith – 19 Days in Napa*. In her forties, Jill faces a conundrum. Her husband, Derek, has broken his vow to love and honor her, but she feels guilty and petrified about leaving him. Jill grew up in a devout, sheltered home that taught her divorce is immoral. She wants to fix her broken marriage, yet is it fixable? She has lived long enough in silence. It is time for Jill to face reality.

Jill's struggles are human and universal. They cut across socioeconomic classes, religions, genders, and ethnicities. As you read this book, I invite you to put yourself in Jill's shoes. Walk, talk, and pour a glass of wine with her. Experience what she has experienced. Please note, there may be triggers in this book. Proceed with caution.

Grab a chair and take a front-row seat through Jill's journey. There, you will witness her muddled expectations, childhood, marriage, parenting. These can be in your life, too – brothers, sisters, parents, husbands, and children.

Are you ready to join Jill in her *19 Days in Napa*? Snag your copy today and discover how she overcomes challenges and finds her true self.

– Nadia J. Crane

PROLOGUE

I married Derek twenty years ago. Our marriage had been rocky for almost that long, starting the night he yelled at me at the top of his lungs.

His voice shrilled down my spine, "You should be afraid of me! I'm in charge here! You better get with the program. Shape up, Wife!"

A jolt zapped through my body as Derek pushed me, his behavior seeming spiteful and out of character.

As I looked back on this outburst, which preceded our vows by less than a year, I remember that it scared me to the core. Then came the collywobbles, slowly and steadily churning into a crescendo as Derek's angry voice resounded in my memory from that day forward.

*****

Another Valentine's Day.

No card, intimate relations, or "I love you."

The clock struck two in the afternoon on the chilly Wednesday in February, a few short months ago. The children were at school, and Derek, at work.

I searched religious texts for treasure. I hoped it would help me figure out this mess.

The pull of two different directions.

I opened my *Bible* to *1 Peter 3:7*.

Intently, I read about husbands treating wives with respect.

Husbands, in the same way be considerate as you live with your wives, and treat them with respect as the weaker partner and as heirs with you of the gracious gift of life...   – 1 Peter 3:7

"Jill, you are not alone. I am here, right beside you. Read these words and find comfort." I heard a voice. A whisper, really. Speaking into my ear, reassuring me that I wasn't alone. To me, this message emanated from God, the source of comfort, my refuge.

The God of the Universe.

The God of Marriage.

The God of all things good in this world.

Then, a tug on my heart. A revelation, in fact. The word "respect." It hit me like a two-by-four: RESPECT. The backbone of a healthy relationship.

Let. That. Sink. In. Jill.

Drenched, at this point, in a holy type of Spirit, I contemplated the institution of marriage.

I stopped.

[iv]

Overcome with an incredible urge to share a glass with the One who changed water into wine, I poured a glass of *Levy & McClellan Cabernet Sauvignon.*

A rich, vibrant wine passed from the bottle to the crystal goblet with the gold rim. The glass glistened in the light.

As I sipped the wine, I asked God to bless it, to make it holy. I reflected on what marriage was supposed to be...

Holy.

Sacred.

Loving.

Kind.

Tender.

Hmm.

Everything my marriage lacked, sorely.

I found myself soaking in a new insight. The red liquid delivered a divine message. Marriage was sacred and not a game of chess requiring strategic moves.

Nor was it a place to live in fear.

Nope.

*****

I flipped to *Hebrews 13:3*, which talked about the purity of the marriage bed. I hadn't felt pure, honored, or respected for a long time.

Maybe even ever.

Sipping the wine, I detected a blend of fruit, spices, and a hint of chocolate, dazzling my tongue.

Gazing into the wine opened my eyes to see scripture in a new light. In the past, my heart and soul had succumbed to the notion of a wife submitting to her husband at all costs. Why? Because my parents and the Church indoctrinated me.

Plain and simple.

Yet, scripture challenged this notion. Not to mention the nudge I was feeling by the Holy Spirit.

Had the Church made a big mistake by overlooking the importance of husbands loving their wives?

It sure seemed so.

In *Ephesians 5:24-27*, the Apostle Paul instructed wives to submit to their husbands. Equally important, he wrote about husbands loving their wives.

I submitted to my husband and still did not feel loved.

Okay, maybe I was on to something.

So, to recap:

I needed Derek to respect me, but I was afraid to do anything.

I did not feel loved by Derek.

Now what? *I had no idea.*

Often times when something is off kilter in life, the ripple effect takes over. Once a card is set in motion, the whole house of cards falls to the ground. I didn't know what to believe.

I had more questions than answers.

I was struggling on all fronts, including my faith.

All my relationships were floundering – even with God. Missing the mark on the bar of a higher standard of spirituality led to feelings of inadequacy. I admitted that I was flawed, like a fine wine that spoils due to improper handling.

And so, I thought, what now?

*****

Multiple battles were blowing up in front of me.

Trapped in a broken marriage threw me to the ground. I had been living a lie, trying to pretend to fit in with the expectations of others. But I had lost myself in the process.

Fighting issues, including stress, adenomyosis, anemia,
and an overactive bladder –
Fighting loneliness, depression, and other matters –
Fighting a long-held belief marriage is,
(or should be) forever – I turned to God.

Tried and true tactics were falling apart.

The direct assault was upon me.

A warning order had been issued.

I cried out for help.

*****

Then something marvelous happened.

"Godcidents."

A made-up word to define divine interventions. Such as angels showing up at random times to guide my journey.

To guide, heal, and transform me.

Grab a glass of wine, or herbal tea, dear reader, and join me on my journey of self-discovery. Hold my hand as we confront painful memories together. And you will see how faith can shift guilt and shame to emotional resiliency—one day at a time.

AMELIA'S INVITATION
INTRODUCTION

As I enter the airport, my heart races with anticipation and trepidation. A storm has been brewing for years. My heart pumps faster and faster.

Pinch me. Is this real? I'm flying. Alone. To California.

Doubts gnaw at me.

My choices.

My worthiness.

The path lay ahead.

A dry, parched desert leading me to the Promised Land. An arm outstretched for a glass of pure glistening water my frail bones slithering on the dusty sand.

Quench my thirst, O God.

*****

Despite my doubts and fears, this journey to the Napa Valley is not a mere escape. It is my chance to confront deep-seated secrets drowning me in a sea of black mud.

Quicksand.

The gasp for air echoes for miles.

The following two and a half weeks will be a delirious ride, testing my courage and grit.

I need to find the answer.

I can't back down.

I have to keep going.

Introspective work will be an integral part of this.

It will challenge me to the core.

The core of my very being.

*****

After adjusting the rear-view mirror of the small, red, compact rental car, I turn around. Fumbling.

Where is the Garmin GPS?

Rummaging in my bag, there it is, *of course, at the bottom,* already pre-programmed with Amelia's home address – my lifeline.

Seatbelt clip – check.

My achy bones settle into the comfy bucket seat.

I shift into "Drive" and the car scoots toward the "Exit" signs.

The engine vibrates.

My feet and legs tingle as the shiny red machine roars to life, gliding down the highway. My hands tighten on the steering wheel as I imagine a roller coaster.

The dips.

The turns.

The pit in my stomach.

It is an emotional roller coaster I would rather avoid like the plague. But I need to confront these demons.

Faith is my compass.

Navigating through the dark, windy road ahead requires the universe to guide the way. Memories, facts, and fiction wrestle, hoping to align the heart with the head.

This trip will be a doozy.

Come along on my introspective meanderings where unexpected epiphanies will delight.

*****

But first, let's rewind to a month and a half ago.

At the last conference of the school year, the guidance counselor told Derek and me, Zola, my oldest daughter, had "respect" issues. Of course, Zola had respect issues.

No surprise there.

How couldn't she when she observed Derek mistreating me on a daily basis? To her, it was normal.

Nisha, three years younger than Zola, spewed off her smart mouth, too. This pattern created tension in the household for everyone.

It was this teacher conference that prompted me to call Amelia.

*****

With the teacher conference conversation still fresh in my mind, I felt at a crossroads. I saw a pattern. Derek did not. My good kids were morphing into out-of-control kids. As a mother, I had to fix this problem.

But first I needed clarity and would only get it if I took the time to think about this far away from home. So, I decided to call Amelia and finally take her up on her offer for a visit.

"Namaste, Amelia. How's life treating you?" I asked, making the call I should have made sooner.

"Life is great. What about you, dear friend? What's up?" Amelia's tone exuded warmth.

"Remember your offer to come for a visit?" I hesitated, hoping she'd remember and still be open to the idea.

"Sure, when are you thinking?" Amelia asks.

"I'd love to come on the last day of the school year, in the middle of June, and maybe stay for two weeks-ish? The kids have summer programs, and Derek can handle the household. I'm at the end of my rope and need a break."

"Of course! I know the feeling, Jill. Of course, you can come.

"It's about time you are taking me up on my invitation."

"I'm just so glad you asked me, Amelia. I wouldn't be at your place the whole time. I also want to track down a few of my cousins while I'm out there, too."

"Jill, you know my house is your house. Sure, find a flight. Let me know the details. I'd love to see you; it's been too long."

"Thanks, we are way overdue for a long girls' talk," I said with a smile.

Of course, Amelia said, "Yes!"

Life at that moment changed.

A respite.

A glimmer of hope.

Giddy with delight, I smiled as I put a plan into action for the visit. She had been my next-door neighbor in Henderson, Nevada, and we shared a sister-like bond from the moment we met. After divorcing her husband five years ago, Amelia lived alone in a cozy chalet deep in California wine country.

*****

A gut-wrenching decision about my marriage lies ahead. Lucky for me, Amelia understands my plight and knows the gravity of my situation. Opening up her home to consider the pros and cons of my dilemma lifts my spirits.

A true gift of friendship.

For years, we had cheered and cried with each other. It is only fitting to spend time with her as I process the questions in my head.

Amelia.

My rock.

Supportive, kind, and a great listener.

Amelia's open-mindedness makes her a great choice to share my two secrets. I sure hope she will be able to provide me with her insights.

But first, I have to face my own shame and guilt.

The first secret started at age twelve.

The second slapped me in the face at twenty-eight.

Three years after I married.

Note to self: Buy extra tissues in Napa.

*****

When planning my trip, I decided to make the most of it. I have family and friends scattered all over California. Let me see where everybody lives. I don't want to impose too much on Amelia.

Who do I know in California?

The page of the atlas turns to California.

Cousin Lata lives in Thousand Oaks. She is a hoot.

Well, that looks nearby.

Cousin Sophie, her husband Pavan, and two of their three adult children are in Sacramento. I haven't seen those guys in a while. It must be five years or so.

Hmm.

A hop, skip, and jump.

Their son Manny and I would hang out with our cousin Vijay as kids. Our shenanigans regularly led us to trouble. It will be great to see how our maturity has changed us.

And then, there are my mother's friends, who are retired missionaries. Marty and Binita, Helen, and Eve. Something told me they would help clarify my situation.

In fact, I was sure of it.

The gravitational pull toward these people proves powerful. Not having seen them in ten or fifteen years.

The Spirit is moving and guiding me.

No surprise. God works in mysterious ways.

They live in the same *Cumberland Missionary Village* in Fort Bragg.

Not far at all. And so convenient.

One summer, right before my thirteenth birthday, I lent a hand to Binita at the church's parsonage as a mother's helper.

So, catching up with her and her family will be comforting, too.

*****

Flipping up the top of my computer, I log into my inbox to email these precious people about my upcoming trip to California in a few weeks. Can we schedule a short visit?

For my mom's friends – it will be a one-day visit. They live only a few houses away from each other.

I ask Sophie to squeeze in a visit with her sons, Manny and Tarus, which should be fun. I hope to stay a day or two.

Lata, in Thousand Oaks, divorced years ago and lives alone. I'd love to stay with her for a few days. I wonder if her son, Ryo, still lives nearby.

I look forward to spending quality time with Lata, as we haven't seen each other in years. She is usually full of good humor. *I can use a little humor.*

A few days later, confirmations arrived in my inbox.

Yes. Full speed ahead! A busy itinerary will keep me on my toes.

*****

I'm Jill.

I met my husband, Derek, during my senior year of college when earning a four-year degree topped my "Things to Do List."

[xvi]

College meant attending classes while working to pay for tuition, leaving little time for a social life. I kept up my dating skills during school breaks, so I wouldn't rust.

Before college, I completed a massage therapy program and worked in a spa for three weeks. My back-to-back clients felt like an assembly line with no time for breaks. It sure differed from the glamorous job I had expected it to be. After that "factory" fiasco, I enrolled in college.

Meeting new people is invigorating.

They inspire me to be creative.

To think out of the box.

It is no wonder I ended up in the hospitality business. Managing people and events eventually segued into full-time motherhood.

With a household of six: three girls, Zola, Nisha, and Rebecca; one boy, Kobe; Derek, and me, I hardly have time to sit.

Let alone enjoy a cup of hot coffee.

My dad says, "Idle hands are the devil's workshop." So, keeping busy is important to me. I teach massage therapy one night a week and once a month on Saturdays. Teaching is so much better than working in a factory.

The usual tasks of laundry, food shopping, meal planning, and cooking consume my world.

Mothering is a formidable job.

If I am not nurturing or tending to my garden, you can find me at a school activity, Bible study, cooking, or chauffeuring. Watch out for the white Toyota mini-van with a green university decal on the rear window.

Yup. That's me!

*****

Our personalities were polar opposites. Derek's calm demeanor often masked his explosive outbursts. My even-keeled manner contrasted with my behavior of leaving in a huff when I was angry. I would define this as conflict avoidance.

Derek's communication was strategic. He paused when he spoke. I could almost see the wheels turning in his head. Derek consistently weighed the pros and cons before speaking, his tone authoritative.

I, on the other hand, tended to say whatever was on my mind, not taking too much time to think about it.

Derek spoke deliberately and stiltedly. If he had wanted to apologize, he would have said, "I. Am. Sorry."

But he rarely said that. Only once did he say it to me. In therapy.

We clashed about how to intervene with our children's behavior. I wanted to suggest alternative behaviors, "teachable moments," if you will.

Derek, on the other hand, would scold our kids harshly for their mistakes.

Our contrasting styles were a mystery to me and created more distance and resentment between us.

After Zola's birth, it wasn't so bad. Even with Nisha, Derek communicated when necessary.

Then, the twins came.

Having four kids under eight years old caught us off guard for the first few months.

Yes, sir.

Quite the change.

Luckily for us, Great Aunt Ati came to the rescue.

Derek's great-aunt from Zimbabwe came to help during the first six months. We call her, Aunt Ati.

She was a godsend.

Having an extra set of hands with the babies proved invaluable. Since her bones were brittle, she used a cane to climb stairs. But she fed and loved the babies, which she did well. Keeping an eye and ear on the twins while I showered was a heavenly gift.

With Aunt Ati, life bloomed like flowers in a garden. Her superpower of deflecting conflict had not gone unnoticed. With her around, Derek's behavior won awards. Which meant that I had a reprieve from the emotional hammering of daily life.

So, when Aunt Ati's tourist visa was about to expire, the collywobbles wiggled more.

I began to prepare for life without her.

*****

In retrospect, the pace of my life back then was racing at incredible speed. Transporting Zola to elementary school and Nisha to preschool with twins in tow made a circus ring leader's job look easy.

Was this the way life was supposed to be? It seemed to be full of unmet expectations.

I had hoped and prayed for a happy marriage all my life. A loving husband and a peaceful family.

But reality shattered those dreams long ago. I was trying to accept my lot in life and, at the same time, consider what change might look like.

Maybe there was still a chance for love and peace.

Maybe there was a reason to keep going, but, going forward, I would need encouragement and love.

Instead, in actuality, I was receiving rejection and criticism, which, more often than not, left me miserable. Derek didn't appreciate me for who I was.

It hurt like a pin in the eye.

I didn't know how to cope with it. I hated conflict. So, I would walk away rather than confronting Derek or standing up for myself. Instead, I remained silent. At night, I would cry myself to sleep, hoping for a miracle.

*****

Over the next nineteen days, I had some serious thinking to do.

Faith.

Love.

Marriage.

Separation.

Wow.

A lot to think about!

FRIENDS IN STRANGE PLACES
DAY 1

Las Vegas, Nevada

S melling the garlic and onions upstairs, I take one more peek in the mirror. I haven't traveled by myself in about ten years, so I want to make sure I look like a regular person, not a frumpy housewife.

Hair – a little shaggy.

Praying hands earrings – a bit eye-catching, but, okay.

Teal sleeveless cotton tank – okay.

Lightweight, long gray wool tweed jacket, black yoga pants with bell bottoms – okay.

Black loafers – easy slip on, slip off for the plane, sure hope they'll be comfortable – okay.

An early lunch of shiitake mushroom burgers with a side of corn bean salad had been prepared and cooked.

*****

"Jill! Get Going!

"Jill! Get Going!

"I do not have all day, you know. You do not want to miss your flight," Derek shouts up the stairs.

[1]

"Okay! Okay! Hold your tigers! Be down in a minute," I shout down the stairs.

Picking up the pace as my stomach knots up, there were the collywobbles again. I take a deep breath and double-check my black bag. One last visit to the powder room.

I grab my carry-on bag and cellphone and run a checklist in my head. The plane can't come soon enough. It's time to fly away from all this drama.

Suitcase? – Check.

Black carry-on case? – Check.

Cellphone? – Check.

Wallet? – Check.

Airline Ticket? – Check.

The black van marked "Casino Properties" is in the driveway, waiting for me to settle into its passenger seat.

Derek drives the twenty-minute route to the airport as I gaze out the window. I am anticipating nineteen days of total bliss.

He rambles on about his latest casino project while on a work call, but I don't listen. I nod and smile, pretending to care. As I expected, it lasted the entire drive to the airport.

He pulls up to the "Departures" sign and stops the vehicle. Reaching for the door handle, he pivots his long legs to reach the pavement.

Derek walks around the rear, opens the van's back doors to retrieve my suitcase, and lowers it onto the curb. At this moment, I feel like a suitcase kicked to the curb.

*****

Yesterday.

"Jill, what in the world are you doing?" Derek's tone exuded disbelief.

"I'm packing," I said calmly.

His arm jutted out, and his fingers elongated as if he was stopping traffic.

"Stop packing!"

The harshness of his voice made the hair on my neck stand up. My heart beat faster.

"You are not going anywhere. Who do you think you are?"

It was a preposterous question.

Derek's demand seemed on the verge of insanity.

I took a deep breath and looked into his eyes. "You TOLD me to go to Amelia's." I reminded him. "You and Dr. Kate agreed, remember?"

"Are you kidding me?" Derek shook his head. "No! I don't remember."

"Your exact words were, 'Go, run to Amelia. See if I care.'"

"I cannot imagine I would say that!"

"Well, Derek, you did."

"I did not mean for you to take me literally. Are you stupid, Jill?"

"No, I'm not stupid, Derek. Are you saying I shouldn't believe anything you say? Because it sure sounds like that. It was you who said you didn't care."

"I really cannot believe you did this, Jill. You planned this whole trip without asking?! Go. Go. Go. Get out of here! Good riddance."

Derek stormed out of the bedroom in a huff.

*****

Dr. Kate
Our Marriage Counselor
Specialty: Couples Therapy

Six weeks ago, a tall, slim woman in her early thirties endorsed this trip. How strange that Derek agreed. That was even more weird.

Hmm.

But, of course, he thought it was his idea.

I remember how the whole thing unfolded in Dr. Kate's office. We were arguing about the kids.

"Derek, I can't take it when you disrespect me in front of our children. Don't you get it?"

[4]

"There you go again, Jill," Derek replied. "You are mentally ill! That is why you feel the way you do. It is all in your head, my dear."

I saw a vein pop out on his forehead.

"No, Derek, it's not in my head. You disrespect me, and you do it all of the time."

"Jill, you are imagining all of this."

"No, Derek, I'm not. I really need a break from our constant fighting."

"If you really want a break, just get the hell out of here. Go cry to your friend, Amelia. Go! Run to Amelia. See if I care. Then I will not have to listen to you babble on and on."

My head spun.

Was I hearing Derek actually giving me permission to go to Amelia's?

"Well, Derek, what do you think?" Dr. Kate interjected. "Would it be okay for Jill to take a break? A getaway to her friend might be just what she needs right now."

"That is ridiculous," Derek muttered. "But, if you think it is a good idea, Dr. Kate, well, then, I guess so."

Turning to me, Dr. Kate asks, "What do you think, Jill?"

"Sounds great!" I chimed in. And so, I scheduled a trip to Napa.

Derek thought I was mentally ill. Well, truth be told, I felt the same about him.

*****

The porter tags my suitcase for its destination.

San Francisco, here I come.

Derek tips him as he circles to the van's rear. He hugs me and says, to me, barely audibly, "Keep your guard up. I will have eyes on you – the whole trip. Do not do anything stupid!"

Then, abruptly changes his tone, and says, "Enjoy your trip. Cheerio."

Noticing the police officer staring at Derek's coffee-brown skin, I felt a sense of urgency to quickly say, "Goodbye."

Then, with another hug, I bend my head and whisper in his ear, "Don't worry. I'll be good. Take care of yourself and the kids. Cheerio."

*****

Through the revolving door of the airport, the security line is my first destination. Belt first, and then, bracelets come off mid-stride, then shoes. Three large plastic bins hold my belongings. The security device scans without a beep.

Passing with flying colors and sighing in relief, I run a checklist in my head.

[6]

Belt? – Check.

Bracelets? – Check.

Shoes? – Check.

Black carry-on case? – Check.

Cellphone? – Check.

Wallet? – Check.

Airline Ticket? – Check.

A window ledge is across from the end of the security check-in. I walk toward it to lean on, so I can reach my phone to check on Derek. Concerned for his safety, the collywobbles strike again.

"Hey, Derek. It's me. I'm checking to make sure you are okay. Did you have any trouble getting out of the airport?"

"Eish! Jill.

"I am fine.

"I am on my way to the office.

"I have a meeting in twenty minutes.

"I have to go!" The call ends.

Okay, at least he is safe. Now, my knotted tummy can relax.

Strolling down the corridor, I place my cellphone back into my black bag. Glancing at the various shops along the way to the gate, I hold my head high.

A glimpse of a book catches my eye.

[7]

Stop.

I take a few steps backward, peering through the window to read *The Great Gatsby's* title on the book cover. Oh, what a classic. I stepped inside and bought it for my flight.

The gate is in sight. Then several eateries. One. Another one. And another. Then, a small market displays snack bars at the register. I buy one and also a water bottle. I'm in no mood to sit since boarding will be soon and the flight will be long.

One bite into the food bar, I taste coconut and feel my nose wrinkle. Ewe! The texture makes me spit it out into my napkin. I read the label. The ingredients check out alright– or did they? My cheeks turn red.

I had read the ingredients – I must have missed it.

I remind myself that it's not the end of the world.

*****

"Flight 283 to San Francisco is now boarding at Gate C."

The announcement signals it's time to head to the gate and board the plane.

Suitcase. Black bag. Cellphone. Wallet.

Clenching my belongings, I head to the line of passengers standing under "Gate C." A sign reads "San Francisco." A flight attendant mentions the airplane had landed from Stockholm.

The jet bridge leads the way to the aircraft. The top of the door frame is low.

Airplanes are not suitable for tall people.

Passengers file through the narrow aisle in search of their seats.

*****

After finding the aisle seat marked "22A," I sit next to a woman I had seen earlier checking in. She is wearing turquoise capri pants with a 1960s vintage print top. Speaking Spanish on her cellphone, she greets me with a nod and smile.

Entrenched in a book, another woman at the window seat does not even peek up as I plop into the aisle chair.

With the window shade up, the bright sun pierces my eyes like a razor blade.

As I pick up my book and settle in, the brassy-dyed blond woman beside me ends her call.

She starts speaking English.

Confused, I hadn't realized she was talking to me.

My fuzzy brain needs to catch up in comprehending the language change. I didn't want to be rude, so I returned a warm greeting.

*****

Neck, head, eyes – I'm a wreck. Ordinarily, I enjoy a good chat. But right now, a headache is coming on. Sad to say, the mere thought of paying attention to a conversation is bothering me.

Ah. Read a little. Rest a little. Close my eyes a little. Not too much to ask. Is it?

Yet, I turn my head to the left to engage in conversation. The blinding light is making matters worse.

Carmen, my seat neighbor, introduces herself as a mother and grandmother. She is sixty years old and lives in Napa. She appears calm and collected.

We exchange niceties.

My head lies back on the seat to rest for a few minutes.

I smile, remembering a scenario from earlier in the day.

"Zola. Nisha. Rebecca. Kobe," I bellowed from the bottom of the stairs. "Wake up! It's time to get up and get ready for school. It is the last school day before summer break."

The morning routine ticked like a clock.

I woke up, then woke up the kids, dressed, prepared breakfast and lunches, and scooted the kids out the door.

How blessed I am.

*****

Derek and I were born two years apart in Henderson, Nevada, believe it or not, in the same hospital. Of course, it was the only hospital there, but nonetheless, what a kawinky dink.

We grew up in the post-hippie seventies amidst a changing world. Our paths hadn't crossed yet, even though we attended the same high school.

Derek's medium-dark silky skin came from his grandfather, Edward, who had a tall tale to tell. In the 1920s, Edward, on his paternal side, immigrated to the United States, leaving behind a life of service in the South African Government in Johannesburg.

Derek spoke fondly of his grandfather's adventuresome spirit, which was still alive and well at family gatherings.

As for me, my olive-toned skin stemmed from my missionary grandparents, who had ventured from Calcutta, India. They had worked hard building schools to share the good news of the Gospel. Their love for education influenced me to work through college and spend a semester abroad in France the year before graduating from the University of Colorado.

High school was a joke for Derek. He did the minimal amount of work required to graduate. But when Derek enrolled in an electrician apprenticeship program, he discovered working with his hands brought a sense of satisfaction he hadn't encountered before. He found his groove and graduated at the top of his class.

Happenstance finally brought Derek to me. Our marriage, like most, ebbed and flowed. The joy of bringing children into the world overshadowed some dark spots. Our commitment to our marriage kept us moving forward.

So did our love of family for a while.

Then; the tipping point came.

The moment I said, "Enough is enough."

Although Derek had found his groove, our relationship had not. The realization that our relationship had transformed into something unhealthy gnawed at me.

It was time for me to consider a different path.

To break free from the shackles.

To reclaim my life.

My strength.

A new beginning.

*****

A decade and a half ago.

With Nisha's birth, my job title changed from special events director to stay-at-home mom. Three years later, my maternal resume added two more love bundles. When the twins arrived, Nisha was three, and Zola was eight.

*****

Once all passengers are on the plane, it rolls down the runway. Quick departures are unheard of at *McCrakin International Airport*. It is infamous for planes to sit on the tarmac for hours.

Not today.

The plane prepares for take-off within a few minutes after the final boarding call.

"Flight 283 from Las Vegas to San Francisco. Please prepare for take-off," announces the pilot.

I open my eyes and see Carmen. From the nervous look on her face (I'm sure it's similar to mine), it is clear neither of us likes to fly. We both show anxious expressions as the plane takes off and gains altitude.

Carmen speaks fast, and some of her words run together, making it hard for me to follow. Once the airplane evens out, we become more relaxed and continue our conversation.

My takeaways are: Carmen is divorced, her ex-husband has a week heart and she took him to the emergency room once. She is a Christians and is a health nut, like me.

Hey, head – will you please feel better? Stop pounding.

*****

As the plane descends, the pilot broadcasts, "Please remain seated with your seatbelts on. We will be experiencing turbulence for the next few minutes."

Oh boy. This is not going to be good.

Sure enough, the plane hit turbulence.

Bump!

And then, the plane jerks upward.

Carmen reaches for my hand, which I grasp as we confess to one another our stomach aches and fear of flying.

I can't wait for the airplane to land.

Finally, the plane touches down.

The "Fasten Seat Belt" sign turns off. I stand up to retrieve my black bag.

Carmen asks, "Do you see my red suitcase?"

"Yes, I see it."

"Jill, while you are up there, please retrieve it?"

"Of course," handing her suitcase to her.

Sliding back into the dull gray leather seat in the upright position, I double-check the pouch in front of me. I gather up my wallet, cellphone, and black bag and run a checklist in my head.

As passengers disembark the plane, I scan my phone to check my messages. There are several texts from Derek.

They will have to wait. I can't read my phone and carry my bag at the same time.

I dig into my wallet, grab my massage therapy business card, and hand it to Carmen as we walk down the jet bridge and into the main airport. She takes the card and places in the back pocket of her snappy pants. My new friend waves goodbye as she tugs on her bright red suitcase.

I wave back, raising my voice so Carmen can hear me say, "Goodbye. Can't wait for our date at Wild Bill's. Cheers."

Carmen walks toward the "Exit" sign. I turn to follow the sign to the "Baggage Claim" area.

Upon arrival, an airport employee announces its temporary closure due to lightning.

"How long do you think it will be closed?" I ask.

"Perhaps an hour, Miss. This is quite typical with summer storms in San Francisco," responds the courteous employee.

I glance down at my phone to read Derek's text messages.

"Where are you?"

"Call me."

*****

San Francisco, California

Through the automatic doors, a path leads to the rent-a-car counter.

"Good afternoon, how can I help you," greets the agent.

"Good afternoon," I reply. "I'd like to fill out the paperwork for my rental car while waiting for my baggage to drop."

"I'm not sure that is a good idea." The agent challenges.

"How come?" I wonder.

"Well," the agent sighs, responding robotically. "A twenty-minute clock starts ticking after the paperwork is complete. Once the twenty minutes are over, we can no longer release the keys. The transaction voids."

How silly.

The check-in process becomes a moot point without an estimated time for the baggage carousel to reopen.

It is now four-thirty, so there is plenty of time to meander around. But first, I call Derek.

"Derek, I'm glad I caught you. I wanted to let you know I arrived safely and I'm waiting for my luggage. I received your text messages; what's up?"

"I expected you to call earlier," he scolds. "I was worried about you and wanted to make sure you did not get lost, or talk to strangers." Then switching his tone, he asks "So, how was your flight?"

"It was a bit rocky, and I have a headache. How was the rest of your day?"

"My meeting went well," says Derek. "The casino will be undergoing another renovation, which means more work hours for me."

"What else is new?" I ask, rolling my eyes as if he can see them.

"Well, Jill. I hope you remember what you have here. You don't know how good you have it. Maybe think about that while you are away?"

"Sure, Derek. Whatever you say."

"I have to go, Jill. I need to pick up Zo from dance lessons."

Click.

*****

The next destination is up the escalator to the second floor to browse the storefronts.

But first. Snack time.

My hunger pangs were talking to me. A small zippered plastic bag from my black carry-on contains peppers, celery, and carrots. There is no rush since Amelia is working until seven o'clock. Her hours are usually ten to seven, with Thursdays and Sundays off.

Working long hours in a hospitality-related business is oddly familiar. Years ago, when I worked at *Lake Meade*

Cruises, Amelia and her then-husband Dan owned and operated a boating business on Lake Meade.

An hour later, the luggage finally drops down the chute. The suitcases jiggle onto the conveyor belt and circle around. The fluorescent yellow tag on my black bag stands out like a spotted giraffe.

The walk through the doors and down the path is oddly familiar.

(*I sense doing this before. Oh. Yes, I have, déjà vu!*).

Rental car counter. Long line. Ugh.

*****

After I sign the paperwork, the rental agent hands me the keys to the compact rent-a-car – a red Kia Rio. Before leaving the counter, I run the checklist in my head.

Suitcase? – Check.

Black carry-on case? – Check.

Cellphone? – Check.

Wallet? – Check.

Rental Car Keys? – Check.

The sun begins to set, and the day's activities catch up with my weary body.

Wandering aimlessly in the parking garage, I see the rental car – right in front of me.

*****

Napa Valley, California

Ameilia's office in Napa Valley, California, is the next destination. The drive on Interstate 80, or as the Californians say, "*I-80*," to her office takes a little over an hour. A gigantic sign with yellow letters reads "Heritage Resort and Conference Center."

I pull into the corporate office parking lot. Amelia is waving goodbye to the security guard at the front door.

Rolling the window down, I clear my throat. "Hi, Amelia!" I wave, "I'm over here."

"Hey, Jill! Impeccable timing. My car is over there. Wait where you are. You can follow me home, okay?"

I don't have to get out of the car – which is great because I am so tired.

I wait for Amelia to start her Mercedes and follow her home.

We enter her driveway, and I steer to the right as Amelia drives to the left into her garage.

After parking, I yank my suitcase and place it on the ground, running the same checklist in my head as earlier.

I walk behind Amelia.

She's wearing a dark grayish snappy tailored herringbone blazer. Under her blazer, a dusty pink silk blouse peeks through. Neatly tucked into a pair of black linen slacks.

[19]

Taking a moment to admire the Gothic door with an oil-bronze handle, I roll my bag into the guest room.

I return to the living room to plunk onto the cream-colored leather couch. Comfy.

*****

Half-dead after a long day of traveling with a headache, I am hungry as a horse. Amelia orders a half-no-cheese pizza. After a glass of water, I'm revived, certainly, enough to phone home and chat with Amelia later.

And gab, we do.

"How are the kids?" Amelia asks.

"Say no more." I whip out my wallet to share a cherished family photo, "Here, see? Last Christmas. The kids are growing like weeds. Zola is driving. Can you believe it?"

Returning the picture to my wallet, I continue, "Zola likes Irish dancing best. She is so graceful and synchronous in liturgical dance. She has mastered the Bharatanatyam and is now working on Messianic folk dancing." I catch a breath.

"Nisha loves swimming.

"Rebecca enjoys acting, and Kobe likes soccer. Not surprisingly, he also enjoys South African dance. I'm guessing it is the beat and thumping he likes best.

"Amelia, I'm so proud of them. Each performs well above average in school. They stay busy with choir, sports, and

[20]

other activities, certainly keeping me on my toes." I change the subject. "Enough about me and the kids. How is your new job? Tell me all about it."

"It is fantastic." Amelia's eyes sparkle. "I finally get to make impactful bottom-line decisions. Last year, we made fifty million; this year, we are on target to make seventy-five. The best part is customizing and catering directly to guests and corporate groups. By seeing each client as unique, we provide them with a personal experience geared toward their wants and desires.

"The registration software is top-of-the-line, cutting-edge technology. Jill, get ready for this. It uses artificial intelligence (AI) to make recommendations and create options for each booking. How cool is that?"

"Amelia, that is so cool. I'm glad your company is using AI." Speculating, "The companies who don't embrace it will be left in the dust."

Amelia stares at me, marveling as if I had been hiding under a rock for the past few years.

"I'm surprised you know about AI, Jill."

"I make it a point to stay current with the latest technology. Don't forget, I have a teenager in the house."

"Oh, yeah, I forgot. Of course, that makes sense."

"I'm glad you found such a progressive company where you can shine and earn what you are worth. Your compensation package doesn't look shabby, either," I say, glancing around Amelia's home.

"I have risen one rung on the food chain," Amelia replies. "Speaking of food – how's your mom, and did you bring any of her famous apricot date flatbread?"

"Mom is good. She adjusted well to her senior living community and assists their staff with activities. She has become a different person since moving there.

"When Dad died, she had a hard time living alone in her creepy old house. She became a recluse, so I am overjoyed she is now with people and making friends. She even leads a weekly quilting circle, which is cool because you can do meditative coloring if you don't quilt. Can you believe that is a thing?"

"Sounds fun, Jill. I'm glad your mom is adjusting well to her new place. I have fond memories of your mom; sometimes, you would tag along. I remember how kindly she treated me when I moved in next door on Dogwood Street. She would bring over a thermos of coffee and her amazing bread on Saturday mornings. We would sit on the front porch at the wrought iron bistro set. Remember?" Amelia asks.

"I sure do. Mom made the best apricot date homemade bread. She doesn't bake much anymore – it's a good thing I have her recipe."

Time is flying by.

It is forty-five minutes later.

The pizza delivery person rings the doorbell. Answering, we hardly skip a beat.

Beer bottles are in our left hands, and pizza slices are in our right hands.

"I almost forgot. Guess what? We do have some of Mom's famous flatbread – I made it yesterday. It's in my suitcase. Let me grab it and put it in the refrigerator," I yawn, announcing the good news.

"Sure, Jill – sounds great – can't wait to have some in the morning." Amelia agrees.

I retrieve the apricot bread, double-wrapped in wax paper and foil, and put it in the fridge.

We continue chatting until midnight.

Suddenly, I am so tired I can't keep my eyes open any longer.

In a soft, quiet voice, I whisper, "Goodnight, Amelia."

"Goodnight, Jill. Sleep tight. Let me know if you need anything," Amelia whispers back.

I walk down the hallway toward the guest room.

[23]

Plunking my head on a fluffy pillow, I settle under the blankets.

I sure miss my kiddos. It has been a long day.

Feeling safe for the first time in years, I drift off to sleep in peace.

SECRET NUMBER ONE
DAY 2 ~ MORNING

S huffling into the Tuscany-style kitchen, I open the pantry door. Behind the cereal boxes, I find bootstrap molasses and organic apple cider vinegar. I grab and carry them to the counter.

The molasses is precisely the right brand. It is the kind with twenty percent iron. Not the brand with only fifteen percent. And certainly not the brand with no iron at all.

Measure one tablespoon of molasses.

Pour into the water bottle.

Add one tablespoon of vinegar.

Shake vigorously.

Drinking the concoction suppresses appetite. As a bonus, it makes hair fuller and thicker. Plus, it supplies my body with iron. It's hard to argue with its benefits.

*****

Time to change into my swimsuit.

I pause.

It is going to be a glorious day. My head feels great.

Refreshed, I'm ready to call Derek.

Pushing the numbers on the cellphone screen, I hear it ring.

Derek answers, "Hello?"

"Namaste. Good morning, Derek," I greet him with an upbeat, positive tone. "Guess what?"

"Eish. I am not a fan of guessing games, Jill. You should know by now."

"I fit into my pink polka-dot bikini." I announce bursting with joy.

"Really? I cannot believe you are wearing a bikini with a birthmark the size of Mount Kilimanjaro," Derek teases. "What are you trying to do? Ward off the entire animal kingdom? Are you sure you want to sunbathe? Your skin is wrinkling and appearing older – you already look like an old sack."

Ignoring his jests, I respond, "I plan to sunbathe and ponder the meaning of life." Then, changing the subject, "I'd love to talk to the kiddos to say hello."

"Fine, I will get Nisha – she is right here."

"Hi, Pookie. How did you sleep?"

"Fine. Kobe and Rebecca suck," Nisha hisses, "I have to do chores. Come home."

"Pookie, chores build character. Toughen up. I'll be home before you know it and will check in later. Listen to your

[26]

dad, and please be kind to Rebecca and Kobe. Can you give the phone to Kobe?"

"Hi, Ko-man. How are you, Pookie?"

"Hi, Mommy! I miss you so much. Please come home soon. Nisha smacked me again while I ate my breakfast, and I didn't even do anything."

"I'm so sorry, Pookie. Nisha should not be smacking you. It's wrong. Try to stay out of Nisha's way. Be good. I'll talk to you later. Can you hand the phone to Zola, please?"

"Hi, Zo. Thanks again for driving Nisha to her swim practice yesterday. How are you? Are you managing, okay?"

"Yes, Mom. I'm fine. Everyone is fine. Fine. Fine. Fine!" Zola snarls.

"Okay, Zo, can you put Rebecca on the phone?"

"Hi, Pookie. Are you thrilled to pieces? I sure hope you have fun at your theatre camp today. I can't wait to hear about it."

"Thanks, Mom. I am excited. A little nervous. But I'll be alright. Talk to you later. Bye, Mom."

I press the "off" button.

*****

Stepping onto the private patio to catch a few sun rays, I head toward the chaise lounge. Lowering my body onto it, I raise my face toward the sun. It feels so good.

[27]

Amelia opens the slider.

"Good morning. The date bread strikes again. Toasted and buttered, it tasted delicious. I hope you enjoy it as much as I did.

"I'm leaving for work, and don't forget I'll be home late. There's a budget meeting later today, and I'm taking my team to dinner afterward. Have a nice day – don't forget to put some sunscreen on; I'm running a bit late and gotta run," Amelia urges lovingly as she heads off to work.

"Okay," I reply, "Play nicely with the other children in the sandbox."

*****

After I shift my weight, and wiggle to get comfortable in the chaise, I contemplate Dr. Kate's suggestion.

"It might be a good idea to tell your mom your secret," Dr. Kate advised me several months ago.

I imagine confiding to my mom about the decades-old abuse, one of my darkest secrets.

Very soon now, the cat will be finally out of the bag.

*****

Secret #1

Nelson, a trusted family friend, molested me when I was twelve. Yet, it wasn't until decades later that I began to understand its enormous impact on my life, especially in my marriage and other relationships.

It was the fourth of July.

Nelson and his wife Bina had invited the entire church congregation to their home for a pool party. Their brick mid-century house sat on an acre of property with an inground pool. An ideal location for a large gathering.

Adults mingled and chatted in the house while most children were in the pool.

Several families from our church were there.

Near the pool stood a tree house with a tall ladder. Off to the side sat a life-size doll house with white shingles. Pretty pink flowers cascaded from the window box. The red door of a small guest cottage stood out at the end of the property and beckoned me to enter.

Wandering in, I faced a wall of books, hundreds sitting on the bookshelves. As an avid reader, I felt I had won the lottery. I scanned the titles, pulling out a few books that piqued my interest. I was so engrossed; I didn't hear anyone enter the room.

*****

That afternoon, the unthinkable happened. Nelson began touching me inappropriately.

I remember the stroking.

The scent of his cologne.

The way my body tingled.

He said I was a good girl and told me to be quiet. Stunned, unsure of what to do or say, I said nothing.

My eyes closed; my body rigid with fright.

I froze when I heard him unbuckle his belt and unzip his shorts; the sound seared into my brain.

*****

Over the next year and a half, there were about a dozen of these types of episodes when I looked after their dog. Nelson instructed me to never tell anyone.

This nightmare ended, or so I thought, when I started dating my first boyfriend, Jasper. Then, the abuse vanished from my memory, receding into my subconscious for decades.

Despite being physically free from the abuse, I did not feel liberated internally. I kept silent, unconsciously wearing a scarlet letter on my forehead as if to say, "Hey predators, come and get me."

The molestation experience as a twelve-year-old profoundly affected my marriage and parenting. After my oldest daughter turned twelve, these dormant emotions triggered something inside me. Like a light bulb suddenly going on, although I didn't know why.

[30]

I no longer trusted other adults, my daughter, or her friends.

Again, I didn't know why.

*****

Looking back all those years ago, I realize this trauma had changed how my brain processed and interpreted information. Not to mention the unspoken expectation that would silence me about what had happened. I understood I could never tell anyone. Feelings of guilt and shame permeated every inch of my being.

Somehow, I knew from a primal place within me how profoundly wrong it was for an adult man to touch me that way. My prepubescent brain could not process the sensations I felt. My body aroused with pleasure – as if drinking a glass of champagne. Bubbly and exciting.

Yet, my brain reacted to the dirty, sinful act I had engaged in.

It had harmed me.

Violating my innocence – and contradicting everything my church upbringing taught me about being good, right, and pure. I felt anything but that.

The strange comfort and attention that I'd received from Nelson confused me. For the first time in my life, I felt I mattered. The deep-seated feeling of being a burden (to my parents) had melted away.

What a complicated mess.

What had just happened?

Even now, I'm not sure.

But, as Dr. Kate explained to me, my twelve-year-old brain had done what it needed to do for self-preservation.

It locked the memory.

Into a vault.

Quite common in child exploitation, this "*dissociative amnesia*," the term Dr. Kate used, was a defense mechanism preventing me from remembering. It seemed to make sense to me.

To further complicate the story, I continued to experience physical sensations of arousal. Again and again, these feelings caused me more shame and guilt. My constant attempts to suppress them lurked in my consciousness.

*****

I rise from the chaise lounge, stretch my legs, and sit on the chair with my legs on the stucco ledge. Still, on the patio, the cool breeze against my legs.

Closing my eyes, I remember how my suppressed memories impacted my life. Past actions and reactions come keenly into focus.

[32]

I'd unconsciously buried the sexual abuse deep within my soul until Derek punched the wall in a moment of anger.

The violence triggered my decades-old dormant memories. Causing them to come flooding back.

My reaction overwhelmed me.

Yet, once I told Dr. Kate, I sensed release from a prison of sorts. Yet, from that session forward, paranoia seeped in.

Wounded.

Damaged.

Derek could care less. He used all this as an excuse to tell me I was unstable. Mentally ill.

Nope! Wrong!

I had experienced trauma.

Nothing more. Nothing less.

*****

Telling this to my eighty-three-year-old mother still seemed incomprehensible, even then. I didn't want to discuss a complicated topic with one of my closest confidants, my dear old mom. Months go by without a word about this.

Finally, after booking the plane tickets to Napa to see Amelia, the time had come.

[33]

Before getting on that plane, I knew I needed to see my mom. It was such a weird feeling. It's so strange how the Spirit works.

A few days before my trip, I drove to Mom's place for a quick impromptu visit. After pulling into the parking lot of her apartment complex, I found a parking spot close to the entrance. As another resident entered, I slipped through the main entrance door unnoticed. This avoided having my mom "buzz" me in. She had no idea I was coming.

Down the corridor, the elevators were on the right.

Ding.

Mom excitedly greeted me as she answered the door, blurting out that she had a doctor's appointment in an hour.

Whew.

This one-hour window of time was music to my ears.

Thank you, Lord. I will finally say what I came to say and get out quickly.

Anxious.

I watched the clock as we chatted about the weather and last week's annual Holi festival. Waiting for the right time when there was no right time to tell a secret like this one.

I took a deep breath.

Time was running out.

[34]

So, I took forty-five minutes to muster up the courage to spew out the secret I had carried the longest – *Secret Number One.*

"Mom, I need to get something off my chest. It happened a long time ago."

"Was it something I did or said?" Mom asked, bewildered.

"No, Mom, it wasn't about you. It was about me. I endured inappropriate behavior by an older man when I was twelve."

Whew. The words flew right out of my mouth.

With a sigh of relief, I planted my feet firmly in front of myself. I leaned in, waiting for a response. Worry, fear, anxiety, shame, blame, and abandonment shot through my veins. It was like a bolt of lightning.

"By whom?" Mom inquired.

"Nelson."

"I am so sorry," Mom said. "Tell me about it, Pookie. I love you and will love you no matter what."

"Mom, it is embarrassing. I really don't want to discuss the details with you. All I am comfortable saying is this abuse has affected my relationships without me realizing it. Looking back, it was an awful experience."

A few moments of silence passed. The color drained out of Mom's face as she absorbed my words. She took a moment to compose herself. Then, in a hushed voice, Mom slowly articulated, "This must be hard for you. I am so sorry you had to experience this, Jill. No child should ever have to go through this. Ever. You should consider talking to Nelson about it."

"I don't think so," I answered abruptly.

My fight-flight instinct kicked in, and I immediately wanted to fly out the door. I needed time to process this, but not here.

What good would it do to talk with Nelson about it now?

I stood up, kissed Mom goodbye, told her I loved her, and wished her luck at her doctor's appointment.

And that was that.

Whew. That was a quick exit, indeed. Now, I have to figure out what Mom meant about talking to Nelson about it. Eww.

*****

After the door closed behind me, I skipped back to my car.

A weight had lifted.

It was a miracle!

The butterflies that had been in my stomach were no longer there. It was as if they were now inside the car, flying around. It was freeing.

During the journey back home, I reflected on my jumbled feelings. Exhilaration, jubilation, and, at the same time, marginalization. While these emotions suggested conflict, they had a calming effect on my soul.

This thirty-three-year-old burden began to fade, making me wish I had told my mother sooner.

Dr. Kate nailed it!

Telling my mom *Secret Number One* lessened the burden I had carried for decades. Even though I thought she would have reacted differently.

She could have been more sympathetic.

Or remorseful.

Why did she want me to talk to Nelson about it?

I had no clue. It was so strange; it threw me for a loop. Mom wanting me to talk to Nelson seemed like a brush-off.

Although sharing my past trauma with my mother wasn't easy, opening up to her brought me a new sense of peace. Something, quite frankly, I wasn't expecting.

Opting for a quick visit may not have been the best decision, but I am glad to have had the opportunity to share it with her.

I did regret not asking my mother to tell me more about why she thought I needed to talk to Nelson. That was definitely a mistake on my part.

*****

Lost in thoughts about my visit with Mom, I drift back to the present. Stumbling into the kitchen, I grab a bite to eat. I return to the patio and shift my thoughts to Amelia. I was six when Amelia moved next door. She has been my rock and steadfast support ever since. Despite the ten-year age difference, we were friends.

Yup.

Two peas in a pod.

*****

A few years ago, after the finalization of Amelia's divorce, she moved to California. We kept in touch by phone with visits around the holidays. I had told her about my fragile, out-of-control marriage on several occasions, the last one two years ago. I still remember one of our conversations.

"Namaste. Amelia. Is this a good time to talk?"

"Yeah, how are you, Jill?" Amelia asked.

"Not great. Defeated. Yup. I'm going to explode. Zola wants to go to the ninth-grade dance – which will be fun for her. But then she wants to go to Lake Meade with friends afterward, stay over, and have a day at the lake. I was happy

[38]

to drive her up to the lake in the morning. What I have a tough time with, is agreeing to an overnighter with boys and girls who are fourteen. Am I being unreasonable? I'm trying to get a third opinion here."

"Jill, you are absolutely right about feeling uncomfortable about this. Remember the time you went to Lake Tahoe? You were only fourteen – and you know how that ended." Amelia reminded me.

Cringing at the idea of Zola alone with a boy, my imagination went wild. I collected my thoughts and blurted them out.

"Derek gave Zola permission. What in the world was he thinking? He disregarded my opinion. Again!"

Amelia knew, almost innately, that I needed a break for self-preservation. She suggested that I come for a visit and kept bugging me about it each time we talked on the phone.

Until, I finally did.

*****

Standing up and leaning against the stucco wall, I gaze into the distance.

How grateful I am for Amelia.

Her home is lovely. But I hadn't expected it to be so fancy. The perfect hostess furnishes a most tranquil space. It really is such a treat for me.

[39]

The teal-colored guest suite includes a king bed and a massive clothes closet. Across from the bed, I slide the doors open onto a screened-in patio overlooking a vineyard. A private sunbeam streams from nine to eleven in the morning. The patio has a chaise lounge chair with a custom-made Victorian rose-patterned cushion.

Like a princess from a storybook.

This is one of my favorite places to read and write.

*****

Amelia and Dan had a son, James Michael, born with a hole in his heart. They were extra careful with James. As instructed, they scheduled an appointment with the cardiologist at the six-month mark.

An extensive check-up coupled with several tests followed. All of which confirmed James had an atrial septal disorder. The baby had acquired thrombotic thrombocytopenic purpura (aTTP) – a rare blood disease. He needed a heart transplant.

Generally, this heart condition becomes a non-issue when the gap closes within the first six months of life.

Yet – not in James' case.

Soon after the transplant, James' near lifeless body rejected the heart. He became gravely ill, spending three months in the hospital. One morning, James didn't wake. He had slipped away from this world to another sometime during the night.

*****

No matter what trials and tribulations life has for us, even the strongest marriages incur rough patches. Amelia's cross weighed heavily. The loss of baby James nearly killed her. Dan was devasted as well.

Grief and loss bring couples closer together or pull them apart. As it turned out for them, their marriage deteriorated. It had suffered irreparable damage from this tragic ordeal.

Why do some couples make it while others don't?

CHRISTIANS DO NO WRONG
DAY 2 ~ AFTERNOON

Growing up in a calm, no-yelling environment, I had only heard my parents disagree once. That had been over twenty years ago. Now, they were celebrating their fiftieth wedding anniversary. This brings me to the question: How do couples live in peace? Ruminating on my upbringing will provide answers, I'm sure. Still on Amelia's patio, I start with my childhood.

The unwritten rule in my parent's home had been:

"Peace. At. All. Costs."

Unkind words were unacceptable, let alone spoken. Because of that, my parents' house served as a sanctuary, and my bedroom was a place of solitude. For homework. Or to tiptoe up the stairs after drinking too much at a high school tennis party.

A refuge.

My space of safety.

Free from bullies chasing me in middle school.

Or making fun of my thin hair or bucked front teeth.

Or birthmark. Oh, how I loathed the locker rooms.

Returning to the memories of my childhood home, the deep forest green-colored house stretched fifty feet on Dogwood Street. A macadam driveway paralleled the railroad-styled aluminum-sided abode. A yellow milk can anchored flowers on the front lawn. The house sat on the left, and a porch jutted from the side.

The driveway led to a two-car garage. Up the four stairs, onto the deck, and through the back door stood the kitchen that my dad had remodeled. Oak cabinets lined the wall while white counters sparkled. The round oak table took center stage.

Beyond the kitchen, to the left, the stairs to the second floor led to three bedrooms. With the black shag rug on the right, my gold-colored room was past the green bathroom on the left.

*****

Muffled voices comforted me from the first-floor bedroom of my childhood home. The sounds were amicable, although I did not actually hear specific words. My parents' pillow talk, directly beneath my room, soothed me to sleep.

But now, Derek's and my bedtime ritual resembled a horror show.

*****

Our going-to-bed routine was repetitive and disappointing.

"I'm going to bed now. Why don't you join me?"

"No, Jill!" Derek would say dismissively. "I have electrical plans to go over for my meeting tomorrow."

The next evening, in the hallway.

Near the living room. Where Derek played video games.

"I'm going to bed now. Why don't you join me?" I asked suggestively – although it was more like begging.

"Are you doing this dance with me again?"

"Yes, I am. Don't you want to go to bed?"

"Jill, you are so irritating. Why do you need so much attention?"

"Maybe because you ignore me all day?"

"I have no idea what you are talking about. I work hard all day so you can buy the kids all the clothes they could possibly want. Get over it, Jill. I need alone time."

"So do I! Are you sure you don't want to come to bed?"

"Eish! No! I am in the middle of a game. Stop whining."

The absence of comfort led to a cold and lonely bedtime. I longed for harmonious sounds to lull me to sleep like they did in my childhood.

This early-to-bed/night owl tension added another layer of marital strife. As I slipped under the bed covers each night, I asked myself why Derek didn't want to spend time with me.

Was he gay?

Having an affair?

Did he not like sex?

Were video games more enticing than me?

Feeling baffled, unsexy, and lonely, these thoughts left me all in a tizzy.

*****

Huge age gaps between my siblings gave each of us a very different experience with our parents. I had four older brothers and a younger sister. With my hyperactive brothers, my parents, kept their eyes sharp. My parents were older when my sister and I came along.

More lenient, too.

Sure, they had quirks like most parents. These were some of our house rules: No playing cards. No going to dances. No drinking alcohol. No boys alone in the house. No bike riding on Sundays. Be home by ten.

Although I didn't realize it then, my parents had a feeling of malaise about the secular world. Undercurrents of emotional abandonment and low self-esteem permeated my childhood. I felt like a burden to my parents, not a blessing.

My childhood revolved around school, church, and church activities.

As I got older, my parents' expectations seemed pretty straightforward. Once eighteen, you were on your own; pay rent or leave.

Hmm.

It didn't strike me as godly at all.

My memories were pleasant and harmonious enough.

But what was stirring beneath it all?

Parents who didn't want to be parents and kids who simply wanted to be kids.

That was why a home was so important to me.

*****

Mostly, I parented my younger sister and myself. Presuming we were attending a church activity or hanging out with a group of church kids, my parents would not interfere. One of my favorite activities was hiking with kids from my youth group to the quarry. I'd make a sandwich, grab a drink, and carry it in a knapsack. I'd ride my bike three-quarters of a mile to our church, then start our adventure.

Railroad tracks, dirt roads, gravel roads, and tall mountains. We were a fearless group of kids with God on our side. What could possibly go wrong?

[46]

It was a miracle we were safe. Especially knowing a man in his fifties had fallen to his death from the top of the quarry.

If my kids ever did what I did, I would have grounded them for a month.

*****

Displaying a lack of attunement to their children, my perception of their under-zealous parenting skills was not unfounded. They could have been more concerned and responsive to my needs. In fact, if I needed anything, they would say, "Get a job. Pay for it yourself."

My parents weren't interested in a parent-child bond. They did the least expected of parents. I'm sure it had something to do with Proverbs 13:24. "He that spareth his rod hateth his son: but he that loveth him chasteneth him betimes." *[KJV]*

When my sister and I came along, my parents were older and more tired. They didn't have the energy to be responsible adults. Instead, as long as we did something "Christian," they permitted us to do things we probably should not have done.

Like spending the weekend with my first boyfriend.

Jasper, a senior in high school, invited me to his parent's lake house on Lake Tahoe. I was a freshman. Since Jasper had driven up a few days earlier, his brother Jake agreed to drive me up with his pregnant wife, Annie.

Thursday before Labor Day.

Three in the morning.

I closed the back door of my house without making a sound. Walking down the driveway, I ducked my head, entering the back seat of a compact yellow Datsun B210.

Jake drove.

Annie, four months pregnant, sat in the front passenger seat. We were on our way up to their family lake house for a long weekend.

Somewhere along the route, the car flipped over three times. It felt like it had hit a large pothole in the road. I suspected Jake dozed off and then overcompensated by jerking the steering wheel.

The car hit the median in the center of the highway.

Finally, it came to a stop.

Then silence.

I leaned against the inside of the vehicle in the back seat, stunned. Moments later, a truck driver who had seen the accident pulled his rig off to the side.

It felt like an eternity.

Running over to my side of the car, he opened the crushed back door with the window blown out. He reached for my arm.

I stumbled out of the car as he pulled a handkerchief from his pocket to place on my bleeding face.

Other good Samaritans stopped after the accident and tended to Jake and Annie.

The siren wailed in the background. Getting louder and louder. My heart raced as I glanced back. In utter shock, I stepped into the white box on wheels looking back at what remained of the crushed B210.

It wasn't pretty.

Off I went in an ambulance to a hospital in the obscure town of Yerington, Nevada.

It was a miracle everyone was okay.

After seeing the car, it was hard to imagine three people and an unborn baby walking away, for the most part, unharmed. I broke my nose, and my back hurt. Annie and her baby were fine. Jake had broken a rib.

Alone in the emergency room, I wondered how my parents allowed me to visit Jasper. The experience left me with more questions than answers.

Reflecting now, *where were my parents?*

Shuddering to think –

[49]

Why in the world did my parents let me go in the first place?

I was fourteen, in ninth grade. How insane!

Why?

Because, in a nutshell, my parents trusted me.

No, actually.

The word "Christian" is what they trusted.

They were fine knowing I had met this guy at a church-affiliated youth event. That is all that mattered to them, leaving me to wonder about their myopic view of anything "Christian."

Later, Jasper picked me up in his blue pickup truck with a white roof. He drove me back to his parents' lake house, where I rested for several days.

Looking back, I'll ask it again. Why?

How screwy was that?

It still didn't explain why my parents didn't drive up to bring me home.

*****

The day is inching along and going down memory lane has worked up an appetite. I make myself a late lunch and return to my quiet space on the patio where I pick up where I had left off where more memories flood my mind. This one happened only a few months after the car accident. I was a teenager and attending a youth group.

I hung out with older kids who expected much more from someone my age. Most of the kids were juniors and seniors. I, a lowly freshman, didn't notice their lack of emotional intelligence. I remember a specific meeting that still sends goosebumps up my spine.

It was fall.

That evening, a cool dampness hung in the air as leaves fell from the trees outside the small basement window. We had met friends from the *Teen Spirits* group at Steve's home, ten miles from mine.

I sat cross-legged, wearing a black cotton woven knit shirt and designer blue jeans I had bought with babysitting money.

A dozen youths were all in a circle, taking turns massaging each other's backs. I was rubbing Linda's back, neck, and shoulders. Rusty was behind. Linda was in front of me. Rusty placed his hands on my shoulders. He rubbed them in a circular fashion. A few minutes later, I felt a sensation between my legs.

Baffled by this, I wondered if my hormones were overactive or if my body got excited more than other kids my age? Whatever the case, this memory inked in my mind forever.

Thankfully, no one else noticed this embarrassing moment. But how could this have even happened?! Unthinkable. After all, this was a Christian youth group, for goodness' sake.

There's that word "Christian" again.

It was a turning point.

From then on, a red alert went off in my head when people touched me. I never was the same.

*****

As I grew older, the dismal feeling of being unwanted surfaced again while dating Dimitri, my high school sweetheart.

He caught my eye in the gymnasium.

Tall.

Thin.

Wavy hair.

Intense jawline.

So handsome. Drop-dead gorgeous.

His backhand aimed flawlessly toward a painted cement target.

His boyish grin and kind eyes made me gawk at him. One day, I sheepishly asked him to teach me how to serve.

Yes, it was a pretense.

He stood behind me, reaching for my right arm.

Dimitri held the tennis racquet, and we lifted it with his hand guiding mine. Tossing the tennis ball into the air with his left hand. A spark had ignited.

After that first encounter in the gym, we started to work out and play tennis together.

Soon, our friendship turned into a whole dating thing.

Slow. Like a smoldering flame.

Glowing softly.

I owed my passion for tennis to Dimitri.

His exceptional coaching skills made me a better player. My medals tucked away in a memory box proved it.

*****

Whether education, sports, or spirituality, Dimitri's parents cheered him on. They expected their children not to go to just any college but to one of the best colleges in the country. Money deterred them not.

Once, his mother chimed in, "Jill, if there is a will, there will be a way. Dimitri will apply for scholarships, plus we expect to take out loans if necessary."

Dimitri was Cinderella, and his mom was the Fairy Godmother.

This was so foreign to me.

[53]

Crazy.

*****

Dimitri's enthusiastic parents were a stark contrast to my "Negative Nellie" parents. Mom and Dad seemed content with a laissez-faire attitude toward parenting, whereas Dimitri's family would go to the ends of the earth for the well-being of their children.

Growing up without a Fairy Godmother was hard. I felt like an obligation, as if weighing my parents down like some invisible force. They had to buy more food, more clothes, and exert more energy. It was like my existence made their lives more difficult.

College? That was out of the question.

Why?

Because it required resources which my parents were unwilling to provide. I certainly don't want my children to feel this way.

No sir.

They will feel appreciated. Affirmed.

They won't worry about the cost of trade school, college, or whatever they choose. My children will know they can stay at home for as long as they wish.

They will have no doubt in their minds that they are blessings.

[54]

*****

Taking a deep breath, I close my eyes and rest for a few minutes. My mind switches gears and returns back to my parents. I realize that to some degree, my parents influenced my own marriage.

They didn't discuss problems in front of me. Had they done so, I could have honed my conflict management skills.

Did they even have any issues?

Or did they sweep them under the rug?

My parents were not transparent. They were tight-lipped, much like Derek.

I had no experience with them being angry or handling anger.

They were emotionless yet easygoing as long as I obeyed them and/or acted "Christian." If I was going to attend a Christian event, or be with "Christians" they didn't care what or where it was. I thought Christians were supposed to care. This confused me growing up.

I might have gained better judgment and homemaking skills if they had been more involved.

Or not.

Would've, could've, should've. I needed clarification.

Didn't I?

Not knowing what to think conflicts with my soul. It is like a pressure cooker waiting to explode.

One thing is sure: My home *now* is far from what I had hoped for.

It feels like Derek's house.

Not mine.

I'm a stranger.

"HELPER" – ARE YOU KIDDING ME?
DAY 2 ~ EVENING

The shadows are widening, and it's time to take a break, change scenery, and grab a water bottle. On Amelia's comfy couch, I lift my legs and cross them as I settle in. My mind drifts to Derek, remembering our first encounter, at the bar.

Derek's magnetic allure captured me from the moment I saw him. As did the intricate tattoo on his forearm, a masterpiece, to say the least. A tapestry of colors and symbols drew my attention like a magnet.

The intrigue of it left me with questions.

Full of vibrant colors, a gold crown lay atop a coat of arms with a shield. Red dragons danced on either side. On the shield were four quadrants, each with a symbol.

A lightning bolt.

A rifle.

A deer.

A pair of dice.

Derek's eyes, which had initially drawn me in, held a depth of loyalty. Beyond attraction, his genuine love for family and ambition truly aligned with me. Gathering around the kitchen table, it was easy to imagine him playing cards. I could see him with his family and friends, shuffling a deck of cards, chatting the evening away.

Kindred spirits, we were both at a similar stage of life. We had grown weary of the dating scene, searching for "the one." We were ready to settle down and build something meaningful.

*****

The chemistry between Derek and me struck a chord, like plucked harp strings. As if the heavens were playing a high-pitched celestial sound.

He exuded charisma and charm.

That first glance was irresistible.

Derek's eyes sparkled like diamonds.

His cowboy boots glistened with a metal band between the boot and the heel. They rested on the wooden crosspiece of the bar stool. His warm and inviting smile melted the world's worries away. The noise of the environment disappeared into the walls.

In front of me stood the most handsome man I had ever seen. His presence filled the room with an intensity that was impossible to ignore.

*****

I readjust the pillow on the couch, close my eyes and smile, remembering the first time we met. Home from college during winter break, I met up with my friends Linda and Rusty at the new Bonfire Casino and Lanes. I entered behind Linda as Rusty opened the glass front door.

A waft of tobacco smoke hit my face.

A hint of sweat and alcohol permeated the air.

The sound of bowling balls hitting the pins echoed through the space.

Dressed in a black silk tank top and jeans, I followed Linda to the bar.

Deep blue eyes twinkled like stars against a black button-down shirt. To my left, a man sat, shoulders back, sleeves rolled up, revealing a large forearm tattoo. With a slight tip of his cowboy hat, he smiled at me.

As Linda and Rusty immersed themselves in conversation, suddenly, I felt like a third wheel. I turned and introduced myself to the man next to me.

"Namaste. I'm Jill. Nice place. Have you been here before?"

"I am Derek, fine lady," he nodded without taking his eyes off of me. "Yes, I have been here before," he replied with confident eyes. His shirt fit perfectly across his slightly narrow shoulders. Dressed in tight designer jeans and cowboy boots with pointy toes, Derek leaned in to sip his drink.

"This place opened about a month ago, right?" I asked, noticing the deer's head on the wall.

"Yes, it opened six weeks ago. I was the assistant electrician on the project. By the way, the deer did not see it coming," Derek chuckled with flair, flashing his pearly white teeth against his darkened skin.

The neon lights cast a soft glow on the bar counter.

Our conversation flowed effortlessly.

"Oh, so you undoubtedly know the ins and outs of the place," I laughed.

"Yes, I know most of the casinos inside and out, too. As an apprentice, I worked behind the scenes at most casinos here in Vegas. I guess you can call me a gambling man. Blackjack is my game. And I am mighty good at it."

We clicked from the start. I was sure my honesty attracted Derek. My praying hand earrings added a bit of spirituality to the dynamic. A bond had begun to form as we dug deeper. We told each other about ourselves and how we each valued family.

"Mr. Derek, tell me. Do you have a special lady in your life?" I held my breath in hopeful anticipation of an "eligible" man.

"No, I don't, little lady. It has been hard dating the last few years. I have been working long hours to advance my career and set myself up for the future."

"What does that future hold for you?" I asked.

"I see little rug rats running around a home filled with the smell of apple pie and coffee brewing. What about you, Miss Jill?"

"My first priority is to finish up my degree. As long as nothing crazy happens, I expect to graduate in May. Then, the sky is the limit.

"Finding a job before graduation would definitely be a plus. Then, I'd consider settling down once I work a year or two. Don't tell anyone, but I am a homebody at heart. Sounds like you are, too."

I may have found a fellow homebody like me.

*****

We talked about God, faith, and family. Derek described himself as an open-minded "Christian" but not a churchgoer. In fact, I remembered something odd. When I asked him about God, he told me to ask his uncle.

Something felt off.

Why would a sincere Christian not want to talk about God? Or why did I need to ask another person how Derek felt about God? It made no sense to me. Was he hiding something?

Was it an early warning sign I missed?

I brushed it off at the time because his easygoing personality invited connection. And our chemistry felt undeniably promising.

What an unexpected surprise this serendipitous encounter was.

Could HE be the ONE?

*****

Derek, a master electrician, loved hunting elk and deer. He had finished his apprenticeship several years before we met. Now that his career had trended upward, settling down could be an option.

I would have described him as a "ladies" man. Having dated several girls in high school, it was hard to imagine this rugged creature not clicking with any of them. It struck me he had been a one-night-stand type of guy. But now, apparently, Derek wanted more.

*****

It seems like a lifetime ago.

I married Derek, the same silky, smooth-skinned man from the Bonfires Casino and Lanes. Six months of dating followed by six months of engagement.

Through the years, Derek rose up the ranks to head electrician. He worked for the most prominent casino and luxury resort in Las Vegas.

Our modest home was on a quarter of an acre at *The Whispering Woods* in Summerlin. A quiet neighborhood within the city limits of the southwestern part of Las Vegas.

Even though Derek's hard work and success supported our family, we had grown apart over the years. The lack of affection between us was palpable.

The last time I remember Derek saying he loved me was before we married. This emotional distance translated into a lack of love. The whole idea of marriage was to love someone and receive it back.

Wasn't it?

Love was fundamental – it grounded me.

Truth told; I was in love with love.

And, when I loved – I loved hard.

I was all in.

No matter what...Until I wasn't.

This *"in love with love"* stemmed from early childhood wounds. Trauma, if you will. My secrets and a lack of parent-child attachment.

My parents had attached to each other and to their church. But this had left little room in their lives for me. I felt insignificant. Like I didn't matter.

Did I feel loved as a child? To some degree, yes.

But it was a minimal, obligatory type of love. Not the love parents feel when they think their children are a gift from God. It was confusing.

These complex issues impacted my self-esteem. And now, somehow, they were affecting my marriage.

That was why love was so important to me.

Love was light.

It was hope.

I wanted someone to love, yes.

But even more, I wanted someone to love me…for me.

*****

After years of marriage, the collywobbles appeared more often than not. Our differences seemed to create a wider and wider gap between us. As the years flew by, Derek was going hunting more often. Which of course, led to more angst.

Derek loved hunting. Buck fever.

Yup.

That is what Derek called it.

"Derek, it looks like you are packing for a weekend of hunting."

"Yes, Jill. It does look like that."

"Another weekend away?"

"I know, but you know how short the season is, right?"

"But, Derek, we have stuff going on. The kids have soccer practice, and we were going to look at the kitchen redesign."

"I do not want to disappoint the guys. Like I said, I forgot. Leave it be, Jill. Just handle it."

"Derek, you know I like us to spend the weekends with the kids as a family."

"I spend enough time with the kids, Jill. Give me a break, will you?"

"I wish you would care. I'm sick of having to beg you for some attention. Our marriage is in trouble, and you are going off hunting."

"Jill, you are so melodramatic. Get a grip, girl."

*****

Around this time, my self-esteem plunged into the black hole of Calcutta. I met depression for the first time.

It would rear its ugly head after I dropped off the twins to school. I began to cry uncontrollably. Not knowing why I was so sad, stumped me.

I had no idea.

Or did I?

Why did I feel this way? Was it because I tried to hold myself together for the kids' sake and fell to pieces when they left? Could it be due to Derek being so controlling? Was his job in jeopardy? (Would he even tell me if it was?) Was Derek having an affair?

It was pure conjecture.

Plain and simple.

My husband rarely shared his thoughts and feelings with me. If he did, it was in bits and pieces, like a *"fill-in-the-blank"* game.

And the game was getting old.

*****

I sip from my water bottle as my thoughts now drift to my precious children. They truly are the bright spots in my life. They lighten the darkness of the valley I find myself in. They keep me going, each one excelling in school and full of energy.

Zola, my oldest daughter, is a risk-taker.

She loves dancing and can be sassy. Academically, she is off the charts. Zo doesn't have to study – she has natural talent. Same for dancing.

Nisha, my second oldest, is my swim girl.

She loves swimming as much as I do. I recall her first lessons in the Goldfish class at the community pool in

Summerlin. I would swim laps while Nisha had her lesson in the training pool. She advanced through three levels that first summer.

Nisha also does well in school. She has a photographic mind and scores incredibly high on standardized tests.

Rebecca, one of the twins, is my artsy-fartsy kid.

She loves anything drama.

Rebecca is my *"Sarah Bernhardt."* The famous 19th-century French actress, Ms. Bernhardt held the record of having the earliest birth on the Hollywood Walk of Fame. Of course, Sarah didn't live to see her induction in 1960. But it unquestionably conveyed a sense of significant professional accomplishment for a woman.

Kobe, my other twin and only son, is my sports team kid.

He loves everything about soccer.

Soccer balls, soccer shoes, soccer socks – who knew such a market for soccer anything existed? What is the difference between a running sock and a soccer sock, anyway? If there is one, Kobe will know.

Blessed. Yes, we are. Derek and I have happy, healthy, positive, upbeat kids, despite their few reprimands at school. Each has a different personality and a contagious spirit of awe and wonder.

*****

[67]

Clearly, our children were not the cause of my unhappiness. One day, a few years ago, I found myself wanting to search for answers. Derek's office would be the best place to find a clue, starting with his desk. Most of his papers were under lock and key. So, I started with his desk.

Receipts?

Nope – none.

Bank statements?

Nope – nowhere found.

I remember sitting at Derek's computer and thinking I was sure to find an Excel file with something incriminating, but saw nothing out of the ordinary. The receipts all looked in order.

No jewelry or perfume.

No unfamiliar restaurants.

Nada.

That was a relief. Or was it?

I was back to square one.

*****

Emerging from my memories, I stretch my legs and stroll into Amelia's kitchen for a snack, like a happy hour. As I forage through the refrigerator, the almond milk and a wedge of Wisconsin cheddar cheese with cherries call my name.

Paired with crackers, I add a banana from the fruit bowl and protein powder from the pantry.

Good smoothie fixins.

As I prepare a plate, the heaviness of my marriage troubles me. I grab a wine bottle, head into the guest room, sit in the velvet-padded rocker, place my plate and wine on the side table, and stare out the window.

Oh, how I long for a happier marriage.

All the searching, reading, and meditating on scripture I had done in the past and before this trip to Napa made me realize my marriage is so off base. It's so far from what God intends, it is ridiculous. Saving my marriage at this point can only happen by the grace of the Almighty.

So, I decide to look at another passage to ease my collywobbles. I get up from the rocker, grab my *Bible* and the bottle of wine, and bring them to the living room.

The empty smoothie glass is in the sink, and the cheese and crackers are now next to the wine. I open the *Shafer Cabernet Sauvignon Hillside Select* and pour a glass.

On the couch, I read and contemplate a Bible verse. It is *Genesis 2:18*. It talks about Yahweh speaking to Adam needing a suitable helper.

Hmm.

I desire to be Derek's suitable helper, but I don't feel like a helper.

I feel like a slave!

With another sip of wine, I notice the hint of fruit.

Black cherries and licorice.

It is smooth and delicious.

I think about how Yahweh doesn't want Adam to be alone. What about the woman?

I can't speak for Eve, but I don't want to be alone either. Yes, I want a suitable helper too.

What would it have been like to whisper my wants and desires to Derek?

*****

Home is not supposed to be a place to fear.

But I do.

I fear anger, rejection, and not being perfect. For me, these fears are genuine. Family therapy or an intervention may help.

Yes.

But who knows?

I am feeling defeated.

I ask myself, *why do I endure this unequal marriage?*

Well, first of all, divorce is against my Christian upbringing. Until now, it hasn't even occurred to me it might be an option.

Second, Derek can't help himself – he has no idea how hurtful and disrespectful he is. That is what he experienced growing up. So how could he act any other way?

Our kids are another reason.

Loved.

Cherished.

Growing like weeds with necks that smell so sweet after a shower or bath.

I think of their lunches that need to be prepared and brought to school if left on the kitchen counter.

I can't imagine not seeing them each and every day.

*****

Time flies, as I grapple with my thoughts, questions, and memories. It is almost time for dinner. Amelia is working late. So, I order steamed shrimp and vegetables with white rice from an Asian restaurant.

Ten minutes later, plugging the address into the navigational system, I ran a checklist in my head. Cellphone. Wallet. Keys.

Pulling out of the driveway, I head down the road and make a right onto Railroad Avenue to pick up the order.

When I return, I turn on the television to *20/20*, pour another glass of wine, and eat my dinner peacefully. Evening reminds me it's time to call the kids.

"Hello, this is Zola speaking – the Princess of the Universe."

"Hello, sweet Princess of the Universe. Is the Princess behaving herself?"

"Yes, Mother dear," Zola replies. "Oh, I meant to tell you, I'll be babysitting the neighbor's twins for the summer. Miss Esther picked up a client and asked if I could drive her twins to and from camp with Rebecca and Kobe. Dad says it is fine.

"Is it okay with you?" Zola asks.

"Sure, Zo, please be extra careful driving; I love you to the moon and back. Can you hand the phone to Nisha, please?"

"Nisha is at Kim's house."

"Okay, can you get Kobe, please?"

"Sure."

"Hi, Pookie. You, okay?"

"Yes, Mommy, I'm fine now, but Nisha picked on me today. Zola pushed Nisha so hard that she fell and bumped her head. I miss you, Mom. I need you. When are you coming home?" Kobe asks in his sweet angelic voice.

"I love you to the moon and back. I'll be home before you know it. I have an idea. How about finding Mr. Cow and taking him to bed tonight, and when you cuddle him, think about me cuddling you. Sound good?"

"Mr. Cow is on the chair in my room. I'll take him to bed, but it won't be the same, Mom," Kobe sniffles.

"Goodnight, sweet boy," I add before he hangs up.

"Can you put Rebecca on the phone?"

"Okay, Mom." He says in a disappointed tone.

"Hi, Mom!" Rebecca answers with delight.

"Hi, Rebecca. How was your first day of drama class?"

"It's rad. I'm so happy! We are working on *The Sound of Music*, and I am auditioning next week for the role of Maria." Rebecca giggles, "I sure hope I get it."

"I sure hope so, too. Good luck, Pookie. I love you to the moon and back. Have a good sleep," I say, pressing the "Power-off" button on my cellphone.

*****

Lying in bed in Amelia's guest room, my mind drifts to the topic of parenting. In an instant, I flash back to the Parenting Workshop debacle.

It began when I unzipped the backpack Nisha left on the kitchen chair. I reached for the homework folder where notices and papers from school went.

[73]

I opened the princess-stickered powder blue folder and read a fluorescent yellow flyer:

PARENTING WORKSHOP
Tuesday, 7 p.m. – 8:30 p.m.
Summerlin Community Center
Topic: Who is the Tween in your House?
Workshop Leader: Marita Sanchez, Ph.D.
A parenting expert from the National Association for Parenting.
Sponsored by: The Parent Association.

This was the answer to my prayer.

That night. At dinner.

Keeping a blank look, I glanced at Derek and asked, "Derek, the school is sponsoring a parenting workshop on tweens. You feel like going?"

"What night is it?" he asks.

"Tuesday, at seven o'clock at the community center." I replied.

"If you want to, I will go. Does it count as a date night?"

"Sure, Derek." I said warmly.

Positivity and optimism filled my soul when he agreed to go without cajoling. It seemed a bit out of character, but I was willing to bask in a moment of bliss.

We finally agreed to do something together. How nice.

Later that evening, I completed the registration form and laid it on the table beside the front door as a reminder to deliver it to the community center.

I woke up the following day and felt better than I had in a long time. I slept well for a change, thinking about this workshop's possibilities.

Better parenting.

Better partners.

Better communication. It sounded perfect to me.

After dropping off the kids at school, I hand-delivered the piece of paper to the assistant at the office. Again, a splash of optimism sprinkled over me.

I felt a glimmer of hope. These workshops could miraculously fix our conflicting communication and parenting styles.

A week passed, and the night of the Parenting Workshop was ahead of us. Derek's younger brother, Willem, came to watch the kids. While waiting for the pizza delivery, Derek and I went upstairs to get ready.

"Do not wear heels – you'll look like a giraffe. Do not wear those sandals either. Your feet are ugly," Derek uttered as I dressed.

"I'll ignore your insults, thank you," I nodded as I returned to my closet rummaging to find acceptable shoes.

*****

An odd-shaped wood-paneled room. Two empty seats. We slipped through the rear door and tiptoed in. I wore a skirt, a top, and my funky low-heeled shoes. Derek wore jeans and a lavender button-down shirt.

We settled into our seats and listened to the speaker's introductory remarks. Half a dozen other couples were already there. A petite woman with a dark, wavy pixie haircut stood in the front of the room next to a whiteboard.

Ms. Sanchez welcomed the group, provided an overview of the series, and discussed the consequences of poor behavior.

I took notes.

"Making a case to link behaviors to consequences is critical during the tween years. Consequences resemble SMART goals.

S is for specific.

M is for measurable.

A is for attainable.

R is for relevant.

T is for time-based."

The presentation emphasized that parents must: Learn to be firm. Talk about children together. Discuss parenting styles. And, establish a middle ground.

Leaving the one-hour workshop, the outside door shut behind us.

We ambled down the path to the dark, creepy street where Derek's black van stood.

Uplifted and positive, I parked my rear end on the van's seat. Wondering what Derek had gleaned from the workshop, I hoped he had heard a similar message.

So, out on a limb, I asked, "Derek, what did you think of the workshop?"

"Well, you know, it is all psychobabble. Goals. Talking together. What is the point? Our kids are fine."

"What did you think about the speaker? She was so spunky. Too bad you thought it was psychobabble. It isn't. It is based on solid research," I shared.

I had hoped Derek would be more positive. Or reflective.

He doesn't get it, does he?

Can't he see that he is too authoritarian?

It was his way or the highway, which left me feeling like chopped liver.

Even with the psychobabble remark, Derek seemed in a good mood, at least for a few days. Life was bearable for a change.

Until workshop number two, when Derek abruptly left in the middle of it and didn't return.

I'm guessing the topic of boundaries set him off.

Embarrassed, I stayed through the lecture and learned the importance of: Setting clear rules. Ignoring mildly irritating and annoying behaviors. And the idea of writing down house rules to display in a common area.

Heading out the door that night, Ms. Sanchez motioned me over. Gazing concernedly toward me, she whispered, "I am so sorry. It must be difficult when parents are on different pages."

I thought so too, and she didn't know the half of it!

To top it off, Derek didn't pick me up. I ended up walking home alone in the dark.

*****

That's when the uncontrollable crying started. Tears were like uninvited guests who showed up at my doorstep. At first, my tears were like raindrops tapping on the roof. Then, like a torrential downpour.

Why was my heart still so heavy?

I roust my butt out of bed and sit on the patio, watching the moon rise over the vineyard. Here, in the stillness of the night, I am in awe of how a change in scenery can shift perspective. Here, I can think more clearly. Looking back now, it's easier to pinpoint when these episodes began.

My bouts of crying started right after the parenting workshop. Which seemed to get worse when Derek would tell me he was going hunting. Now, I can see my body was calling out for help. I had been trying to mend a marriage when Derek wasn't even there.

What was I thinking?

It hadn't occurred to me that it takes two people to repair a broken marriage.

Until now.

*****

Six years ago.

Suni, a former lawyer, now a full-time mom, was the first person, besides my college roommate Carla, to whom I spilled my guts.

One scorching summer day, through a mutual friend, I met Suni at the high school track field. She was new to town and had moved from Colorado.

Her daughter, Nisha's age, was in first grade at the same school. We bonded and soon became regular walking-talking buddies.

While trying to help me figure out my uncontrollable crying, Suni became a pillar of strength.

A refuge to whom I disclosed my innermost thoughts.

An angel, for sure!

[79]

Why?

Because she kept my secrets and encouraged me to seek professional help.

My marriage and parenting issues festered like a sore full of puss, unable to heal.

*****

Dr. Victoria
My Therapist
Specialty: Cognitive Processes

With Suni's gentle nudge, I decided to go to a therapist. Pastor Don, a friend and confidante, referred me to Dr. Victoria.

I remember her specifically asking me about Derek's behaviors.

So, I told her about Derek walking out of the parenting workshop, not wanting to be intimate, demeaning me regularly, and calling me mentally ill.

"Ok, Jill. That's good. Now, think of these situations and use one word to describe each."

I focused on the behaviors and thought for a few minutes.

"Cold. Disrespectful. Angry. Distant. Belittling."

She labeled these behaviors as "*bullying*." I had a hard time wrapping my head around that.

Dr. Victoria continued, "Now, Jill, I want you to tell me how you felt when he treated you this way. Use one-word answers."

I replied,

"Fearful. Hurt. Dehumanized.

"Marginalized. Angry. Sad.

"Unappreciated."

Then, a recognition of truth.

Oh, my goodness! I had not considered bullying behavior before – at least not from my husband.

This was a wakeup call for me.

I couldn't wait to return home to research this for myself. I entered *bully* into my laptop's browser.

According to www.dictionary.com, a bully is "a blustering, quarrelsome, overbearing person. Who habitually badgers and intimidates smaller or weaker people."

Yes, this sure sounded like Derek.

I needed to figure out where to go from here.

Dr. Victoria had the answer. If only temporarily, by teaching me specific visual techniques to help my brain process information differently.

So, when Derek would be mean to me, I would try to break the pattern.

And when I did, it boosted my confidence.

*****

This newfound knowledge brought a renewed sense of confidence.

Good thing I'm learning how to handle Derek.

It's about time.

Soon after, I remembered having an enlightening conversation with my neighbor Esther. She lived around the corner in the *Whispering Woods* community. I remembered it like it was yesterday.

"You hoo! It's Jill," I announced, walking toward her back door and seeing her in the kitchen.

"Come on in. The door is open," Esther howled back through the window.

I entered her farmhouse-decorated kitchen. A floral apron covered her t-shirt and jeans. She greeted me with a bear hug. *Wow. How did she know I needed one so desperately?*

A mother of twins, too, Esther signaled me to sit at her lace-dressed table. Teacups, saucers, and dessert plates took center stage. Home-baked cookies adorned a large decorative platter. The gold rim glistened on the antique teapot. Small and dainty.

Esther poured and saw the anguish on my face.

"I see you are hurting, my friend, and I want you to know I am here for you."

Finally, someone noticed me. My feelings.

I sighed, a sound of relief.

Esther, with her delicate porcelain cup, sat across from me, her eyes attentive. As my secrets spilled forth, my tea turned tepid.

She leaned toward me, "You know, Jill. This sounds a lot like NPD."

"NPD?" I asked.

"*Narcissistic Personality Disorder*," Esther explained. "They are people who manipulate others to get what they want. People who have these tendencies tend to feel more successful than they are. They want to be recognized as being well-liked. They have a need to feel they are deserving. Entitled. They often lie to create this persona of being more successful than they really are."

"I didn't realize you knew about this stuff, Esther."

"I took a course for my Doctorate in social work, and I was fascinated by this topic," she explained.

Grateful to learn about this new concept, NPD, I decided to shelve it for now, noticing the time slipping away. It is two fifty in the afternoon – time to pick up the kids from school. Oh no.

I stood up, reached for my keys, blurting out, "Thank you for listening and the lesson. I gotta go."

"Okay, Jill. Slow down. The kids will wait for you."

"Thanks for the tea and cookies. Cheers."

Walking out the door, Esther handed me a slip of paper I put in my back pocket.

Down the steps, across the path, and into the driveway, I opened my car door. I fumbled for my keys in my right front pocket.

Voila.

I pulled them out, started the engine, and put the car in "Reverse," to back out of the driveway. Clicking the shifter into "Drive," I drove toward the grammar school.

I am so grateful for Esther's friendship.

She is an angel!

I am trying, trying, and Derek is not, not.

Everyone seemed to know about Derek's personality but me.

Parking on the side street in my usual spot, I reached into my pocket and read Esther's note while waiting for the kids. She had remembered the barbeque shrimp recipe.

I chuckled to myself.

I had requested it at the neighborhood party the previous weekend.

[84]

Why can't Derek remember, like Esther? He didn't even remember Valentine's Day, nor did he remember to say, "I love you."

Folding the recipe back up, I noticed writing on the other side.

What? A divorce attorney's phone number?

Oh, no! I'm not ready for that.

I quickly placed it again in my back pocket. Simultaneously, the side door slid open, and the neighborhood kids and my twins piled into the car.

After all, it was my turn to carpool.

*****

Fast forward six years, in the middle of a therapy session. Derek turned to me, almost spitting, "You drink too much and have relationships with old boyfriends. You abandon our children when you are at your so-called religious studies."

I remember feeling dumbstruck.

Where were these false accusations coming from?

Were these his demons?

I had no idea. They were not mine because I took marriage vows seriously.

Why?

Because they were sacred.

Derek blurted, "I am only in this marriage because you are the mother of my children."

This was a pivotal moment.

It finally hit me.

Right then.

On the couch in Dr. Kate's office, I realized Derek did not love me.

Wham.

Punched in the gut.

What happened to the "I promise to love and cherish" part of the marriage vows? Except this was me. Remember? Hopeful, cheerful me.

"Well, that came out of nowhere," I muttered on our way back to the car. By this time, we weren't speaking to one another. When we did, we usually ended up arguing over something stupid.

"How, how cou-cou-could you say that, Derek?" I sobbed, quivering and stuttering, holding back tears.

"Jill, this should not come as a surprise. You are a different person. You have changed. All you do is go to Bible class. You are not pulling your weight around the house. You are bringing nothing to the table. It is quite simple, Jill," Derek sputtered. "I. Do. Not. Care. What. You. Think."

[86]

By this time, we were in the car, driving home. Shocked, I had no idea what to say. So, I said nothing.

Crying softly. Trying to keep my tears from flowing too much.

Reluctant to accept a broken marriage covenant, I held on to the hope of transformation. I simply wanted Derek to speak to me – not as a parent scolding a child, but as a husband wanting to love and honor his wife.

That was not happening.

*****

Seeing the stars in the sky above Amelia's patio reminds me of my family. All those who came before me and those in my life now.

The love in my heart should run through my veins like blood through my body. Yet, instead, it squirts out like a cut artery. With that, a shiver runs down my spine as if to hear the chilly air whisper, "Return to bed."

God loves me and for that I am grateful.

earing my kids on the phone each day is now part of an enjoyable routine. After calling them and grabbing a coffee, I walk through the glass sliders onto the patio. Leaning against the short, three-foot stucco wall, elbows on the ledge, I gaze out to the valley. For a moment, I appreciate the majestic view.

Emotionally drained from rehashing memories of yesterday, I stare at the light blue sky as, once again, memories start flooding my soul.

My mind drifts to the topic of spirituality.

Organized religion went by the wayside in my late teens and early twenties. My thirst for discovering what life and death were all about began after losing my Aunt Bet.

Aunt Bet died two years after I married.

I loved my Aunt Bet. We were close, which sparked my desire to have Zola experience some sort of loosely structured church upbringing. Derek and I didn't want to force anything down her throat. But we agreed to expose her to church or at least some religious teaching.

So, locating a loving, accepting and open-minded church (unlike the church of my childhood) was essential. This would be like looking for a needle in a haystack.

Stuffy churches with tattered draperies did not make the "go back to" list. Nor did those with tiny congregations.

Then, I stumbled upon the *Religious Cultural Center*.

Oh, how interesting.

It offered liturgical programs for children and adults, including different religious and cultural dances.

I pictured our kids' reading books about their Indian and South African heritage. Expressing worship through dance intrigued me even more. I might even convince Derek to take a class with me.

Music played an integral role at the *Cultural Center*, offering weekly programs from preschool through middle school. Anyone older joined the Adult Choir, under different leadership.

This seemed promising.

They call their Sunday service "Education Class."

After listening to Pastor Don, I knew it was the right place for my family.

It was welcoming, and it focused on the love of nature and how we are all connected. Plus, Aunt Bet would have loved their music program. It would be an honor to remember her in this way. She loved music and often sang solos at her church.

We started attending the *Cultural Center* shortly after moving into our new home. At first, it was only Zola and me. I would drop Zola off in the toddler room and then listen to the sermon in the main auditorium.

Later, when Zola reached first grade, I became her class's regular Sunday School teacher. By then, Nisha was a toddler herself.

The children were growing up, and my marriage was still floundering. I popped in regularly to grab a short chat with Pastor Don, a gentle-spirited man.

After Nisha was born, I spent more time at the *Center* and ran into Don more often, leading to a special bond between us. He soon became my kind, warm-hearted friend. Safe. Trusting.

He listened compassionately and showed fatherly concern. At one point, he recommended Derek and I see Dr. Jack.

*****

Dr. Jack
Our First Marriage Counselor
Specialty: Couples Therapy

Dr. Jack was a certified counselor, psychologist, and ordained minister. As it turned out, I followed up on Pastor Don's suggestion.

When the time came, I told Derek how unhappy I was. Making an appointment with Dr. Jack sounded promising.

Our marriage needed help.

To my surprise, Derek agreed.

So, we met with Dr. Jack for the next year and a half. Dr. Jack listened and Derek and I mirrored back what we said to each other. I didn't see any real progress. I expected Dr. Jack to provide action steps Derek and I could try out in our relationship.

However, we spent most of our time discussing parenting issues in his office. This was the only place we had a give-and-take conversation. Home didn't work. We needed a referee.

I did open up once about Derek's harsh, condescending tone. It was good to get that off my chest. Of course, Derek said he had no idea what I was talking about. According to him, I was oversensitive, and that was that.

*****

Marriage counseling brought more questions than answers. *Lake Meade Cruises,* where I worked before Nisha was born, offered an ecumenical Bible study. The group met in the conference room each Tuesday during lunch. It fed my mind and heart in a way that was hard to explain. It brought me a sense of peace. The various faith perspectives were captivating. And, it gave me hope.

Hope in myself. Hope in marriage. Hope in God.

Take Joelle, for instance.

She believed in reincarnation. Joelle was one example of a wide range of beliefs I encountered, which differed from mine.

*****

After Nisha was born, I realized I wanted and needed more spiritual nourishment. So, I signed up for two Bible studies. Pastor Don at the *Religious Cultural Center* led one on Wednesdays in the upscale neighborhood of Canyon Ridge.

The other, *Ladies at the Well*, met on Fridays at the *Spiritual Community Center*, one town over in Sun City. Over one hundred women participated in the *Ladies at the Well* program. It offered child care. These were younger ladies with growing families. Like myself, except they seemed to have healthier relationships than I did.

I knew a tribe was essential for my sanity. Thus, blending in with the group was my priority; it served as an escape from the nonsense at home.

Each week, the group met in an auditorium for refreshments and fellowship. Then, it would break into smaller groups for more intimate discussion and prayer time. There, I met Luna.

Luna went out of her way to make me feel welcome and comfortable. It was miraculous, actually. Right from the start, I felt the presence of God in her.

One day after Bible study, Luna asked, "So, Jill, you want to take a walk?" It was a lovely invitation.

"I'd love to," I replied, grinning ear to ear.

When the doors opened, the sun poured into the foyer. Its brightness beckoned us to come outside as if Almighty God were summoning us. The air was cool, and the sun warmed my face as I looked up at the heavens.

Down the community center's steps, we walked around to the rear of the building, which brought us to a cemetery. Luna knew it would be the perfect place to talk. A flower-lined path circled the sacred space. It was a mystical encounter.

Luna had been an answer to my prayer for a spiritually-minded companion. Her soft-spoken, loving spirit melted my heart. She reminded me of Mary, the mother of Jesus.

Her gentle openness invited me to share my innermost thoughts with her, and she did the same with me.

It turned out that Luna had yearned for a confidant, too. Which was no surprise in our *"Godcident"* friendship.

We talked about doctrine, intimacy, parenting, and whatever else was on our minds.

In our hallowed space, we were learning more about loss.

Loss of spirituality.

Loss of faith.

Loss of confidence.

Loss of self.

We laughed. We cried. And drank lots of herbal tea. The wisdom and prayers we shared blessed us both.

Luna was an angel!

A former lawyer, too.

*****

After listening and keeping a low profile at Bible study for the first few years, I gained more confidence and started sharing my marriage woes. Initially, I asked for general prayers, gradually becoming more specific.

*****

A lifeline.

Ladies at the Well was a group of caring women who supported and uplifted one another. They shared struggles, triumphs, and faith concerns.

[95]

Not only did they accept me, they invited me into their tribe.

Finally, I felt heard.

I found a place to be in my own skin.

Hallelujah!

It didn't matter what my marriage was or wasn't.

Or about my kids.

It was all okay.

Why?

Because God loved us.

We were the daughters of the Almighty God. Who could argue with that? An unstoppable power brewed in this tribe. Prayer summoned Angels.

"Deliver us from evil," we prayed.

Angels swooped to deliver us from demonic shackles.

Chains dropped off our hands and feet. God was doing a mighty work.

Faith wasn't about rigid doctrines. It embraced the essence of love, where compassion transcended religious boundaries. These prayer warriors became my sounding boards. My friends.

Together, we embarked on a spiritual journey, contemplating the meaning of scripture and sharing our personal reflections.

Our ups and downs in life.

Our stories, experiences, and concerns for our children.

We prayed.

And prayed some more until a spiritual presence intertwined us like a fine tapestry.

*****

As the weeks turned into months, I found food for my mind and spirit. A kind of Eucharist. Something to soothe my soul and provide spiritual nourishment.

The group seemed like a living expression of this beloved sacrament.

Spirituality overflowed in my heart seeping into every inch of my being. Much like Holy Communion.

It gave me the strength and courage to face the marital challenges I'd avoided for too long.

*****

A profound transformation occurred. The layers of judgmentalism that had once clouded my vision peeled away. This cleared a path for more empathy and understanding.

Yet, my marriage was still weighing on my mind.

I had to focus on my faith.

I had to trust in the Divine to figure this out.

[97]

Like someone lost, I was wandering in the desert. Trying to find water for my soul. There, at the *Ladies at the Well* group, I could be myself.

Each week, renewed to face a new week.

Thirst quenched.

*****

Eight years later, my twins were in kindergarten. It was time to return full-time to the workforce. With my marriage disintegrating, I updated my resume and tested the waters. Earning more money would offer me options.

Initially, I had hoped I would fix my marriage by staying home after Nisha was born.

Why?

I wasn't sure.

But I suspected Derek had wanted me to stay home after having Zola. He seemed to resent the fact that I hadn't.

So, I decided to become a stay-at-home mom after having Nisha.

Looking back now, I missed this red flag.

Red Flag #1

Consumed in our careers, Derek and I hadn't thought to speak to one another about our first child, Zola. We didn't discuss what returning to work, or not, would look like after she was born. How would this affect our careers?

It was a failure for both of us.

I had the feeling Derek wanted me to stay home. Yet, I had a good job that I loved. I juggled Zola and working full-time until I had Nisha. Then I became a stay-at-home mom, working part-time.

Three years later, the twins arrived. And then, about two years later, the whole "fixing my marriage" part unraveled. My marriage was slowly sinking into quicksand.

Returning to work might help re-balance my spirit and loosen our family's financial bind.

But how exactly would that work?

My paycheck from *Lake Mead Cruises* had gone into a joint account I could not access.

Why didn't I have access to it?

I hadn't a clue.

Derek had decided I should have an allowance. That's right, an "allowance."

What was I, a twelve-year-old?

I knew early on there would be a massive difference in our respective earning powers. Whether it was Derek, Larry, Moe, or Curly, he was a man, and for that reason alone, he made more money than me. That was life.

Female salaries were lower than male salaries.

Hands down.

And, God help us, they still are.

Generally speaking, of course.

So, this whole "equal pay" crap goes out the window in the real world.

In marriage, you hope you have a shot at a fifty-fifty relationship. But, back then, the math didn't add up.

It still doesn't.

But something wasn't adding up. In the past, I had received stellar job performance appraisals. Then, at the time, I was waiting for callbacks from the hundreds of resumes I had sent out. Yet, I only landed three interviews in six months. Which left me discouraged, depressed, and esteem-deprived.

I tried looking at the bright side but couldn't see one. That was until I thought about launching a massage therapy business.

How paradoxical (and excellent) it would be to channel my negative energy into something positive that had been in front of me all along!

Why not?

My experience teaching massage therapy part-time for the previous eight years should count for something.

And then it occurred to me:

I could network and begin building a client base.

So, after all my employment applications hit a dead end, I realigned my energy.

*****

It was early in my marriage on a random day in the kitchen. We were cooking a holiday feast when eighty-year-old Aunt Ati (oddly) said,

"Take some of the food money and hide it. Someday you'll need it."

She warned me privately.

I hadn't mentioned this to anyone. In fact, I did not even know what Aunt Ati meant.

Or why in the world would she even say that?

All I knew was this. She was warning me about something. About what, I had no idea.

She has since passed into another world. For the rest of my days, I will wonder what life experiences taught Aunt Ati this gem of wisdom.

*****

Derek had been the primary breadwinner for our entire relationship. So, it was no surprise when he conveyed a strong impression that *"our"* income belonged to him. And he thought it was up to him to decide what to spend it on.

"Jill, don't you think I earn enough money to run this household?" he asked in a huff.

"Yes, Derek, of course I do. But starting my own business will take money."

"I don't understand why you feel the need to go back to work, Jill. Working part-time is enough. Why do you always want more and more?"

"Derek, I don't always want more and more. It's time for me to invest time in building a business. Soon, the kids won't need me as much."

"Look, Jill. I am doing the best I can around here. I don't see you working your ass off, like me," he snapped.

"Oh, are we going down that road, again Derek? Really?"

"I'm out of here. I need to clear my head!" he said storming out the door.

As usual.

I wanted to start a business to get out of this hellhole. Without Derek's help, I wasn't sure how it would happen.

Then, it dawned on me why Aunt Ati cautioned me about saving money.

Ah ha!

Realizing I didn't have any, it all made sense. That's when I decided to use some of *"our"* money to enroll in a "Start Your Own Business" course.

But who was I kidding?

There was no *"our"* money.

*****

My stomach is rumbling; it's time for lunch.

Lunch?

I still need to eat breakfast.

I forage through Amelia's refrigerator and heat up the shrimp and vegetable leftovers. Adding a scrambled egg to the skillet would make it become more of a brunch.

As it cools on the plate, I dart into the bedroom and pull a thin, pink hardcover book from my suitcase. It is the journal I created during my pregnancy with Zola.

I flip to a note from a few years ago.

Dear Journal,

I am the glue that keeps all my loved ones together. My parents, my aunts and uncle, my siblings, my children, and my in-laws. But emotionally, it is such a heavy load. I am hanging on by a thread.

The collywobbles start when the kids say the exact same nasty words Derek does. And, each time the collywobbles roll around in my stomach, it takes longer and longer for the anxiety to go away.

After lunch, I head back to the patio and try to make sense of my life.

On the patio, the warm breeze encourages me to stroll through the valley. Tying my sneakers and putting the key in my pocket, I heed its call.

Walking and thinking go together like peanut butter and jelly. Keeping on the sidewalk, I hold my head high, nodding at a few people walking their dogs.

It is such a nice neighborhood with friendly people. The air is different here; it has an earthy smell.

Thoughts drift back to my life, my marriage, and my collywobbles.

*****

My marriage continued to be a battlefield, unlike my safe places. Pastor Don's bible study and the *Ladies at the Well group* were my refuge from the verbal missiles and emotional bombshells flying through the air.

One day.

It was fall.

It was chilly. The leaves were falling on the ground from the giant oak tree in the backyard. We were in the middle of a heated discussion in the kitchen.

[104]

"Derek, please leave. Let me take care of the children, and you can stay with your cousin, on the other side of town. Oh, I forgot, you can't stay there because you haven't spoken to him in three years! Why is that?"

"Jill, you know my cousin cheated me out of five thousand dollars, the swine." Derek's voice was becoming shrill.

"Derek, you gave him money to bet on a horse! What did you expect?"

"He said it was a sure thing, Jill. I trusted him."

"I'm sorry, Derek. Go back to your parents, maybe they can help you. Just. Get. Out! Our constant arguing is hurting the children."

The veins in Derek's neck started to pop. His face turned red as he spewed, "I will not leave this house, Jill."

He pointed his finger at me, waving it up and down in my face, blurting out, "Whether you like it or not, you are stuck with me. You know that, right? You know you cannot leave me because you need me, right? If you leave, you will never be able to see the children again."

My eyes filled with tears. My body shook as I sobbed uncontrollably.

I grabbed the car keys, ran out the door, climbed into my car, and drove to the police station.

My safe place.

In my car, in the parking lot. I cooled down and returned home.

Not saying another word.

*****

The following day, Phyllis, a divorced parent of one of Kobe's classmates, saw me drop the twins off at school. We waved "Hello" to each other.

The next day, she hand-delivered *Divorce for Dummies* to me in a plain brown paper bag. She told me that she instinctually sensed something was a bit off yesterday. I call it a woman's intuition.

Although Phyllis' situation differed from mine, she thought the book could be helpful. She was right.

Phyllis, a registered nurse, worked full-time. So, at least she had income.

But wait a minute.

She might not have had access to it if she was like me.

The story goes that her husband, charged with insider trading, was now in prison. He had ruined his employer's reputation along with his family's finances.

In a way, she was lucky. Phyllis didn't have to separate herself from him. The state had taken care of that for her.

Not so for me. Which left me with two choices to consider.

[106]

Leave Derek and move into a shelter with the children. Or, leave the children with Derek, and find a temporary place to live.

Was I really thinking about splitting up with him?!

A shelter didn't sound like a good idea. Not only would it be far from home, but the logistics of getting the kids to school seemed daunting. I was already falling to pieces.

My goal was for them to have the least disruption. Thus, the best solution was for them to remain in their home with their own bedrooms and belongings.

In my heart, I knew Derek would provide for their material needs. After all, Derek was a gambler. A good one, too. Over the years, he had accumulated gambling winnings I simply did not have.

Derek managed our bank accounts, and only he knew how to access them. Unable to withdraw any money, my well had dried up.

Not only was this arrangement untenable, it was wrong, wrong, wrong.

I felt stuck.

To get unstuck, I read *Transitions* by William Bridges. His message to me was clear.

Before anyone could move forward, there had to be closure. Meaning I needed to resolve personal issues, situations, or problems.

That made sense. Leaving the marital home might be the only option.

But not today.

*****

Back home from the walk, I return to Amelia's patio, appreciating the view of the serene valley. The breathtaking vista and the ugliness of my life contrast sharply.

Quite the disconnect.

Gloom and defeat descend on me. It is as if Derek had squashed me like a bug. This is not unusual. His criticisms often lead me to shut down. It's my defense mechanism for coping with his hostility and negativity.

How can I regain my self-esteem, self-worth, and free spirit?

To me, these are oxygen that I need to breathe. I'm sure of it.

Leaving the marital home is the only way I have a shot at this actually happening.

It will not be easy.

But that is a risk I am willing to take.

It is time to break the cycle. I should have ended things years ago. Again and again, I tried to make it work, but Derek wanted no part of it.

I have to do this, whether I like it or not.

*****

Two years prior, Lorina, a friend from our Summerlin town pool, offered me a room in her empty nest home. It had three bedrooms, two bathrooms and was less than a mile away.

Hoping the offer still stands, I am ready to consider it. At the very least, it could be a place to stay while Derek and I try to work out our marital woes.

As my stomach growls, I head into the kitchen for an afternoon snack.

Peel a banana and plop it into the blender.

I add almond milk plus protein powder.

After a loud whizzy whirly noise, my smoothie is ready. I pour the drink into a tall glass with ice and visualize taking Lorina up on her offer – what an angel!

She was such a generous person to offer me a safe place. Not only that, but her close relationships with the members of her blended family suggests a reason to feel hopeful.

Hope sure sounds good.

There is something special about the sun beating down on my body, as I return to the patio. The warmth caresses my skin like a cozy blanket. Beads of sweat run down my neck as I reach for the iced tea on the side table.

Seeing the ice in my glass made my body shiver. Instantly, I remembered a specific time in my pregnancy with Zola.

I had felt alone.

Uncared for. Even though Derek lay beside me.

It had been Labor Day Weekend. A few hours earlier we had checked into Milo's Bed and Breakfast. It was a significant work event I had planned for months. A certain anxiety filled the air.

It was a major fundraising event for the corporate board of the Boulder City Hospital. As the special events director at *Lake Meade Cruises*, I oversaw the entire Rediscover Research Weekend. Since I was pregnant, I wanted to ensure perfection for this event. I didn't want any special treatment because of it.

I chose a dude ranch venue. There would be horse trail rides, horseback riding lessons, and a crystal cavern tour. Some free time, of course. Varied meal options and the highlight of the weekend, the gala dinner cruise.

The cause supported research on craniosynostosis, a rare congenital birth defect. The bones of the skull knit together, causing severe deformity. It was my job to pull this event off without a hitch.

I could not sleep well the evening before the gala because Derek had turned up the air conditioning. Four months pregnant and shivering. I was shaking under the sheets. It seemed like Derek's new mantra was, "Thou shall not make love to your pregnant wife."

*****

Condensation drips from the iced tea glass onto my neck. It tingles.

I rub the glass on my face, then sip.

The contrast of the cool drink against my hot cheek reminds me of wild pregnancy hormones.

The food aversions. The arousals. The emotions all over the place.

It was natural for a pregnant wife to feel aroused.

Wasn't it?

But there I was night after night, wondering when Derek would touch me again.

I remember having a hard time processing that.

Especially in the context of my expectations; after all, my dad said that all boys want sex – all the time.

*****

The nuances of intimacy confused me.

I was brought up with the notion that sex before marriage was wrong. Yet, I wondered for years what that really meant.

Did that mean the actual act only? Or Parts of it?

Or the whole process of getting there?

Pastor Juan, didn't seem to have a clue, either. I remember asking him about pre-marital sex when I was sixteen. He said, "Sex is between a husband, a wife, and God. Young people who are not married should absolutely not be alone."

Well, that was that.

His answer left me to fend for myself in trying to figure this whole sex thing out.

*****

Today is flying by, and it is now mid-afternoon. After a quick shower, I decide to meander around to find the farmer's market. It's supposed to be somewhere around

Amelia's home. I'll explore the vicinity in the process and stay close by. I don't want to get lost.

I run the checklist in my head.

Cellphone? – Check.

Wallet? – Check.

Keys? – Check.

After a short drive around town, I spot the farmer's market. I follow the narrow street that winds through the park. The market is easy to spot.

The vibrant colors.

Bright red tomatoes.

Deep orange carrots.

Royal purple eggplants.

And, of course, local wines. It really is a sight to see. I pick up a few fruits and vegetables for dinner. Of course, a bottle of local wine, as well. After returning, I grab my pink journal and head to the living room.

*****

Keeping a journal aided me in processing information. It served as a sounding board.

Isolated from friends and family, there was no one to talk with nearby. So, keeping a journal provided comfort. Not necessarily for Zola but more for myself. It served as a safe place to record my worry, fear, and anxiety.

[113]

The commute to work in Boulder City back then was about an hour's drive. By the time the weekend came, physical and emotional exhaustion had set in.

Writing in a journal was something I looked forward to.

*****

Clutching the tattered pink book, I settle in on the cream-colored loveseat. I flip the pages and begin to read my thought of long ago.

Dear Baby,

Lately, I have been a little sad. I'm scared for the future of your dad and me. We may not have what it takes to be a happy family.

I have been lonely, as your dad has ignored me for many months. I know I should respect how he feels – but I also think getting no physical attention is ridiculous. I feel resentment, knowing I'll have to alleviate that emotion myself.

I thought life would be different than it is now. I want a soul mate – not a housemate…

My work fills a void. Why am I afraid of giving it up? What should I follow, my head or my heart?

Regardless, your father and I will love and care for you.

Love, Mommy

Remembering the anxiety I felt, writing to my unborn child, a shiver runs down my spine.

I was pregnant.

The newness.

[114]

The unfamiliar.

The heightened senses.

The morning sickness was not only in the morning.

It was in the morning, noon, and night.

I thumb through a few more pages to three days later, precisely one week before Zola was born.

I had written my thoughts to God.

Dear God,

Why is Derek appalled by my big tummy?

Growing a human within is a sacred experience. Yet, I feel as though I have the plague. I never imagined this! I expected more compassion, respect, touching – caressing, and kissing. Being pregnant doesn't mean I have lost my physical urges. If anything, they have intensified. Maybe I'm trying too hard or expecting too much. What if my "condition" turns off Derek? All I know is it makes me so sad.

Please help me to understand why Derek is this way. Guide me, Oh, Lord. Fill my heart with more love and patience. Thank you for the miracle of life.

Amen

I pivot and put a pillow behind my back. After closing the pink book, I place it on the side table.

✳✳✳✳✳

Glancing up at the ceiling in Amelia's lovely home, a waterfall of memories cascades through my mind.

Not all was gloom and doom.

For instance, there was a time when Derek and I bought butter pecan ice cream in different stores. We came home at the same time and laughed our heads off.

Then, there was the time he bought me a thoughtful gift. It was a curved pillow for my back when commuting from Boulder City when I was pregnant with Zola.

It did not take much to make me sparkle. A little sex, a kiss, a cuddle here and there, and helping with the dishes now and again.

Was that asking too much?

*****

Back to reality. It's time to hustle and make dinner.

Into the oven at 350 degrees goes a vegan meatloaf with the vegetables I bought earlier.

Amelia walks through the door fifty minutes later as the timer goes off and asks, "What smells so good, Jill?"

"It's meatloaf," I reply, grinning. Waiting for the wine to reach halfway up the glass, I ask, "It does smell heavenly, doesn't it?"

As I placed the wine bottle down, Amelia put her briefcase on the counter, and I handed her a drink.

We sit down for dinner at the table with fine dinnerware from the hutch.

"Fancy, shmancy, Jill," Amelia accentuates exaggeratedly. "The table looks great. Thanks for dinner."

I giggle, "Don't thank me yet; wait until you taste it first."

"Well, why don't I do just that?" Amelia laughs as she reaches for the silver fork beside her plate. "Lovely, Jill. How do you make meatloaf taste so good? What is your secret?"

"Since you are almost family, I'll tell you. It is three things: red wine, cocoa powder, and oatmeal."

"I wouldn't have guessed that at all," Amelia said, fascinated by the ingredients. She adds, "I'll have to write those down – they are different, that's for sure."

Changing the subject, Amelia asks, "How are you settling into the guest room?"

"Fine, in fact, it is magical. You have a lovely home, and your guest suite is well-appointed. My favorite area is the patio, where I can sit on the lounge chair and enjoy a cup of coffee. Thank you again for this. I am beyond words."

"I'm glad you like it, Jill. I know you are going through a rough patch and I want you to feel welcome and loved. Speaking of love, or maybe not, where are you in your thinking about Derek?" Amelia asks this in a caring, sister way.

"I'm leaning toward separating because I can't stand the yelling and the name-calling. What's worse is Zola and Nisha are starting to parrot Derek.

"So, listen to this. Derek and I signed up to attend a series of workshops on parenting your tween. There I was, trying to gain insight into tween behavior, and Derek behaved like a toddler. Walking out the door in the middle of the second workshop was not cool. I had to walk home in the dark! It was embarrassing, to say the least."

Amelia nods her head in agreement. "Dan used to walk out on conversations whenever I suggested he do this or that." She rolls her eyes adding, "Before long came the yelling. He would yell at me and call me dumb."

"It sure does sound like a pattern," I replied. "I know it all too well."

"Dan used to jump my bones, too. Like – all the time. At first, it was fun. Eventually, it became a chore. It was one-sided. I didn't like it."

"Oh, I can't wrap my head around that one, Amelia. I would kill to have Derek initiate sex. It is so weird. My dad told me all men want '*it*' all the time. Not Derek. He has no interest in '*it*' at all. It makes me wonder if I am the one with a problem. Maybe I am. Do you think? Amelia, tell me." I plead for some sort of answer.

"Sex is a hot topic for most couples, Jill. What does your therapist say about it?"

"Good question. Dr. Kate recommended Derek have a physical to determine his hormone levels. I'm sure you can guess how that went. Men!"

"No argument here, Jill," Amelia empathizes.

We take a breather as we clear the table. I excuse myself to call and check in with my family.

*****

"Hi, Rebecca. How was your day?" I ask, hesitating. "Everything okay?"

"Hi, Mom. After theatre camp, we all went to the zoo and had fun with Dad and Grandpa. Grandpa Ro fed the penguins. Those penguins were so funny, all dressed up in their black tuxedos. Mom, it was hysterical seeing Grandpa feed them. Ha-ha. That was funny – right, Mom? I gotta go – I have to practice my lines for the audition. Goodnight, Mom."

"Goodnight, Pookie – love you to the moon and back."
I hung up the phone.

There was no other news to report on their end, making the call shorter than expected. So, Amelia and I go for a walk.

*****

[119]

"Amelia, I don't know how long I can go without affection. The lack of physical attention is driving me mad," I confess as we walk around the neighborhood.

"You can't make someone want to be intimate," Amelia explains. "Do you think he is seeing someone else?"

"I don't know; Derek says he has been taking weekend trips to the hunting lodge. I want to believe him, but I also want to be smart about this."

"If Derek isn't having sex with you and is going away on weekends, I'm afraid he is doing '*it*' with someone else. It looks pretty clear to me, Jill – I am so sorry."

With quiet compassion, Amelia reaches for my hand to squeeze. The caress of her hand was warm – it was exactly what had been missing.

We return and settle into the living room to watch television.

Two hours later, we say our goodnights, tired from a long day.

After changing into pajamas, I crawl into bed.

Today was emotional – and unsettling.

GOD HATES DIVORCE, RIGHT?
DAY 4 ~ MORNING

Wishing the kids a good day was my first priority this morning. It was a quick call because they were all rushing out the door for their activities. Shortly after, Carmen, my new friend from the flight to San Franciso, called and extended an invitation to Wild Bill's. Excellent. Her call lifted my spirits and made me realize I was a person beyond a mom.

*****

Carmen and I decided to meet after she finished her shift at the hospital. I had one hour to grab something to eat, shower, and change into something respectable. I snap into action.

Into a white skort I wiggle. Then, pull over a sleeveless black top and walk out the door.

Nothing is more elegant than looking polished in a white and black apparel combo.

The first order of today's outing is to drop off a memory card with 467 photos at the pharmacy.

Then, I drive into a nearby parking lot, park at the perimeter under a tall oak tree, and wait for Carmen to call.

[121]

Locating each other by cellphone, we chuckle as we realize we are on opposite sides of the street.

A short while later, we arrive at Wild Bill's.

Once inside, we stroll up and down the aisles together, sharing a grocery cart. Carmen, like me, values a healthy diet.

I like that.

Giggling like teenagers, we rate items on a scale of one to five.

Approaching the one-hour mark, we each leave with an entire bag of groceries. Grateful for the fun experience, we hugged and said our goodbyes.

Back at the photo pharmacy, I pick up the photos. I can't wait to take a peek at them.

*****

After a delightful morning at Wild Bill's, I find my way back to Amelia's. As I unpack the treasures found, gratefulness fills my heart. I grasp each cold item to place in the refrigerator.

Grateful for my new friend Carmen.

Grateful for Amelia.

Grateful for food and shelter.

My heart shifts to the pouch from the drug store. I smile.

[122]

As I finish up putting the groceries away, my heart begins to pound a bit faster.

I can't wait to see what these photos reveal.

The images beckon me to the living room, where I can sit and savor every minute of this task. The photos from the six large envelopes are stacked on the dining room table. I carefully take each picture and place them in a row, one by one. Each one, expressing a significant moment in time, is a story in itself.

Vacations, school events, and activities.

I pause to reflect on a few of them further, with a nagging thought of doubt. Are these pictures telling the truth? Or are they masking the pain of an unhappy family?

Four hundred photographs, I count.

With sixty-seven missing images, where are the rest?

It will take days to figure out which sixty-seven are missing.

I gingerly place them back in their envelopes and head into the guest room to change into more comfy clothes.

*****

With the perfect photos still in my mind, I reflect on the story behind them. Here, in this quiet space, I confront the truth. My mind replays the captured moments.

The forced smiles.

[123]

The sad eyes.

It's all an illusion. Now, it's time to face reality.

And so, I ask myself:

Do I love Derek?

How can I love someone who causes me emotional pain?

If I don't, what is that telling me?

The religious implications of a divorce, not to mention the societal ones, have prevented me from going down the road in front of me.

Continuing my thoughts, it doesn't matter that I don't have all the answers. I'm feeling led to meditate on gratitude. So, that is what I do.

I inhale God's grace and exhale gratitude.

I am grateful for this sacred space. Thank you, God for my health, my children, and for Derek. Please help me come to terms with my failing marriage.

I open my eyes, flip up my laptop, and do an internet search. Since faith is so important to me, I start with this. My fingers type two words on the screen, *"Christian divorce."*

A millisecond later, these words pop up from thelaboroflove.com:

There are some circumstances in which most people would agree that divorce is the inevitable result. When one of the partners in a marriage, whether it is the husband or it is the wife, is physically or emotionally abusive, and unwilling or unable to get treatment for the abusive tendencies, divorce is often the most common result. A man or a woman who is in physical danger from their spouse should not stay with them. Even the most conservative of religions that look at divorce as being taboo tend to see divorce as a reasonable step in the case of physical abuse. An abusive spouse who is unwilling to get help will never change on his own; when this happens, it is probably time to end a marriage.

– thelaboroflove.com

As I read these words, I realize that sometimes faith calls us to protect our own well-being. For ourselves and our children. And to embrace growth, even when it challenges our beliefs.

*****

Protecting my children is paramount. Sure, it would be nice to have kids grow up with a mom and a dad in the same home. But at what cost?

Exposing them to constant arguing and put-downs feels wrong. It makes me sick to my stomach thinking about this. But, despite the turmoil, my faith keeps me afloat. Spirituality offers me solace and eases my soul. Like the Old Testament story about Hannah in the *Book of First Samuel.*

In the story, Hannah is barren. She desperately wants a child. She prays her heart out, and shortly after, the praying woman and her husband, Elkanah, make love. Nine months later, after many years of being childless, she gives birth to a son named Samuel.

There it is.

It's the praying her heart out I attune with.

I identify with her.

Like Hannah, I am a child of The Almighty, who has access to a sense of inner peace. If Hannah can put her trust in God, I can surely put my trust in God to keep my children safe. I will continue to pray as Hannah did. My life and death are in God's hands. I trust my faith will prevail.

SECRET NUMBER TWO
DAY 4 ~AFTERNOON & EVENING

Feeling a bit off after the busy morning at Wild Bill's, an uneasiness sets in that triggers digestive issues. Observing the masked faces behind the photos from earlier today, creates pain for me. It's as if my heart is signaling my brain to wreak havoc on my body.

So, I make a cup of tea and jump back into bed. Chamomile, of course. This tea usually does the trick. It often calms me. As my collywobbles subside, I return to the eggshells I've been stepping around for the past few years. Like, not knowing when Derek would lash out at the children or me. I vividly recall one day, when he had too much to drink, he punched the wall and broke his hand.

The scene seared itself into my memory as it replayed in my mind.

Derek's fury.

My vulnerability.

Why didn't I call the police?

I was a wimp. Understandably so. Ashamed. Afraid.

What might he do to me?

I feared for myself and our children.

[127]

How could I have married such a man?!

In my eyes, I was a failure.

Failed as a mother.

Failed as a wife.

Were the failures mine alone?

How could Derek have so much control over me?

Did some of the responsibility lie with him as well as me?

*****

The hidden truth bubbles beneath the surface.

Meanwhile, the room's silence wraps around me like a warm blanket. A few steps away from the bed, I pull a water bottle from the mini-fridge.

As I consider these questions of failures, fear, and overall turmoil, the secret hidden within the walls of our home starts to emerge. The revelation culminates in a crescendo. It festers like an unattended wound throbbing from the presence of a hidden infection.

Sipping from the water bottle and gazing at the ceiling, a specific memory surfaces in my mind. I call it the "decorative wreath" episode. This memory unfolds as though I were aboard a boat in unchartered waters. Not knowing where the voyage would lead. There was no map to follow.

"Derek?" The sound of his name produced anxiety.

[128]

"What?" Derek responded in a terse yet familiar way.

My voice wavered. "The wreath. Where is the wreath I placed on the front door?"

Silence hung in the air.

A moment stood still.

Derek's eyes grew cold.

Distant.

His face wrinkled with disgust, "I discarded it in the trash, where it belongs. The wreath is hideous! Why do you buy such ugly stuff?"

*****

Secret #2

Derek loved to call the shots. There was no doubt about it. Everything had to run through him. It was as if he got a "kick" out of saying "no" to me.

Initially, Derek's confidence and quick decision-making skills swept me off my feet. He could seize control of any situation and take action. It was impressive to see how he would step into a problem and resolve it with authority. Like when Zola was born. He marched over to the nurse's station, demanded a roll-away bed, and stayed the night.

Over time, however, these same traits revealed undertones of control and manipulation, making me feel isolated and powerless.

[129]

Then, on the rare occasion when we did socialize, Derek would humiliate me.

Dr. Kate said his behavior was rooted in an obsession to exercise power and control. Over me.

*****

You wouldn't think everyday tasks would be a big deal. But, in our house, it was.

After dinner, I would ask, "Zola, please empty the trash can under the sink."

Derek would say, "Your mother is too lazy to do it."

Don't let him get the best of you, Jill.

I remember clenching my jaw, forcing myself to take a slow breath, as Derek's words felt like fingernails scraping on a chalkboard.

"I've told you before, Derek, please not in front of the children."

The next evening would roll around, and after dinner, I would ask, "Nisha, please empty the trash can under the sink."

"Your mother is too lazy to empty the trash," Derek would snap. "Your mother is incompetent. She does not have the time to do it!" He continued his rant, "Boo-hoo. Are you not able to manage your time, Jill?"

This time Derek was more melodramatic than usual.

Mind you, I had worked a half-day, done the food shopping, and picked up the kids from school. I was dog-tired.

Yes, sir.

Dog-tired.

Funny, Derek would ask the kids to empty the trash when I wasn't around. I wondered if they ever thought he was lazy. Why in the world did Derek think I was lazy? What did I ever do to make him believe this? Did I play video games every night after dinner? Or did I clean the kitchen?

*****

Sipping from my water bottle, I recognize how important it is for my children to learn that everyone needs to pitch in and pull their own weight. Derek doesn't. This leads to battles every day. About the importance of the kids picking up after themselves, preparing their own sandwiches, and making their own beds.

Our kids need to learn these things. End of story.

I'm still trying to figure out why Derek disagrees.

*****

Derek has better organizational skills than me. Like making beds, cleaning pots and pans, and knowing where personal belongings are.

Me?

Not so great.

But Derek doesn't help me.

All the while, I'm thinking we ought to work together and encourage each other and our kids to be tidy.

Keys? Glasses? Wallet?

Derek seethes every time I'm searching for an item.

"If you would keep them in the same spot, you would not be wasting time looking for them. You would notice exactly where they are!" Derek would snap.

What are the kids learning from all of this?

Whatever it is, it isn't good.

*****

It's now mid-afternoon. I don't need a clock because my stomach is growling and the afternoon sun is streaming through Amelia's windows.

I turn on the television and search for a station playing classical music. I find a nice one. My belly rumbles as I whip up a tuna salad sandwich on whole-grain bread.

So, there at the kitchen table, eating my sandwich, I reflect further. I ask myself.

What do I expect? Well...It would be nice if my husband acknowledged my homemaking skills. Appreciating me could mitigate some of these horrible feelings I have.

That would be a great first step.

[132]

*****

At the kitchen table, my plate empty, I remember the harsh words Derek said to me with a sigh. With eyes on fire, he called me a bitch. The incident came back to me, as if it were yesterday.

It was a random morning, before school.

We were all in the kitchen.

Derek sipped his coffee, engrossed in a magazine.

I was pouring orange juice at the kitchen table. Zola and Nisha, free-spirited as ever, were throwing their underwear toward the twirling ceiling fan.

The kids were giggling.

My eyes rolled up. I smirked. Thinking, these kids are so funny.

Right then.

Derek glanced up from his hunting magazine, and saw the commotion.

Out of the blue, and out of his mouth came, "You incompetent bitch! You call yourself a mother? Do you see this? The children are running around naked. Do something! Can't you do anything right? Huh? Huh? Huh?"

Dumfounded, I remembered thinking, "What is wrong with him? Let our kids be kids!"

*****

[133]

Shortly after, a new storm emerged, pointing to another red flag. The tray incident.

Red Flag #2

"Derek, where is the wooden tray I bought last summer? I swear I left it in the hall closet."

"How should I know?" Derek replied.

It must be my lucky day. Oh, goody. A scavenger hunt. I need this like a freaking hole in the head.

Down one flight of stairs to the basement, the hunt begins.

Nope. Not there.

Up three flights to the attic, I skim the shelves.

Nope. Not there.

Back down two flights of stairs, and through the laundry room, into the garage. It has to be somewhere.

There it was – in the garage, still in its original packaging, warped from the heat.

I stormed into the house, "WHY is the wooden tray in the garage?"

"I do not like it! It is ugly. Like you! I plan to toss it out on trash night." His eyes pierced through me like a knife. "How many times do I have to tell you I am in charge here?"

Did he say trash?

Maybe my warped marriage needs to be tossed into the trash, too.

[134]

I brew a pot of coffee to enjoy on the patio for a change in scenery. With a fresh cup of coffee, I find my favorite chaise and settle in. Where was I? Oh, yes, the fight over the "wreath." The confrontation over the "wreath episode" was just one example of Derek's control over our home. Another was how he controlled our finances.

Since he handled the checks, it didn't dawn on me to find out how to access the money. I didn't have much in my measly checking account. Due to the fact that, most of it went to pay off college loans and wedding expenses. My weekly *"allowance"* that Derek gave me covered the children's incidentals and personal items.

Bam.

It hit me.

Without realizing it, I had become utterly dependent on Derek.

*****

Money.

Most couples decide what, where, and how to spend their money together.

Don't they?

Wouldn't they discuss buying new fishing and hunting gear or hiring a personal trainer?

Or private piano lessons or private school for the kids?

Or how much money to spend on the basic necessities of food and clothes?

These types of conversations rarely took place. When they did, they devolved into a parent-scolding-a-child lecture. Leaving me empty and void of emotion, with my husband making all the decisions.

It didn't make sense.

My younger sister, Polly, was aware of her family finances. She paid the bills when her husband was away.

So why didn't Derek do this with me?

Why didn't he ask for my input in the decision-making process?

I was independent and savvy; I opened my first checking account at age twelve.

But that was then.

Until a few months ago.

I took my friend Elena's advice. She was a neighbor friend and a former lawyer specializing in couples' mediation. What a godsend. She simplified legal information for me. Her advice and words of wisdom were inspiring.

We agreed on a barter system.

Her professional advice in exchange for massages.

A win-win situation.

I opened up my own banking account. One Derek would have no control over.

It was a big step for me.

Once again, God had placed an angel in my life to guide me through the most complicated decision I ever had to make. Elena pointed out the iron grip Derek had on my life. If I was going to reclaim any of my lost independence, I would have to start standing on my own two feet.

*****

Hearing the garage door open, I jump from the chaise to greet Amelia. She arrives holding a white package with dinner inside – a burger for herself and a vegan burger for me.

"Tada," Amelia announces. "Dinner has arrived."

It had been a busy day, so we were glad to be home and have a bite to eat.

Grabbing two beer bottles from the wine refrigerator and napkins, we sit at the dining room table. I thank Amelia for dinner and spring up to set the table.

After a nice meal together, I excuse myself to check in with my family. Reporting back after a few minutes, I say, "All is good on the family front. They are still alive."

I slide back into the groove. To celebrate that my family is still in one piece, we decide to drink more beer and play cards.

"There is something I want to talk to you about, Amelia," I say as the beer loosens my tongue.

"It's about crying. I'm not much of a crier. But lately, I've been crying every day after dropping the twins off at school and don't know what to make of it. Has this ever happened to you?"

"No, Jill. I must say I have never experienced it. But my mom cried uncontrollably after my dad died."

"All I know, Amelia, is that my body is trying to tell me something I already know. I feel like a broken record, I'm sorry."

"Jill, no apologies necessary. I'm so sorry you are going through this. I know it seems unmanageable. But please trust me, it will get better. Although it will get worse before it gets better, it will get better."

"I sure hope so. Here is another question for you. Did you feel invisible with Dan?"

"I don't think so. Dan was selfish. He only thought about himself. He was oblivious to me and my feelings. My ex didn't want to hear about my life. So, I guess, in a way, I did feel invisible. Do you feel invisible with Derek?"

"Incredibly so. I'll tell you a quick story about my friend, Carla, who was visiting a year ago. We decided to rearrange the furniture in the living room. You know, move the couch from one side to another and place the chairs perpendicular to where they were. We also mixed up the picture frames on the wall. We had so much fun, giggling as we tried pointing the chairs in different directions."

I pause. Then, picking up from where I left off, I said, "After our re-decorating escapade, we went to the grocery store. When we returned an hour later, Derek had moved everything back to its original position! And, when I asked him about it, he growled at me.

"He said, 'I will do what I want. You are not the boss of me! I am in charge here, remember? Good thing I did not make YOU put everything back to where it was before YOU messed it up! Gee willy, Jill, get a life!'"

Saddened yet relieved at the same time, I continue confiding my story to Amelia.

"I felt so unseen right then and there. Like I didn't matter. I have been living with this for many years now."

Whew.

It feels good getting this off my chest.

"Jill, you simply can't continue living in a situation like yours; it'll kill you. You know I have your back. You can stay with me for as long as you wish. I also know you have a family and must figure this out. I wish my bills weren't so high keeping this place up; otherwise, I could help you more. Let's sleep on this, Jill. I'm exhausted, and by the looks of it, you are too. Goodnight. Sleep well."

"Sounds like a plan, Amelia. Goodnight." Walking down the hallway and into the guest room, I turn on the radio to a classical music station.

Hoping it will lull me to sleep.

THE SINGING CARDS
DAY 5

I call my children and check in with each of them. A little later, after hanging up the phone, it dawned on me that, on the day after tomorrow, it would be Father's Day. With four hundred photos to choose from, I'm sure I will be able to find pictures of Derek with each of the kids. Bear in mind, I am the one that takes most of them.

Oh, crap! I don't want to send a "happy" anything to Derek. It is so hard to play this charade. Yet, I still feel obligated to send something in the mail to Derek. He is a father. More importantly, he is the father to my children.

I sit at the dining room table with several large packets of photos. Thirty minutes later, I select four perfect pictures for a Father's Day gift.

These photos were from last year while we were vacationed in La Jolla Shores, California.

What remains, of course, is to shop, find, and purchase photo frames.

Choosing a photo frame is easy for most people but not, of course, for me, the perfectionist. I'm working on that aspect of my life. I am letting go and trying not to "sweat the small stuff."

With that in mind, I begin my search for the perfect frames.

*****

As I gather up my belongings, with the selected images, I wonder why on earth am I even doing this! Then, I realize how important it is set a good example. Despite my ill-feelings I begin the hunt.

My quest at a big box store begins as I search for horizontal, matted, double-hinged picture frames. I see photo insert cards along the way, but my current mission is picture frames. It isn't long before I find some lovely frames, though not four by six horizontal ones, only three-and-a-half by fives. Opening my green knapsack with the orange piping, I take the prized photos out. I try to match them to the frame.

Will they work?

Nope. Ugh.

The images do not fit, so I leave the store and walk next door to another shop. They carry photo frames; it is a hit-or-miss. Today results in a miss.

Yikes.

Ample signs hang from the ceiling as I enter another store farther down the road.

There. To the left. A sign reads "Stationery."

Off I go.

When I arrive, I scour the two shelves of frames.

None of them will work.

Bummer.

On my way out, I take a side trip to their Misses department. My luggage has plenty of room for new treasures.

There is no point in passing up the opportunity to peruse the clearance racks.

Wait a minute. I remember watching Suzie Orman teach women to think of themselves as NOT on sale.

Hmm. Another defect of my personality needs work.

I adjust my thinking.

From: *I **should** get this, so what if it's snug or baggy? It's on sale.*

To: *I will **only** buy them if they look great. It must fit and look fabulous.*

*****

Back in the car, I run the checklist in my head, bringing my search for the perfect frame to a screeching halt.

Time is running out.

I'll miss the post office's four o'clock cut-off time if I don't find something soon.

[143]

I return to the big box store to find the Father's Day cards with the photo inserts. They are the only choice at this point. I'm glad I am solving the gift dilemma, albeit imperfectly, but the photo insert cards will do.

Turning my car around on Napa Valley Way, I enter the parking lot. I skip straight to the kiosk of Father's Day cards. I find the photo insert cards.

What? I am aghast. The cards sing when opened.

This is the last straw.

What on earth will I do now?

I like the singing cards, yet I *know* Derek will not like them.

Noticing a greeting card specialist stocking cards on the rack, in my sweetest voice, I inquire, "Do you have any non-singing photo insert cards?"

"No," the specialist replies. "These are all we have."

I take a moment to digest no non-singing cards are available. Realizing the day is ending, I buy four unique, singing photo insert cards. If I drag this on any longer, they will not arrive by Father's Day.

*****

Exiting the parking lot, I search for a post office. My eyes catch an American flag waving from a giant flagpole.

Indeed, it is a post office.

Reluctantly, I decide to send the pictures in the mail since it would mean a lot to Derek. I am still trying to be the perfect wife and mother. However, more and more, it is becoming challenging to do so.

Walking into the sparkling, spotless post office, I find the rack with supplies. A few people are standing in line.

I need a pen. Why don't I have one?

I usually keep a pen in my bag.

But where is it now?

Somehow, it vanished.

The people in the post office appear frazzled and hurried. There I am, standing alone. An out-of-towner in the post office, combing each nook and cranny for a pen.

How silly.

I search the racks and counters again. Nothing except the express packets and slips. Zippo. Nada. Zilch.

I breathe a sigh of disbelief.

How can this be?

So, out the door, I bolt.

Next on the hit list is finding an ATM. An empty wallet lies in my purse after the shopping spree at Wild Bill's and the Misses clothes department.

Time to refill.

I find a drive-through ATM and withdraw one hundred dollars.

Behold, an idea.

Realizing banks have pens, I become joyous, circle, and park my car. I enter the bank carrying my plastic bag with four photo insert cards and envelopes.

Sure enough, a pen is right there in the bank lobby.

What a relief.

I take the cards out of the bag, open the first one, prepare to write, and it begins to sing.

Loudly.

Time freezes for a moment.

You can hear a pin drop.

Mortified, I don't dare peek at anyone.

How fast can I write? I need to be faster.

Whew. I finish.

Stashing the cards back into the bag and returning the pen to its chained holder, my heart drops.

Once again, my master plan crumbles before my eyes. I will still need to find a pen to fill out a mailing label for the Mail Express package.

I'll cross that bridge when I get there.

*****

I brush the potential defeat off myself and speed to the nearest Mail Express location.

Ten minutes pass.

I ask the salesperson how much it will cost to overnight the cards down to Las Vegas.

"Zip code, please," she replies. A moment later, she announces, "That will be forty-six dollars."

"*I don't think so,*" I whisper to myself.

I ask the helpful salesperson for a piece of paper with a polite smile. Noticing the shocked expression on my face, the salesperson begins to read from notes. She explains how rates are going up every day due to the high cost of gas.

Paper in hand, I thank her and walk to the workstation.

Taking the paper, I write a lengthy note wishing Derek a quadruple Happy Father's Day. I address the label, write in a return address, and voila. It is ready for the mail.

Returning to the car, I insert the photos into the chirping cards.

At least, here, I am embarrassed alone.

Next, I find a different post office – this one is only a block away. It is on the other side of the road, of course.

California is well known for its turn-arounds.

U-turns to some.

Which often proves to be more of a hindrance than a help.

[147]

Once again, turning the car around, I pull into the post office parking lot and enter the building.

Wow, what a difference.

This post office is not only well-stocked, but it is overflowing with pens, tape, and paper. My faith in post offices is restored.

I wait in line and ask how much it would cost to mail my cards to Las Vegas.

"Sixteen dollars," the clerk announces.

"Thank you."

So, there are three options at this point. The first one is forty-six dollars guaranteed delivery tomorrow. The second is sixteen dollars priority with a possible delivery by Father's Day. And, the last one is three dollars and eighteen cents regular snail mail to arrive in three to five days.

A little voice in my head reminds me to check with Derek. Usually, Derek wants me to call him each time I make a financial decision.

This isn't about a home décor piece or rearranging furniture. But I'll call Derek anyway, so he can feel superior to me and stroke his ego. He likes that. He'll probably yell at me, so I better prepare myself.

"Hi Derek, It's me. I have a quick question for you. Do you have a minute?"

"Go ahead, I am listening."

I imagine him rolling his eyes and glancing out the window.

"I need to mail you Father's Day Cards. It's Friday. Should I mail them guaranteed express for forty-six dollars, and you'll get them tomorrow? Or priority mail from the post office for sixteen dollars, and hopefully, they'll arrive on Sunday? Or snail mail them knowing you won't get them until the Tuesday or Wednesday after Father's Day?"

"Send them regular snail mail and spend the forty-six dollars on a delicious meal for yourself. Jill, I have to get back to work."

Click.

So, that is what I do.

Chuckling, I pay three dollars and eighteen cents and release my prized cargo to the postal worker. Derek can be kind and generous when he wants to be.

Are we on the same wavelength at this moment?

Aww. I remember why I had married this man.

*****

On the ride back to Amelia's, I continue to rehash my relationship with Derek and the meaning of Father's Day.

Again, I ask myself *why I am sending Father's Day cards to him.*

Why?

For the sake of the children, of course!

"Do unto others as you would have them do unto you." *(Matthew 7:12).* Taking the next forty-five minutes, I ponder my current level of angst. I realize I am confused.

I have warm feelings towards Derek when he's been acting like a jerk – what's happening here?

On the one hand, he's not all bad. Yes, he can be good sometimes. But he's been mistreating me for years.

So, which is it? Is Derek good? Or bad?

This devious dichotomy is driving me nuts.

It is a black-and-white type of thinking, which isn't me at all. I am a pure gray thinker through and through. Or am I? *This is what I came up with:*

I'm nice – Derek is not.

I'm accommodating – Derek is not.

I try to see both sides of an issue – but Derek does not.

My feelings hurt easily – Derek's don't.

I am spiritual – Derek is not.

I love liturgical dance – Derek does not.

Let me think about this.

I see all of this as black-and-white thinking!

This calls for a readjustment. Now.

Here goes:

Derek and I have moments of kindness, unkindness, and everything in between.

We ebb and flow, accommodating each other's needs – although one of us ebbs and flows more.

Derek and I have communication issues – a gray, murky area. I am afraid to start a conversation with him because it might end with name-calling. Making me feel horrible about myself.

We have different feelings, concerns, and sensitivity levels when disciplining our kids. I try to be composed and work out a solution. He doesn't.

Derek lets me drag him to church to hear the kids sing in the choir. I attend church for the solitude and peace it provides me – if only for an hour a week.

Derek is not interested in dance. But he enjoys attending the children's dance performances.

Derek believes in authoritative discipline, and I prefer to train by example.

Derek has anger management issues. He is not interested in learning alternative parenting strategies.

It's not quite as black and white as I thought.

*****

Back at Amelia's, after my Father's Day expedition, I continue to mull over these questions.

What else adds to my angst?

Cooking three different meals: morning, noon, and night.

But why do I do this?

To accommodate a limited food palate and food allergies. Derek wants me to cook only one meal and make our children eat it, whether they like it or not.

I can't do that.

My parents required me to taste one bite. If I didn't like it, I made myself a peanut butter and jelly sandwich. Which I did from time to time, which makes more sense than tying a child to a chair and forcing them to eat.

Another problem area is what I will call a "social mismatch."

I want to host dinner parties, and Derek wants nothing to do with it. The truth is, when we have company over or go out in public, Derek is on his best behavior. This creates a much more harmonious environment.

Who wouldn't want more of that?

It is a tough place to be, and our parenting styles consistently clash, adding to the angst. I remember trying to have a conversation with Derek before I saw Dr. Victoria.

It went something like this.

[152]

"Derek, why do you need to yell at the kids and scare them to death?"

"It is important to show them who the boss is, Jill. I am. Clearly. It is me who has to discipline them because your wishy-washy parenting style isn't working."

"But, Derek, Zola is having respect issues at school. What are you going to do about it?"

"I'm sure she is fine, Jill. Zola has to stick up for herself. She is a smart kid and gets good grades. Leave her alone."

"All I'm saying is we should balance our approaches. Ease up a bit. Listen to them and encourage them to do chores and take responsibility."

"Why, Jill? Because you are too lazy to take care of the house? Eish, Jill. I am done with this conversation."

*****

Our dinner plans tonight include Amelia and her friends. As I dress for dinner, I wonder why I am reluctant to go. Because, at some level, I think I don't deserve a nice night out.

To me, it is frivolous.

But why am I feeling this way? I have no idea.

It may have to do with my parents.

Hmm. No surprise there.

My parents tried to create an insular world around our family of everything they deemed "Christian." From an early age, I read *The Bible*, prayed, and distributed religious tracts. There wasn't time for anything else.

Movies or playing cards were no-nos.

Yet, I remember buying a deck of cards to play with my mom. My dad was the one who didn't want us to play cards, but I knew I wouldn't go to hell because of it.

I am convinced my dad finally figured this out somewhere along the way, too.

So, why do I feel that I don't deserve to have nice things?

My upbringing had a lot to do with that.

Some time ago, my therapist helped me recognize this, too.

Jill, you seem to believe you aren't entitled to a sense of happiness, pleasure, and joy. You have this idea: every time something good happens to you it must be followed by something negative. So, for example, if you feel happy when you've bought yourself a new dress, you think it is necessary to feel guilty about it afterward. I call that "stinkin' thinkin'", Jill. And I don't believe it's doing you any good.

– Dr. Victoria

As I place the past on the shelf, my mood brightens. I find myself at the restaurant with Amelia and her friend, Joan. Tina, another friend of Amelia's, meets us there for a party

[154]

of five because Louanne, an old friend of Amelia's, might join us a little late. Louanne has a habit of agreeing to come, yet often does not. Hence, our party of five will probably be a party of four.

We order margaritas.

Not too tart. Not too sweet.

I order Ahi Tuna and a salad with no dressing, which is delicious.

Midway through dinner, Louanne arrives and slips into the conversation.

The dinner ends with separate checks for everyone. The waitress splits the drinks across the bills.

How brilliant.

I had yet to see that done before.

I feel like I just fell off the turnip truck.

It is hard to believe this is my first time out with the girls in a few years. Louanne leaves after dinner. Joan checks the schedule online and sees that *The Sentinel* begins at seven thirty-five.

The rest of us drive from the restaurant to the cinema.

"Eight dollars and fifty cents, please," the cashier announces in a high-pitched tone. We sit in the last row of the small theater with a handful of people in the audience.

Toward the end of the movie, my cellphone vibrates. Derek's name is on the screen.

But of course, not knowing it at the time, I think the worst: Derek needs to reach me. It must be important.

I excuse myself and walk to the rear of the theatre to answer. It turns out Rebecca is calling to tell me she is lonely. I sigh with relief and chuckle as I explain I am with Aunt Amelia at the movies.

"Oh, Pookie, I'm so sorry you feel lonely. How about sleeping with Mr. Koala Bear? He loves you and will keep you company until I come home next week. How are your lines coming?"

"It's a slow go, Mom. I've done two read throughs, so far."

"That sounds awesome. Keep reading. The more you go over it, the more you will learn the scenes. I love you. Can I talk to Dad?"

"Okay. I love you, too, Mom. Here's Dad," Rebecca says.

"Namaste, Derek."

"How was your dinner with the girls? I hope you did not overeat. You do know you are fat, right?" Derek says in a half-joking tone.

"I'll ignore your insult, thank you." I snap back. "Dinner was great, and it was a buy-one-get-one-free margarita night."

"Enjoy the rest of the evening, Jill. Say hi to Amelia for me, will you?" Derek replies, trying to redeem himself.

"Sure, Derek. Have a good night. Kiss the kids for me. Cheers."

When the movie ends, a tired Tina decides to return home after a long, tedious work week. She told me she worked in a law office earlier in the evening. She assisted with helping families who had lost their homes in the mudslides.

Oh, my goodness. And here I am, taking a break from my family while other families lost their homes.

It is a somber moment.

As I lay in bed that night at Amelia's, I think: *What a comical yet complex day this has been: The singing cards. Not finding a pen. Derek tells me to mail the cards and use the saved money for dinner. Later, spending the money on dinner with Amelia and her friends. Our night out was so much fun.*

Then, I learned about the families who lost their homes. They must be devastated. Those husbands allowed their wives to decorate their homes. They didn't throw their tables, chairs, or Tiffany-type lamps in the trash as Derek did. I feel sad for those families who lost their physical homes. And for my own family, who live amid emotional chaos every day.

MEAN SPIRITED & GRUMPY PEOPLE
DAY 6 ~ MORNING

I t's Saturday. It is a leisurely morning and too early to call the kids. I shuffle into the kitchen to mix my dark sludge, which I bring back to bed. The soft yet firm mattress cradles my body like a big hug.

My mind wanders to Derek and his brother, Willem.

Derek and Willem are polar opposites, much like our twins are. And, now that I think about it, my brothers as well. If genetics don't play a role in how children end up being alike or different, what does?

Unlike Derek, Willem is a big teddy bear filled with humor, love, and kindness. He welcomes conversation.

Derek, not so much.

What makes someone distant, strict, and controlling?

And others inviting, loving, and kind?

I can't picture Willem giving the belt to one of his children.

Or disrespecting his wife.

I open my eyes, stretch my arms and legs, and close my eyelids again. How do family traits pass from generation to generation?

[159]

Specifically, how can mean-spirited and grumpy parents raise mean-spirited and grumpy children? Who, in turn, may well end up having more mean-spirited and grumpy daughters or sons of their own.

Raised in a grumpy family?

I didn't think I was. Grumpy? No. Strict? Yes.

It is hard for me to be around mean-spirited people. My religious upbringing, my parents, and my faith are probably why.

*****

Mean spirits fill my home – Derek, my kids, even me. This sense of negativity has turned me into something I don't like. The cycle needs to stop.

Take family chores. Derek and I are polar opposites. Since we can no longer afford a cleaning service, Derek expects me to do all of the housecleaning chores. Since I believe we all need to pitch in, and Derek doesn't, our discord further separates us.

For goodness' sake, there is nothing wrong in wanting the kids to help. They are getting older, and I want them to learn to do laundry, cook, and clean. I cannot fathom why Derek feels I should do all the chores alone. Nor can I understand why he doesn't want the children to learn these tasks.

It makes me feel like I am Cinderella.

Kneeling on the floor and scrubbing it while Derek, the stepmother, barks orders.

*****

My thoughts on genetics, family traits, and chores fade as I step onto the patio.

The fresh air will help me think.

As I settle into the chaise I notice the beauty of the blue sky. Okay, it is time to tackle the elephant in the room. Namely, the loss of my mind and my crumbling marriage. I ask myself these questions.

Is Derek maliciously planting evil thoughts of inadequacy into my mind so I will go off the deep end?

Is this his way of trying to control me and my emotions?

Does he want to paralyze me with fear so I will forever depend on him?

Is he removing my financial resources so I have nowhere else to turn? If so, is he doing this consciously?

Are these imaginings true? Or are they a defense mechanism for my own survival?

Is the family dysfunction caused by the devil or some demonic force?

I sure have a lot of questions.

By this time, I am convinced that Derek no longer loves me or even cares.

What a lousy place to be.

*****

Shifting my legs on the chaise, I confront the monster squarely in the face.

One year ago.

The air thickened. It was the hush before the storm, the quiet before the crescendo. The grenade in hand, ready to toss.

Dirty dishes stacked in the sink. The kids were upstairs getting ready for bed. I stared out the window, rinsing the dishes for the dishwasher. Derek called from the bonus room, where he was watching the news.

"Jill, get me a beer. Will you?"

"I'm in the middle of doing the dishes."

"I don't care. I want a beer."

"Get it yourself. My hands are wet."

It was the first time I spoke back to Derek, like that.

Derek rounded the corner and screamed, "How dare you talk to me that way! I am the king, here. You do as I say. You are a pathetic brick!"

My face grew red with anger. I wanted to throw something – anything. I was afraid – afraid of Derek, but, more afraid of the fury rising up in myself. So, I did the most logical thing I could do: I left.

[162]

I grabbed the car keys and stormed out of the house. "I'm taking a drive. I'll be back later," I muttered.

"*You are a pathetic brick,*" played in my head.

Driving to the police station parking lot, I sat in my car feeling safe. But angry. Alone in the dark parking lot, I tried to settle down. Between the tears and the madness, my mind wandered to another incident. It was from earlier that day while I was pruning the rose bush in the garden.

Derek snarled out of nowhere, "You are scum and not fit to be a mother. You are not good enough!" His voice uttered coldness and cruelty as if he hated me. It was the same sharp, scolding, repetitive narrative on an endless loop.

I don't understand why Derek speaks to me this way.

You are scum, Jill, my thoughts answered. That's why.

Stop it, Jill! Stop listening to these lies.

YOU are good enough!

Shame and guilt washed over me.

Jill, get a grip! There is nothing for you to feel shame and guilt about.

I felt like I was losing my mind with all that yelling echoing in my head. How can I make it stop? Panic set in until it occurred to me.

I need help. I need to talk to someone. Who can I call?

Think, Think!

[163]

Carla!

Yes, I can call dear, sweet Carla. She will know exactly what to do.

In desperation, I grabbed my phone to call her, my best friend from college. She was the only person who knew firsthand how Derek treated me.

"Hello?" she sounded surprised and sleepy.

"Carla, it's me, Jill." My voice was shaky and hoarse. "I'm, I'm so, so sorry to disturb your evening. Derek and I had a huge fight, and I am done!" I started to hyperventilate. "I can't take one more minute of this abuse." I heard her gasp on the other end of the line.

"Jill, are you okay?"

"No, I'm really not okay. I think I am having a panic attack."

"Okay, Jill. Calm down. Take a deep breath. Breathe with me. One, two, three. Inhale. Hold. One, two, three. Exhale. Okay, Jill. You are doing great."

My slow breaths started to calm me down.

"Where are you?" Carla asked anxiously.

"I'm, I'm at the police station," I stuttered. "Don't worry, I'm safe in my car in the parking lot."

The tissue from the door's side pocket absorbed the wetness from my eyes.

[164]

"Safe from what?" she asked, sounding alarmed. "Did Derek hit you? Did he hurt you?"

"No, no, he didn't hit me," I answered, shaking my head as if Carla could see me. "He doesn't hit me. He says mean things to me."

"Like what?" she asked softly.

"Right to my face, he told me, 'I'm a pathetic brick and I was stupid.'"

"That's awful. Derek has no right to say that to you. You are not a pathetic brick, Jill. Get that right out of your head. You're an incredible woman and a great mother. You are kind and beautiful, hear me?"

"Thanks, Carla." I sniffled, feeling a little better. "You are a good friend; I appreciate you trying to calm me down."

"You better go home, Jill."

"I want to leave."

"Leave? Jill, think of your children." Carla's voice pierced through my angst.

"I am thinking of them!" I snapped back. "They deserve a happy home, not, this."

"Jill, slow down," she said firmly. "You're not thinking clearly right now. You're very emotional. Take a breath. God knows what's best for you and your family. Let's pray quick. Okay?"

[165]

"Uh-huh."

Carla prayed,

Dear God,

Please wrap your loving arms around Jill and let her calm down. Keep her safe and let her know you are beside her as she figures out what to do about her situation.

Amen

*****

After years of trying to figure out what causes a marriage to fail, I asked Dr. Kate. She explained it simply. My marriage was a generational and psychological disaster of a relationship. Later on, she shared her case notes with me. They said:

Jill's inadvertent and subconscious attraction to Derek stemmed from the sexual abuse she experienced as a child. At some level, Jill felt she was unworthy and was unknowingly seeking mistreatment.

Equally disturbing, Dr. Kate further analyzed:

Derek's subconscious attraction to Jill stemmed from the abuse he saw as a child in his own family. At some level, Derek felt unworthy and was, therefore, unknowingly seeking power and control in the marriage.

Dr. Kate's insights shed light on the deep-rooted psychological dynamics within our relationship.

*****

Carla lived in Iowa and stayed overnight from time to time. Even before Derek and I met, she had been there. Carla related to me on a profound level, understood my dilemma, and knew this would be a hard battle.

She knew about Derek's secret power and control tendencies and was the only non-family person to witness this.

Encouraging me to vent and pray, Carla became my sounding board. Another confidant with whom I could share my woes. She offered unwavering support during this challenging time.

An angel!

*****

Back at the police station parking lot, I started the car and drove to a nearby park just down the road.

I wasn't ready to go home yet.

I didn't want to go home ever again!

I'd better call my mom. I knew it was late, but she would be up.

I was sobbing in my car, when I dialed her number and waited for her to answer. I quickly composed myself.

She picked up right away.

As usual.

"Hello?" She sounded surprisingly chipper at this late hour of the evening.

I said in a crackling voice, "I'm sorry to be calling so late. Mom, I can't believe it!"

I burst into tears.

"Pookie, what's wrong?"

"I think it's over between me and Derek. I can't go on."

Unable to hold back the tears, I poured out my heart.

I explained what had happened with Derek, and everything he had said and done to me. Everything I had been keeping bottled up inside of me spilled out.

"I'm so sorry you are going through this."

"Thanks, Mom."

Mom's tone became serious. "I'm here for you, Jill. Whatever you need, whatever you decide, I'm on your side, now and forever. But I have to tell you something. I wondered when you would call me about this."

She caught me off guard. Stunned, actually. How did she know? What did she mean?

"I've known something was wrong with your marriage for a long time. I saw it in your eyes. Your voice. Your behavior. You thought you were hiding it from me. But I can read you like a book. After all, I am your mother."

I breathed a sigh of relief.

No more hiding.

*****

My mom understood my plight.

It took me years to figure that out.

A few days after spilling my guts to Mom, I called Esther for her lawyer's contact information. Esther said Sarita Sandeep was one of the best attorneys in Nevada.

It took three weeks to get an appointment with her. I met with Ms. Sandeep to discuss what, if anything, I should do next. We agreed telephoning Derek would be a good idea. The call would allow her to gauge the situation to determine how open and receptive he would be to a sit-down meeting.

At the time, I knew I was not ready for a divorce but I wanted the disrespectful behavior to stop. I wanted to protect my children. Separation, not divorce, sounded good to me. I had no idea how Derek would react when he received the phone call.

At that point, I believed he could harm me.

His sheer height, hunting skills, and guns gave me goosebumps.

My concerns were justifiable.

I feared for my life and felt Derek hated me so much he might do something rash.

Whether rational or irrational, my fear felt real.

*****

I turned to my Bible, as I often did when sad, lonely, or at my wit's end, and prayed.

Dear Lord,

I am so fearful right now. I surrender my life to you and ask you to direct my path. Only you know what is in my heart.

Show me, oh Lord, your goodness and mercy. Speak to me, bring me peace, and let thy will be done.

Amen

The Psalms provided encouragement to me.

I pushed my thumbs inside the middle of my Bible. The *Psalms* opened to Psalm 27.

My eyes widened as I read the words.

The LORD is my light and my salvation; Whom shall I fear? The LORD is the strength of my life...My heart shall not fear; ...In this I will be confident.

– Psalm 27:1-3

Ah. I needed not to fear. There it was. What a relief.

Confessing once again my inner struggle, I found a divine confirmation, an answered prayer.

*****

Despite the solace I found in my quiet time with God, tension built within me like a cork jammed into a champagne bottle. Soon afterward, Ms. Sandeep scheduled her call to Derek. I braced myself for what would unfold.

It was a Thursday morning.

After dropping the children off at school, I busied myself with errands, anticipating the attorney's call at nine o'clock. I couldn't bear to be near the house when the bomb dropped.

I had already pictured scenarios where Derek would hire a lawyer, possibly bringing a new and welcome peace to our family. Could this be my ticket to heaven? Would it coax Derek into treating me kindly? It would be a wake-up call, wouldn't it?

As I returned home, my collywobbles began to do somersaults.

Then, the unthinkable happened.

Derek began ranting and raving. He vehemently opposed the idea of hiring a lawyer. "They are thieves!" he roared.

What was I hearing? He didn't want to hire an attorney?

This was not what I expected.

At all.

I thought he would jump at the chance of a separation. Instead, I had to think fast and offer an alternative or we would never get to the root of our marriage problems.

So, hesitantly, I suggested, "Maybe we should consider seeing a mediator?"

Derek reluctantly agreed.

Swiftly, I scheduled an appointment with a mediator named Marcus.

Well-spoken, he got right down to business at our first meeting. He started by asking us some very basic questions. But it wasn't long before the session spiraled out of control as his questions grew more complex as they dug deeper into our marital strife.

Suddenly, it felt like we were in the middle of a warzone. Verbal missiles were shooting in all directions.

Finally, Marcus called a truce. "I cannot help you until you can sit in the same room and act civilly toward each other," he said in exasperation.

Gaining his composure, Marcus turned to us. Tilting his head, he asked if we would commit to another counseling session with his colleague, Dr. Kate.

He told us that she specialized in helping couples with communication issues.

Derek agreed.

What? Again? You have got to be kidding.

I reluctantly said, "Sure." Marcus then told us he would make an appointment on our behalf.

The following week, we found ourselves sitting in Dr. Kate's waiting room. It was our first time at her office.

It was small and cozy with a sound machine making white noise plugged into the electrical socket in the corner. Her Doctorate Degree hung on the wall. It read *Summa Cum Laude* from Harvard.

Wow. Impressive. I sure hope Miss Smarty Pants can work miracles. Am I really considering staying with this guy after he humiliated me in front of Marcus?

"You must be Derek and Jill. I spoke to Marcus and heard an earful about the two of you. Come in." Dr. Kate motioned for us to enter her office and take a seat on the black leather couch.

"It's nice to meet you both." Taking a deep breath, she sat upright and leaned toward Derek. Without missing a beat, she said with a look of disgust, "You screwed up.

"Where do we go from here?!"

Wow! I'm gonna like this lady!

I saw the light bulb go on in Derek's head.

He finally realized he might have something to do with the sorry state of our marriage.

There may be hope for us after all.

*****

[173]

A year had passed, and forty therapy sessions later, Derek and I found ourselves communicating more civilly. Yet despite the progress, our emotional intimacy had evaporated, like a coin dropped into an empty well.

I recounted my childhood traumas, but Derek hadn't confronted the demons lurking in his soul. His lack of introspection hindered our path to authentic connection, leaving us more like housemates than spouses.

The name-calling had faded in my memory, except for the *dumb brick* remarks. Derek was trying to bring me into the decision-making process; yet, at the same time, he was resistant. What he did do was to choose his words more carefully. It seemed he genuinely wanted to please me.

Not in my wildest dreams had I anticipated we would be here, together, in spite of the threats he had made about divorcing me. He still wanted me as his wife.

This left me grappling with conflicted emotions.

As my head spun, I questioned whether I wanted Derek as my husband.

Puzzled by his wishy-washy behavior left me torn between, *he loves me. He loves me, not.*

Well, which one was it? Or did it even matter?

THE BIRD MOMS
DAY 6 ~ AFTERNOON & EVENING

Lifting my head off the chaise lounge, I check the time on the thick, black-rimmed clock on the exterior wall of Amelia's house. It is almost two in the afternoon.

Oh my.

My cluttered mind must focus because today is a special day. I will meet an old friend, Sandy, my former next-door neighbor, for an early dinner.

Emerging from my thoughts, I rise from the chaise lounge and shake off my fuzzy thinking.

I shower, dry off, and slip into a sleeveless sheath multi-colored sundress.

I am so excited.

I haven't seen Sandy in well over ten years. I run the checklist in my head.

Cellphone? – Check.

Wallet? – Check.

Keys? – Check.

Knapsack? – Check.

It is a short drive to the River Bend Plaza, where we had agreed to meet on the Promenade.

[175]

"Namaste, Sandy. It's good to see you again. How have you been? You look a bit tired," I said hugging her.

"Hi, Jill. It's good to see you, too. I am tired. I'll fill you in after we order our meal. Sound good to you?"

"Sure. Let's go."

There is a lot to catch up on.

A short distance away is Grace's Table, a small café with a Boho vibe. We sit on the outside patio overlooking a fishing pier. In the distance, several people fish, and a young boy is on a bike. Seagulls line the railing on the dock, and a fishy smell permeates the air.

First, we each order a Citrus Super Shandy, a refreshing beer mixed with lemonade. The tangy, lemony taste of the Shandy swirls in my mouth as the cornbread wafts a sweet aroma from the hot skillet.

I order a spinach salad with salmon, and Sandy orders a Kobe burger and two sweet iced teas.

Two sweet teas?

My lips button up, and I let the cloud of my own snap judgment escape out my ears. The waterside view washes the atmosphere with a sense of calmness. It opens the doors to a personal conversation that seems so natural for two friends to share with one another.

"Sandy, tell me what's going on?"

"Well, to be honest, Jill, I've struggled a lot lately. I have hypothyroidism, which means my thyroid gland doesn't produce enough hormones to regulate my metabolism."

"Oh, I'm sorry to hear that."

"It makes me feel depressed and lethargic. Like I don't want to do anything. I don't sleep well, either. I've gained a few pounds, which doesn't help."

"That's awful. Sounds a bit like my adenomyosis. It causes heavy periods that wipe me out. It's a constant struggle."

"What the heck is adenomyosis? I've not heard of that."

"It has to do with endometrial tissue in the uterus. Basically, the lining of the uterus grows into the walls and causes the uterus to expand. It is worse during my period."

"We sure have our share of health issues, don't we? Being a woman is complicated, for sure," Sandy says.

"Oh, yes, for sure. Adenomyosis. Derek doesn't understand it nor does he want to. He ignores me and tells me it's all in my head.

"Really? No. My head is not my uterus. Ugh!

"Can't he see how tired I am and how I'm affected by this and the anemia every day?

"Sorry for the rant, Sandy. I guess I'm trying to say I totally get where you are coming from."

"My periods are under control and one less thing to worry about. It's keeping my thyroid condition in check. I have to take medicine, and when I forget, depression hits. Fast and hard," Sandy divulges.

"Depression. Tell me more. What is it like for you, Sandy?"

"Jill, it's hard to explain. It is a heavy feeling all over your body. It's hard to get out of bed in the morning. I feel sad and cloudy as if I were seeing through a fog. It's hard to focus, too."

"Oh, my, Sandy. It sounds terrible. I'm so sorry you feel this way."

"It is. Most people don't understand how debilitating it can be. If only people would see it as a medical condition, which it is. More people would be empathetic. Don't you think, Jill?"

"Well, what I can say is, it reminds me of Derek and people like him who think we make this stuff up. He doesn't want to understand. It's frustrating."

"Derek doesn't seem supportive at all, Jill. Maybe counseling could help?"

"We've been in counseling for years. It is not a healthy relationship. I'm trying to wrap my head around the possibility of separating from him. I think it might knock some sense into him. What do you think?"

"Well, Jill. It might work. Or he'll take it as a threat and attack."

"Attack? What do you mean?"

"I mean, he might get physical and lash out at you. He might try to make you feel guilty and manipulate you into staying. He might say you are being selfish. Or unfaithful. Or he might get violent."

"Violent? Not really. Derek has a bad temper, that's for sure. And he takes it out on the kids, which breaks my heart. He calls me names and throws my things away. He's even threatened me by saying, if I leave, I can never return."

Shaking my head. I continue.

My voice shakes slightly. "It scares me and makes me feel worthless. Not to mention helpless."

"That's not acceptable, Jill. That's emotional abuse. You deserve respect and love, you know."

"Thank you, Sandy. You're a good friend."

"Anytime, Jill. I'm here for you. I'm only a phone call away. You are not alone in this. You are loved, and you have a great support system in place."

"It makes me feel so helpless. Let's change the subject.

"I'm curious. So – Sandy, what happened with Precision Tools?"

"Well, Jill, hang on to your hat. You remember that we met because I had moved to Las Vegas to be near them, right?"

"Uh-huh."

Sandy continues, "Well, then they decided to move to California. Ten years ago, already. My job was safe – except for the fact that it was moving all the way to California. But, since I had nothing holding me back, I decided, what the heck?

"But, five years later, they went out of business, and I lost my job."

"That sounds horrible. I'm so sorry to hear it."

"It was hard for a while because of the struggling job market. I ended up piecing a few part-time jobs together to make ends meet. It was tough. That was when I found out about my thyroid issue."

With our plates cleared, and the bill paid, I suggest a short walk on the boardwalk.

"Sandy, I don't want our visit to end. Let's take a few minutes to enjoy the simple pleasures of life. How about we see the awesome pre-sunset from the pier?"

"Sure, Jill. I could use the exercise."

"Me too, Sandy."

There's a nice walking path to the pier, where we find a bench to sit and admire the vibrant colors before us. Then, we find a set of stairs that lead to beneath the pier, where we stroll and chat more about our lives, where we came from, and where we are now.

*****

Sandy grew up in Red Lodge, Montana, where winters were long and frigid. It was a long drive from Henderson.

She settled into a second-floor apartment on Washington Avenue. And that's where we met. We lived next door to each other in the reddish-brown brick Tudor apartments. The building with the large crank windows hid behind a circular driveway.

We were bird moms.

Sandy's bird was Max, and mine was Millie.

It was convenient when one of us worked late or needed to be out of town for a few days – the other would care for the birds. Knowing Sandy would care for my beloved Millie in my absence, I worried less.

That was a good thing.

*****

The sun is setting, and I sense our time together is ending. Sandy has a long drive ahead of her.

[181]

On our way back to the parking lot, she shared she will move to Colorado soon.

"Oh, Sandy, I'm glad you'll be closer to your sister. When do you move?"

"I plan to move after the summer. I'm really looking forward to being closer to my family. It'll be nice to have more support. Let's make sure we stay in touch better, okay?"

"Yes. Let's make sure of it!"

We hug and kiss and return to our respective cars. As we part company, we promise to do just that.

I go through my checklist. All good.

Sandy drives away, and I head back to Amelia's.

*****

As I turn onto the highway, I notice how calm I feel. The radio is playing classical music. After a busy day, the solitude is welcome. I smile as I reflect on my time with this dear old friend. Even with the challenges that we are both facing, it is clear that we care for one another.

When the radio goes to a commercial break, I turn it off and call the kids. It's good to hear their voices. I say goodnight and toss the phone on the passenger seat.

With the darkness of the night and the glare of oncoming headlights, I focus on the trip home. Each traffic light resembles a firework display with a haze of colors emanating from a central focal point.

Despite the steering wheel feeling sweaty from my tight grip, I return safe and sound.

Walking down the hall, I wave to Amelia and see her watching a movie. She pauses the film, and I tell her about my visit with Sandy. After offering a goodnight and sleep-tight wish, I head to the guest room.

In a flash, I undress and slip beneath the covers, exhausted. Lying in bed, I rehash the conversation I had earlier with Sandy.

I have come to the following conclusion. The man I married: Doesn't love or respect me. Threatens and scares me. And makes me sad.

*****

I roll over, and my thoughts shift to Sandy, Amelia, Carla, and Suni.

My friends. My support network.

I reflect on the past few days and how blessed I am to have friends like Amelia and Sandy. They have listened to me with such compassion. I am very grateful. But, strange to say, I'm also feeling guilty…Maybe it's because our conversations have been so lopsided. Seems like I'm doing all the talking. About my struggling marriage, of course. And

[183]

they're doing all the listening. The thing is, it's making such a difference! Little by little, I'm starting to make sense of things.

I need to keep reminding myself that it's okay. My friends are here to help me.

Why am I this way?

I think long and hard. Then, I come up with this.

I'm like a glass full of water. There is no more capacity in my glass. Not one more drop. I can barely keep myself together. And that is why it is hard for me to talk about anything else.

But I have faith!

Faith that by talking more about this, I will continue to find clarity.

But it will take time.

God, help me be patient.

…Finally, I drift off to sleep.

A SPRINKLE OF WATER
DAY 7 ~ MORNING

It is Sunday, and my heart tugs on me to attend church. After a quick check-in call to my family, I find myself at a Community Church down the street from Amelia's.

The sign reads:

Sunday
9:00 AM Contemporary Service
11:00 AM Traditional Service

I'm early, which is rare. I park the car and enter the sanctuary.

Sitting in one of the rear pews on the left, with a red, velvety cushion, I open the bulletin.

The solitude quiets my body and soul. Glancing upward, I admire the mosaic-colored stained-glass windows. The sheer beauty eases the turmoil within me.

My mind starts to slow down as I bow my head in reverence.

> *Dear God,*
>
> *Continue to quiet my thoughts so I can focus on the magnitude of your grace. Thank you for today and for leading me to this church. Shower me with your peace.*
>
> *Please keep my children safe. I pray they will find kind and loving spouses. Fill me, oh Lord, with your Holy Spirit. Forgive Derek. Forgive me.*
>
> *Please free us from the demons destroying our marriage.*
>
> *Amen*

I glance up and the service begins.

Between prayers and the sermon, an adult baptism squeezed in; what a *"Godcident!"*

How exciting.

The pastor reaches for the glass decanter and holds it upward to receive God's blessing. He proceeds with the sacrament.

He quotes, "Very truly, I tell you, no one can enter the kingdom of God unless they are born of water and the Spirit. Flesh gives birth to flesh, but the Spirit gives birth to Spirit." *(John 3:5-6)*

He asks the man seeking baptism, "Do you believe in God, the Father Almighty, Creator of heaven and earth...." Moments later he begins to pour the water, reading from the Book of Order,

[186]

"I baptize you in the name of the Father, Son, and the Holy Spirit."

As the water flows and washes away human frailty, it reminds me of the forgiveness of sins and God's eternal love.

For Derek, Zola, Nisha, Rebecca, Kobe, and me.

I keep reminding myself God loves and forgives Derek, too. Just as much as the Divine loves and forgives me.

Baptism signifies being born anew from above (or again) of the (Holy) Spirit. It also symbolizes God's forgiveness of sin. The sins I have committed, like thinking ill of Derek.

*****

Derek and I agreed baptism would be solely up to our children.

No infant baptism for them.

Once again, it surprised me. We had been on the same page about this. Which didn't happen often.

As it turned out, Pastor Don baptized Zola so she could complete her confirmation class.

Witnessing Zola's baptism and subsequent confirmation meant the world to me. I was proud to see her publicly accept a spiritual faith for herself.

Zola didn't realize it, but it was the best gift she could have given me.

[187]

Our bedtime ritual was another gift my kids and I shared. My favorite books to read to them were the *Goodnight Angel book* series by Susan Ling. Derek read them mystery stories from *The Hardy Boys* series by Franklin Dixon. We took turns reading each night to our children.

Another ritual we agreed on, too.

*****

I hurry out of the church, still needing to assemble a daypack for my upcoming missionary visit with several retired missionaries, who were very good friends with my mom.

In the parking lot, I consult the checklist embedded in my brain.

Yes. I have my belongings.

Walking swiftly into Amelia's, I compile ingredients for a protein shake. The blender shrieks as I push the power button, creating a nutritious drink. Pouring it into a go cup, I run a new checklist in my head.

With a map and a daypack, I head to Fort Bragg. I know my mom is anxious to hear about my visit with her missionary friends. It will be interesting, for sure!

*****

Marty and Binita are an extraordinary couple. Love oozed from their pores. For each other. And for others.

[188]

No wonder they were missionaries.

Even when I babysat their kids, they treated me respectfully, like an equal. A feeling that still sprinkles over me again, thirty years later. I remembered conversing with Binita about boys, my parents, and God. She had listened, and she encouraged me to seek God's presence.

Not once did Binita judge me.

That stuck with me. All these years.

*****

Fort Bragg, California

"Orange Bloom Retirement Community" reads the sign from the main road. Passing the community center, shuffleboard court, and swimming pools, I see Marty and Binita's modest home off to the side.

The elderly couple stands behind a glass door as I pull into the driveway. Binita greets me as if she is a three-year-old on Christmas morning.

"Welcome to our home, Jill," Binita bubbles.

"In this home, we serve the Lord," Marty adds, smiling ear to ear.

"Amen!" I shout.

Marty embraces me as if I am his daughter, a love I hadn't felt in years. I capture a mental snapshot of it in my mind and hold it tight.

Why is this embrace endearing? Oh, right. Derek hasn't hugged me like this since forever.

Into Marty's arms, I melt and hug him back as if he was the last person on earth.

It is an embrace of a lifetime.

A lifetime of love, hardship, and sorrow.

A lifeline of sorts.

To me, it is air.

Air to finally breathe.

To be myself.

It is acceptance. And forgiveness.

It is the love of God.

Flowing through Marty and Binita.

I don't want this feeling of love to leave.

Marty releases his arms, and Binita leans in to hug me. I feel like her most loved and favorite childhood ragdoll.

And this feeling of abundant love fills my soul.

Fresh. Unadulterated. Pure.

I wish I could stay like this forever, safe and secure in Binita's arms.

Binita steps back and starts bombarding me with questions.

"Jill, how was the drive? How were the directions? Did you have any trouble finding us?"

Abruptly switching gears from feeling loved and secure to the present situation, I collect my thoughts. I smile, nod, and report, "The drive was fine, not much traffic. The directions were perfect."

"Jill, with all your driving, you must be famished. Let's eat!"

*****

Binita had aged gracefully, and Marty's robust shoulders had grown frail. The dining table was set with bone porcelain plates with a gold crisscross pattern. Heavy glass goblets held raspberry tea. A platter of brown rice with vegetables rested on the table.

*****

We sit down to lunch and talk about God. How God shows up in everyday life, including all types of adversity. Marty begins with a prayer.

Dear God in Heaven,

We thank you for this meal your servant Binita made. We thank you for our sister in Christ, Jill, who you led here today.

We thank you for all of the blessings you have bestowed upon us. We ask you to nourish us. To comfort us. To continue to love us.

In the Lord's name,
Amen

"Amen," Binita and I say at the same time.

"Dig in," Binita says.

"I can't begin to tell you how much I appreciate this lunch. It looks delicious, Binita."

"A meal is fellowship," Marty says. "We learn from each other. God designs us to live in community.

"To talk to one another.

"To care for one another.

"To love one another.

"Now, Jill, what you have been up to?"

"Well, I'm not sure where to begin. First, let me start by saying you two make me smile. What you have is something I have been longing for all my life." Shifting from joy and delight to trepidation and angst, I continue.

"Right now, I'm not in a good place. My husband, Derek, is disrespectful to me. That would be marginally tolerable, but he is rude to me in front of the children. He picks fights with me too. Whenever I find myself navigating these situations it feels like I'm walking on eggshells."

Marty and Binita look a bit dazed and confused.

"Let me clarify," I explain. "It's the children. I don't want them to think being rude is appropriate. They are learning bullying behavior. That is not okay.

[192]

"I have prayed and gone to counseling. Derek says I'm crazy. And a mental institution is where I need to be. I am beginning to believe him, but I know I'm not crazy. I can't continue to live such a lie. The lie of a happy home. The lie of a happy marriage. It is all far from happy."

I pause. Then, continue, "Derek finally admitted he didn't love me. Which makes me wonder, why am I married? Marty and Binita, I'm sorry for spilling all this on you."

Marty tenderly smiles, "Jill, God has a way of placing people in your life at just the right time when you need them. Right now, we are here. For you. Remember, Jill, God walks with you through tough times."

The conversation steers away from me and turns toward others as Marty continues, "Like the time there was a fire in our village. It destroyed homes, yet no one was hurt."

Whew.

Glad we are changing gears. I need a little distraction about now.

Binita nods, "We were there for the villagers. Since we were untouched by the fire, we opened our home. I baked tons of bread and made rice and beans for weeks.

"Then there was the time when one of the young village boys went missing. The entire village prayed as they swept the surrounding area, searching for the little boy. Marty gathered the men and led a search party. While I invited the women to our front porch, where we prayed for hours."

Marty chimes in, "As darkness fell, a whimper from a wooded area echoed through the air. The little boy had fallen into a well. It took hours to find a ladder long enough to rescue him."

Turning to Marty, I ask, "What happened to the little boy?"

"God answered our prayers. We found the boy safe. He walked out of the clinic with only a sprained ankle."

I turn to Binita, "God does work in mysterious ways to those who have faith, right?"

"Indeed, he does, Jill. How about we take a breather and peruse some family photos?" Binita suggests.

"Sounds good," I reply, nodding my head.

Binita's disposition shifts. Her thoughts move from her love of her mission community to a mother's love for her children. She reaches for her iPad.

"Jill, go sit on the couch," Binita directs.

"I want to show you my daughter, Leena, and her son, Sam."

Binita sits next to me on the couch and tilts her iPad toward me so I can "meet" Leena and Sam. She scrolls down the device, showing me pictures of her family, and then pauses.

"You know Jill, God is watching over your children right now. Our heavenly Father knows each of them. Like he knows you, Jill. God is with you. God hears your cries."

I start to lose it.

Studying Leena's picture and seeing her face glow hit a nerve.

My outburst becomes more robust, and Binita puts her arm around me. My head rests naturally on her shoulder, and my tears flow like a violent rainstorm.

"Jill, let it all out. Everything will be alright. Scripture says we KNOW that in all things, God works for the good of those who love him and have been called according to his purpose.

"Like I said, Jill. God knows. He knows what you have been going through. God wants you to end the suffering.

"Walk away from the disrespect.

"Walk away from the unbeliever.

"It will be okay, Jill. Your faith will pull you through this." Binita pulls out a linen handkerchief, wipes my eyes, and kisses my cheek.

"God loves you, honey, and we do, too."

Binita, stood up and gestured toward the hallway, "Now, go to the powder room down the hall, on the left, and freshen up."

*****

Next stop. Helen's.

On the way to my second visit of the day, I spot her house at the end of the street.

I park in the driveway and ring the doorbell.

A heavy-set lady answers the door.

Two of Helen's friends from her church, Mabel and Athenia, are visiting too – how wonderful.

*****

Retired missionaries, Helen and her family, served in Guam. Like Marty and Binita, they were missionaries supported by my childhood church. My church took pride in supporting missionaries all over the world. In fact, a world map hung in the church's foyer. Tiny bulbs twinkled in every spot where a missionary served.

Since my mom volunteered to be the liaison between the church and the missionaries, she knew them well. She corresponded with each of them every month. That was why these missionaries knew more about me than I did about them.

*****

Three wrinkled-skinned women radiate God's love in the cozy living room, their smiles weathered by experience. We briefly share about ourselves and how grateful we are to find each other on this day at Helen's. We sip tea and chuckle at how life differs from what we had imagined.

Athenia asks me what brings me to California.

"Good question. To make a long story short, I'm staying at a longtime friend's home in Napa, where I've been doing tons of thinking.

"Reflecting.

"Refining.

"And praying.

"My marriage isn't healthy. Frankly, it is eating away at me."

The ladies nod and smile tenderly. I continue, "I've been praying for more than a decade. My faith prevented me from even considering a divorce. But now, since I found out in a recent therapy session that my husband doesn't love me, I feel he has broken our wedding vows. I can rightfully think about separating and ending this charade."

I sit straight up and lean forward in anticipation.

Will these women be angels sent by God to give me a message?

[197]

With a gentle yet accusatory tone, Mabel turns to me and says, "Dear, I think you are being overly sensitive here. Remember, compromise is essential in a marriage. Sacrifices need to be made for the sake of your children."

"That is exactly what I am contemplating," I reply. "Sacrifices. Absolutely. I AM making a sacrifice for my children.

"I don't want them to spend one more minute in such a volatile home. I'm afraid Derek will hurt me and the kids. If I take myself out of the mix, I know Derek won't kick anyone else around. He pounces on the children because of me, not because of them.

"Of course, I care about the children.

"This is all about them. And their futures.

"I have spent years trying to fix my marriage. Nothing worked. I may have no choice but to leave because Derek refuses to leave.

"There is a lot at stake. If I leave Derek, my kids will eventually see a father who is mean and disrespectful to their mother. And they'll see that he ends up alone."

Helen, who lost her husband recently and had been married for over fifty years, chimes in, "Love is patient and kind. Marriage is about coming together and compromising.

Love is sweet. It is respectful. It should not be stressful. You should feel safe."

Athenia gently follows, "Communication is key, my dear. Without it, you can't have a relationship. You can't keep things bottled up inside of you. Otherwise, you'll explode! No one wants an explosive wife. No, Sir!"

I attempt to absorb the advice. But my heart is torn between feeling scolded and trying to understand what these ladies are saying. Am I being over-sensitive here? I don't think so. I know these ladies have walked in my shoes. Yet have they? Did they have husbands who called them names? Or trash items they bought? Were they denied access to their bank accounts? I don't think so.

"Sometimes change is a good thing, Jill." Helen continues, "God commands husbands to love their wives. If Derek doesn't love you, you have no choice but to leave. Don't let your emotions cloud your judgment. Make sure you have exhausted all of the possibilities to fix your marriage. But, sometimes, you can't beat a dead horse into compliance no matter how hard you try. God commands a husband to love his wife. If your husband doesn't love you anymore, you must leave."

As I listen to the words "*you must leave*," a splash of hope and reassurance sprinkles my skin. I feel validated.

[199]

After a leisurely cup of tea, and losing all track of time, I notice it is getting late. The last hour had gone by lightning fast.

Knowing I have one more visit on my schedule, I spring up and announce my departure. But, before the ladies let me out the door, they pray over me. The ladies place their hands on my head. Helen clears her throat and says, "I'll pray...

Dear Loving God,

We lift Jill up to you. Comfort her as she struggles with her decision when she returns home to Las Vegas.

Keep her and her children safe. Guide her and send angels to help her out of this mess. We can't wait to hear where you will lead her.

Amen

"Thank you, ladies." I hug each of them as if they are adorable fuzzy teddy bears and wave farewell.

Helen points to Eve's house across the street.

"Enjoy your visit with Eve, Jill."

"Yes, thanks, I plan to. Till we meet again!"

Wow. This is powerful stuff. Never underestimate the power of angels. They show up in the strangest places.

N ext stop, Eve's.

Right across the street from Helen's.

A mezuzah, the Hebrew home blessing, hangs on her doorframe. It holds an inscribed piece of parchment paper encased in a decorative metal holder. Hardly noticeable, it measures about four inches. It originates from a bible verse where Yahweh instructs his people to write commandments on the "doorframes of your houses…" *(Deuteronomy 6:9)*.

Shalom reads a sign on the door. I instantly feel the peace. I am bonding with Eve even before she opens the door.

When it does, she is wearing two necklaces.

One is a beautiful gold Star of David with a cross inside.

The other is the shape of Singapore with a cross in the center.

I also catch a glimpse of a menorah in the front window. Entering Eve's home, a wave of peace continues to surround me.

Her house has an Asian vibe mixed with Judaica treasures including a shofar on her bookcase.

[201]

It is beautiful!

Long and sleek, it looks like a natural stone.

This house gives me a sense of belonging here. It feels familiar. Like I've been here before. Even though I haven't. It is a spiritual experience that is hard to describe or explain.

Eve's brown, piercing eyes stare intensely into mine with a profound acceptance. It makes no earthly sense. Yet, I have learned the Spirit shows up in unexpected places.

Without uttering a word of greeting, Eve seems to read my energy and take in the struggles of my soul. Then, after a long pause, she says, "Jill, your worries are weighing on your soul. Put them into the God of Abraham's hands. Your path will become clear in God's kind and gentle way," she promises. "Pray often and trust Yahweh."

"I hope my path will become clear," I reply. "Lord only knows how much I have prayed."

We walk over to her kitchen counter, where she puts on a kettle for tea. The conversation starts with travel, weaves in her missionary work and then circles back to the real purpose of my visit. During our heartfelt exchange, I confess that my marriage is hanging by a thread. I explain to Eve how I am contemplating divorce. The thought of it, I share with her, makes me feel judged.

"Am I going to hell for even considering it?" I ask.

[202]

"Come here, Jill. Sit next to me." Eve motions with her hand, patting the sofa.

Eve takes my hand and says, "I will have none of this! Let's pray right now,"

Dear God,

Father of Abraham, Isaac, and Jacob. We come to you in this time of need. We ask for your guidance and wisdom for Jill. She is facing the most difficult decision about her marriage.

We know divorce must break your heart. But you also love your children. You want them to be free from abuse and oppression.

You are a God of justice and mercy. You are a God of grace. Forgiveness. One who restores the broken-hearted. You delivered your people from slavery in Egypt. You graciously gave us your Holy Word. You sent your son, Jesus, for each one of us.

You are the God of Israel.
The God of the Church.
The God of Jill. And the God of Derek.

I trust, O Lord, you will be faithful to your daughter, Jill.

With her head still bowed, Eve finishes, "Jill, go ahead and pray from your heart."

"*Lord,*" I sigh. Then, collecting my thoughts, I begin,

Thank you for Eve. I am scared and confused. I don't know what to do about my marriage. I think I love

[203]

Derek, but, at this point, I don't know. He doesn't love me. He doesn't care about you. Or my faith. He doesn't want to change. I don't know what you want me to do. Do you want me to stay or leave? Only you can heal my marriage. Or is it too late for that?

I pause.

Eve jumps back in,

Lord,

Only you know Jill's heart. Show her the way. Give her clarity. Help her find courage. Surround her with angels. Because she needs them.

Eve stops.

I pick up where she left off,

Lord,

I trust you, and I surrender to you. Thank you, and keep me and my children in your tender care.

Taking a deep breath, signaling to Eve with my silence, she adds,

Lord,

Thank you for hearing our prayers. Please keep Jill safe on this trip and open her eyes to your light.

Amen

"Amen. And Amen." Sighing in relief.

A weight has lifted. I don't feel like a sinner anymore. A heavenly peace showers me as I rise from the sofa and gather my daypack to end our visit.

Eve places her Star of David in my hand. Her eyes pierce my heart. Seeing my tears, she smiles and says gently, "I want you to have this."

How did Eve know just how sacred the Star of David is to me? How generous! A "Godcident," for sure! I can't wait to take this all in on the drive back to Napa.

Filling up with emotion…I sputter out, "Thank you," as we exchange a lingering hug.

*****

As I drive back to Amelia's, my thoughts return to this most unexpected, joyful day. Despite the tears, the love I felt from these people will live in my heart forever.

Even though their prayers were a bit long, I loved them!

Following the yellow painted lines of the road, my mind wanders back in time.

Thoughts of Judaism flood my soul.

A youngster in Sunday School listening to Bible stories, and as a teenager volunteering at the Jewish convalescent home. All of this prompting questions about the relationship between Christianity and Judaism. After all, hadn't Jesus himself been Jewish?

[205]

Growing up, I immersed myself in the stories of Creation, Adam and Eve, Noah and the Ark, as well as the Tower of Babel, Daniel and the Lion's Den, David and Goliath, and Ruth. Yet, as I ponder these parallels, I can't shake the feeling of: *Why I am being drawn to all things Jewish?*

I'm not sure why I feel determined to bridge the gap between Judaism and Christianity.

But I do. ...But not today.

*****

Napa Valley, California

As I get closer to Amelia's, sermons from my childhood in church pop into my head.

Specifically, about the concept of evangelizing.

Spreading the gospel. Sharing the Good News of God's love with other people.

Pulling into Amelia's driveway, I take these thoughts to the guest room. And mull them over some more.

Evangelizing gets a bad rap, doesn't it?

Some see it as trying to change people and make them more religious.

Because they are defective.

Is that what it is?

But wait a minute. Aren't we all broken?

I don't think "defective" is a good word here.

[206]

I am definitely not "defective."

Broken is what I am. Meaning, I am not perfect. Because no one is perfect except God.

Which brings us back to the question of evangelizing.

What is it?

Well, it tells a story about one's faith experiences with God.

Doesn't it?

And that could help people.

It helps them realize they are not alone in this world. And that is a good thing.

Settling back into the guest room, the question of sharing God's love with others versus trying to shove it down their throats has gotten me all riled up.

I still feel shame and guilt.

What if I have had it wrong all this time?

I still can't believe I "preached" about sins and the need to repent to others in my teens. It was part of our church teaching. It was what we did.

But don't we, as Christians, need to love one another?

Not hit one another over the head with doctrine.

I need to sort this out.

As I pour myself a glass of *Tablas Creek Esprit de Beaucastel Panoplie* and pull out my *Bible*, I search for more answers about my faith journey. I flip to the end of *Mark,* the second book of the New Testament, and read:

Later Jesus appeared to the eleven as they were eating… [Jesus said,] "Go into all the world and preach the gospel to all creation." – Mark 16:14-15

Well, there it is.

Preach the gospel to all creation.

A pretty specific directive. Except what gospel?! And, what creation?

"Creation" is an odd choice of a word. The word "humans" would have worked better there. The "gospel." It means "message of good news."

Hmm. What good news?

The good news of salvation?

The good news of the Trinity?

The good news of baptism?

The good news of love?

I have no idea.

But the conviction in my heart is compelling me to spread something. But I'm unsure of what it is or why.

Growing up, my church instilled this sense of *preaching the gospel* to those who didn't believe the way we did. Namely, Jews, Muslims, Buddhists, Catholics, and

Mormons –and all religious people who, we believed, were not "saved."

Yes, that is what I learned.

But this is what I think now:

Our place is to love one another. It is not to judge.

*****

The guilt and the shame of *Secret Number One* strike again. Nelson told me not to tell anyone. So, I obeyed out of fear. For more than thirty years, I said nothing, and it tore my insides apart. That very same ingrained mindset has chipped away at me ever since, causing me to remain silent.

To not question Derek.

To not fight back.

I had become a doormat.

After telling my secret number one to our therapist, Dr. Kate, and my mother, I felt a sense of freedom and perhaps, victory.

I finally had a voice.

Once I confronted my demons head-on, I was able to be more forthcoming. My mindset began forming a new belief: Telling secrets can be good. It took the burden off of me – and it felt freeing. Now, I am convinced God wants me to use my voice.

To help others.

[209]

To share God's love.

*****

Sipping the fine red wine with the dry, earthy flavor, my thoughts drift toward the significant presence of Jewish people in my life. Is it possible that my love for Judaism began with my first best friend?

Rose. She was six, and I was five.

Walk one house to the right on Fifth Avenue and Ferncliff Street. Turn left and cross the road. Pass the green lawn. Go to the next house, a white one on the left, where six-year-old Rose lived.

Her complexion was olive – like mine, and she had brown curly hair. Little Rose was Jewish, and I loved her.

She moved almost a mile away about a year later, which felt like a hundred miles when you were five or six. At that juncture, my mother seized the opportunity to discourage me from being friends with Rose.

Why?

Because...oh my goodness...she was Jewish.

*****

My early exposure to Jewish culture and friendship paved the way for the spiritual encounters that were to come. I found myself drawn to it during specific times in my life.

[210]

First in middle school. Then at my first job. After that, it was a friend who married a Jewish man.

In middle school, I was too young to be a candy striper at the local hospital. But I was old enough to be a sunshine girl at a nearby nursing home.

Beth El Shalom Home for the Aged.

There I fell in love with all things Jewish.

An indescribable peace washed over my whole being while I was there. I didn't know why.

Perhaps God inspired it.

Fast forward a few more years.

Hired as an office assistant at the local Jewish Vocational Center, I worked there during one of my summer breaks. Most of the employees were Jewish, and many thought I was Jewish, too. Again, it was another place where I felt comfortable in my skin. Then, one of my church friends from childhood married a Jewish man. They had a daughter and brought her up in the Jewish faith. It was the first Bat Mitzvah I had ever attended.

Another significant religious encounter.

The Temple.

The Torah.

The Rabbi.

Everything Jewish felt strangely familiar.

[211]

*****

My thoughts shift to religious rites of passage. Specifically, the roles they play in shaping beliefs and family traditions. Like confirmation in the Christian faith. Like Bar and Bat Mitzvahs in the Jewish faith. Why do families stop attending religious services after their children finish their spiritual training and others don't?

During my formative years, our family attended three services each Sunday.

Yup. Sunday School plus two church services every week.

Even in the summer.

My father said, "God does not take a vacation."

Yup. Every Sunday. No matter where we were.

So, this concept of not attending church regularly was foreign to me.

*****

Helene and Saul were my Jewish neighbors. Yet, in my mind, their unwavering friendship exemplified the love of Christ. They shared a deep mutual respect and understanding for one another. They were angels, too, right in our *Whispering Woods* community. Despite their older age, this couple celebrated their extraordinary youthfulness. Helene attended Temple, yet her husband, Saul, of almost fifty years, did not.

Helene lent me a book called *Jewish Observances*. I wanted to learn more about high holy days, especially in preparation for our family to celebrate our first Passover with their family. They had grown surprisingly close to Derek and me. The four of us attended religious events and family celebrations with one another. The bottom line was our two families were close despite our religious differences.

*****

Open-mindedness. This topic is important to me. As I try to wrap my head around the fact that my upbringing was anything but that. Reflecting on this, and about religion more generally, brings Derek's parents to mind. Especially when it comes to matters of faith and how accepting they were of mine.

I continue to mull this over while I brush my teeth and get ready for bed.

Looking back, I realized that Derek's parents had surprised me.

Their open-mindedness was new to me early on.

Hmm.

In my world as a child, if you didn't believe the way my parents did, well, that was simply not good enough.

Yup.

You were going to hell to spend eternity in darkness.

That had been my assumption, too.

Yet, as I matured in my faith, this notion disturbed me more and more.

How could I profess to be a spiritual person yet be so close-minded? It was hard to leave acceptance and judgment to the one and only Judge (God). My old way of thinking was hard to shake.

In spite of that, little by little, day by day, I am becoming more broad-minded and more accepting. And for that, I am grateful.

Taking the time to appreciate where I have been is a gift. Broader perspectives and a sense of connection, are what community is all about. Whether it be Saul and Helene, Rose, or the staff at Beth El Shalom Home for the Aged.

The bed calls my name. The soft comfort of the mattress awaits me. It has been a long day. Before I close my eyes, I pick up the phone and call the kids to say goodnight.

PINK GOGGLES
DAY 8

Leisure. What exactly is it? To me, it is a time when there are no expectations. It is a time when I can let down my guard and enjoy the moment. And this is precisely what I am going to do today.

The only thing on my agenda is dinner with Amelia. Later, when she returns from work, we will dine at a nearby Thai place. I love Thai food and can't wait to try a new place. The thought of it makes my mouth water.

But first, I need to check in with Derek and the kids to ensure they are all safe. Then, I will relax, swim laps, and enjoy every moment.

Thankfully, all is good on the home front.

Thank you, God, for keeping my family safe.

*****

I make a smoothie and nurse it on the patio, where I daydream of a peaceful life with a husband who honors and adores me. It feels good yet sad to think about what life could have been.

[215]

I change into my suit and head to the pool. I remind myself this is a day to enjoy. I take a deep breath. Shhh. It is quiet. I can hear the birds in the trees as I open the gate to the pool. I slide into the water and slip on my pink goggles.

Swimming laps is good exercise - great for the mind and the body. It calms me, protecting and swaddling me in a sea of soothing tranquility. The birds singing and the hum of the pool pump work their magic, taking me to a serene place. Maintaining a rhythmic breathing pattern, I sink deeper into relaxation.

A mantra of sorts.

Inhale, hold, exhale.

I lift my right arm out of the water, stretch it as far as possible, scoop, and glide.

Fears and anxiety melt away.

Each stroke refreshes like a glass of cool water.

Twenty minutes later, I pull myself out of the pool. Wrapped in a pink polka-dot towel, I slide into a lounge chair, shut my eyes, and nap.

Upon awakening, I can't get "pink" out of my head. Turning toward the chalet, I sense that the goggles and towel are trying to tell me something. I bring my lunch to the patio and sit at the table and, in so doing, I remember:

Pink reminds me of my wedding day.

[216]

How could I have forgotten?

I know why. But before I go there, I grasp the memories resurfacing in bits and pieces.

It was a sunny March day with temperatures in the low seventies. Violins played softly in the background as I entered the church, a veil covering my face. Walking down the aisle made me feel like a princess from a storybook.

At the reception, gold-rimmed plates shimmered on the tables. Pink roses in glass vases released a fragrant scent, filling the air with romance. Tiny lights glowed in the dark.

As I remember it now, it was a joyous occasion, like a fairy tale sprinkled with pixie dust, although short-lived.

The storybook wedding had turned into an ugly charade.

*****

Christianity and divorce don't mix well. Theologians have been wrestling with this dichotomy for centuries. My childhood church adamantly opposed divorce, as did my parents. It was time for me to find out for myself why divorce was so sinful.

It took twelve months to search for and reflect on these words in scripture: "wife," "husband," "love," and "marriage." It was no easy task, but I had done it. For that, I was proud.

[217]

To my surprise, I learned no direct statement prohibited a woman from divorcing a husband. Although some passages suggested that a husband should not divorce his wife.

This encouraged me.

Along the way, I discovered that it is better to get married than to remain unmarried. Why? Because burning with unfulfilled passion and desire sounded horrible.

*****

I retrieve a *Kenwood Vineyards White Table Wine* bottle from Amelia's cellar. I pour a glass and read a passage from *The Bible.*

...A wife must not separate from her husband. But if she does, she must remain unmarried or else be reconciled to her husband. And a husband must not divorce his wife.
— 1 Cor. 7:10-11

In verse 14, which follows, the passage continues, *"For the unbelieving husband has been sanctified through his wife...."*

Wait a minute. I have questions.

Am I responsible for Derek's salvation?

That would be a heavy burden to bear. My actions have not "turned" Derek around. I don't think I have sanctified him.

Not one bit.

[218]

So, am I the one who is behaving in a "non-Christian" way?

I read a little further.

...God has called us to live in peace. How do you know, wife, whether you will save your husband? Or, how do you know, husband, whether you will save your wife? — 1 Cor. 7:15-16

I pause, soaking in the words. I allow them to pour over me and wash away my preconceived notions.

"God has called us to live in peace."

That doesn't mean *peace at all costs,* as my father would say. No, we are called to peace. But neither a troubled heart nor a contentious relationship with my husband is peace.

Then, it hit me.

Bam.

Strangely, this might just be my *get-out-of-jail-free card.*

Lifting my head up, I begin humming *Amazing Grace.*

Hmm. The Spirit fills my soul.

Peace.

Knowing in my heart that God has ordained the notion of living in peace has now opened the door to separating from Derek.

I can almost taste it.

*****

Derek's words cut deep.

"You are not good enough to be a mother!" Derek had roared at me one day. I don't trust you, either. Plain and simple. You are mentally ill, and you need help."

Derek threatened to install security cameras to keep an eye on me at home to protect our children. Leaving me baffled and wounded.

Why? Protect them from what?

Had I made a mistake I was unaware of?

Was he worried I would walk out one day, take the children, and not return? Or was he, without realizing it, afraid of himself?

*****

Two hours slip by as I read, pray, and sip my glass of Amelia's light, refreshing, peachy-tasting wine. I pour myself another. To me, the amber liquid reflects the turmoil of my soul.

Confused like a deer blinded by a beam of light, waves of disappointment, failure, and shame come and go.

I read Mark 7:21-23.

For from within, out of the heart of men, proceed evil thoughts, adulteries, covetousness, wickedness, deceit, lewdness, an evil eye, blasphemy, pride, foolishness. All these evil things come from within and defile a man.   – Mark 7:21-23 KJV

The passage is bone-chilling in its directness.

I meditate on the words, "evil thoughts come from within."

How does this relate to Derek and me?

Generally, I want to see the good in people and typically do. Yet, I can't see the good in Derek anymore. All I see is his destructiveness.

Is God trying to tell me something?

Sometimes, I think our fractured marriage is unfixable.

But doubt lingers. It gnaws away at me.

There are so many unanswered questions. Is our marriage an unsolvable puzzle?

How can we possibly move forward when the words between us have become weapons?

I can't live like this anymore.

It is eating me alive.

*****

Tick tock.

Time is flying by.

I hop into the shower and change into a black skirt and a casual pink t-shirt.

Yup, pink is definitely the color of the day.

Amelia wears light gray capris and a teal knit shirt.

[221]

As we head out, I perform my mental checklist of cellphone, wallet, and knapsack.

Off we scoot in Amelia's Mercedes to dine at an elegant place where the décor is authentic. Reds, oranges, and browns landscape the interior. Even the dining chairs are a dark mahogany brown. Metallic and ceramic artwork adorn the golden-hued walls.

Amelia and I both order Diet Cokes.

She had heard that their Pad Thai is superb. So, that is what we plan to order. We have high expectations.

We eat our dinners while chatting the night away.

Amelia asks, "How was your visit yesterday in Fort Bragg?"

"It was a lovely day visiting my mother's missionary friends. It was weird because they knew me way better than I knew them. Mom still writes them regularly.

"Eve, who had been a missionary in Japan, was my favorite. Her love for Jewish people was endearing. Amelia, how do you feel about Jewish people?"

"That's an interesting question no one has asked me before. I'd have to say Jewish people are God's children. I want to be a good neighbor to everyone regardless of their religious beliefs, Jill."

"Me, too, Amelia. For me, it is so mysterious. A sense of peace sprinkles over me whenever I see something Jewish, like a mezuzah or shofar. For me, these objects are sacred. I'm so drawn to them it feels like I was Jewish in a past life. It is weird but in a divine, cool way."

I take a moment to ponder my Jewish connection.

"Spirituality is different for each of us," Amelia says. "We experience God in different ways. No one way is better than another."

"Yes, I'm glad we are both spiritual in our own way and live our faith as best we can. You, by playing keyboard in your praise band, and me, well, by cerebral thinking," I say with a laugh.

The Pad Thai lived up to our expectations. It really was delicious.

*****

Enjoying Amelia's company after so many years makes me warm and fuzzy. At home, we settle in to watch *Dancing with the Stars* in Amelia's indoor theatre. When the show ends, we say our goodnights.

I ponder life, marriage, and the meaning of divorce. How will a divorce affect my family – my children? Who will get my children? How hard will Derek fight to take them away from me?

[223]

I fall asleep thinking about how to kidnap them. Figuring out a way to move to a foreign country undetected shouldn't be too hard.

Yikes! What am I thinking?

CEREAL & THE BOOK
DAY 9

E ight o'clock reads the timepiece on the nightstand. Still in bed, the morning ritual begins with a phone call to the kids. Their voices comfort me, ground me, and somehow make me well aware of my insecurities.

Reaching for the pink journal on the side table, I read an excerpt of a note I wrote to three-year-old Zo.

Dear Zola,

I am afraid of your dad. I am worried if we separate, he will want custody. He earns lots of money and can afford much better things than I could provide for you as a single mom. It is a shame we cannot live on love alone.

Relationships are imperfect; you will find this out for yourself one day. If I stay in my unhappy marriage, that might be okay if it allows you to have a mom and a dad in the same house. But I am afraid your dad is going to hurt me – he has such a bad temper. I'll try to persevere. For you, I'll try anything. Sweet dreams, my little girl!

Love, Mommy

Feeling anxious, laying the book aside, I reflect on the words written that day to little Zo.

[225]

It seems like a lifetime ago.

If Zola was three back then, it was thirteen years ago. Here I am, imagining separation – this time with three more children to consider.

Wow.

Think of the cost of meals, clothes, and so much more over the years. That is a lot of money!

*****

I join Amelia in the kitchen for a cup of coffee before she goes to work.

"Good morning, Amelia. Thanks for making the coffee. It smells great."

"Good morning; your cup is beside the coffee maker, and the creamer is in the refrigerator. Oh, yeah – sorry, I forgot you don't take creamer," Amelia remembers.

"Just black," I nod.

"You look a bit worried this morning – what's up?" Amelia detects anxiety in my frowning eyebrows.

"When I woke up, I read a passage in my journal I had written to Zola when she was little. It was about separating from Derek and how there was no way I could afford to leave him and take her with me. My mom and dad were living alone on a fixed income. My siblings had their own families. None of them were overflowing with discretionary income.

[226]

I wasn't earning enough money to support Zola and me. I felt hopeless and helpless with nowhere to go."

"Heavy thinking for so early in the morning, Jill," Amelia shoots back. Adding, "Gender pay inequality makes my blood boil. I can't believe it is still an issue – after all these years. I thought it would have been a non-issue by now. But it's still out there, don't I know it. My predecessor at Heritage made well over six figures. I'm not quite there yet. We had similar education with the same years of experience."

Amelia continues, "I'm so sorry you felt that way thirteen years ago, and I'm sorry you are feeling so miserable now. You and the kids are welcome here, Jill. Anytime. For as long as you need a place to stay. I have to get ready for work, but I want you to think about my offer."

"Okay, Amelia, I'll think about it." I retreat to the bedroom, adding, "I'm going to lie down. Have a great day at work."

*****

Climbing back into bed, I feel overwhelmed. Thoughts about money and supporting four children swirl in my head. This intense thinking zaps the energy right out of me.

Rolling on my side, my mind shifts from supporting the children to racking my brain about red flags.

[227]

First red flag: Not discussing with Derek \whether I'd stay home after Zola's was born.

Next flag: The random disappearance of items I had purchased.

What else did I miss?

Were there any other red flags?

Hours later, I wake up from an unexpected nap. A tuna sandwich quells my hunger pangs.

Then, off to the pool.

As I swim, my mind returns to the red flags. Looking inward, reflecting on my marriage, I noticed signs of distress. Long before I even walked down the aisle.

Red Flag #3

This was when I asked Derek about God.

He smirked, "Go ask my uncle."

At the time, I thought, "Why would he say something like this?" Foolishly, I had brushed it off.

As time passed, I learned how private a person Derek was. He didn't talk much about his past or anything personal. Looking back, this signaled a lack of emotional intimacy. Something I wish I had thought more about at the time.

Red Flag #4

This appeared when Derek's siblings called me about our wedding reception. Maybe it wasn't because they ganged up on me. It was about how it made me feel. Like my feelings didn't count.

I felt infinitesimally small.

It brought me right back to middle school, where relentless bullying made my life a living hell.

They tried to convince me to have our wedding reception at one of Las Vegas' lavish casinos. This might be attractive to someone else.

But not to me.

I wanted a reception at the golf resort less than a mile from home. I had dreamed of this since I was a little girl. And the golf resort offered a premium wedding package at a reasonable cost. A win/win.

Friction from the *sibling gang-up* permeated the air for weeks.

That was when my marriage started to sink into the sand.

Even before it started.

*****

Turning from these red flags, I wonder if I am missing any other signs. What else could I have overlooked?

I glance at the clock, realizing it is time for dinner.

Since Amelia's meeting will run late, I plan to eat alone. Since I have no appetite for dinner, a bowl of cereal will suffice.

[229]

Afterward, I pick up a book I had meant to read earlier and plop down on the guest bed. It is *The Unexpected Legacy of Divorce: The 25-Year Landmark Study* by Julia M. Lewis and Sandra Blakeslee.

Separation and divorce complicate lives no matter how you slice and dice it. The priority is to lessen the impact and create a path forward for a more peaceful future. I curl up in the dense book for the evening. Knowing the subject will not be cheerful, I press on, sensing that now is the right time to read this. If my marriage is coming to an end, I better get prepared. After all, knowledge is power.

Learning that children of divorced parents are much more likely to go down the wrong path scares me to death. I want to devise a plan to keep them on track since they are all doing well in school. Let's keep it that way.

So, uprooting them and moving to California is not an option. Maintaining as much normalcy as possible is critical. Ensuring that they know how much I love them matters above all else.

The book posits that grown-ups must make hard decisions and that living peacefully is in kids' best interests.

Parents must put their children first.

*****

I hear Amelia come in at nine. With a raised voice, I sputter "goodnight" through my door.

Reaching for my cellphone, I call home to touch base with the kids and spend a few minutes chatting about their day.

After I hang up, I hear Amelia puttering in the kitchen and join her.

"Amelia, how are you?"

"I could use a drink," she replies. "How about a beer? Will you join me?"

"I need something a bit stronger, Amelia. I'm going to have a scotch on the rocks. You?"

"No, I'll stick to the beer. You go ahead and have a scotch."

Amelia asked me how my day was. I tell her I'm almost finished with the *Legacy of Divorce* book.

"*Legacy of Divorce?* What does that mean?"

"It is a well-known longitudinal study of children from divorce. I think it is important for me to read this."

"Good thinking, Jill," Amelia said. "So, what have you learned so far?"

"Well, that is a good question. I can tell you this book scares me. It is about the high probability of divorced children having behavior and mental health issues, including breaking laws, becoming drug addicts, or committing suicide. It is not cheery at all. It's quite ominous, in fact."

"That does sound scary, Jill."

"So, I must get this right to avoid these potential issues. My kid's lives depend on it."

"Jill, you have good kids. I think it is smart for you to learn about divorce and prepare for all types of scenarios."

"Good point. I don't want a divorce, but I can't stay in this marriage as it is. Demons are possessing my soul."

"What do you mean?"

"I'm becoming mean, miserable, and angry, and it is affecting every bone in my body."

"A bad marriage tends to have that effect," Amelia chimes in.

"I am worried Derek might divorce me. Then, I'll truly be in trouble. Okay, I'm getting ahead of myself here."

"Yes, Jill, let's slow down just a bit."

"Amelia, you are right. I think Derek and I should separate and see if we can figure out how to move forward. Amicably, of course. To start rebuilding our family."

"That does sound like a good plan, Jill. I've known you for a long time. You've been through a lot with Derek and your kids. I know you are trying to prepare for all possible outcomes."

"I'm trying, Amelia. Lord knows I am trying!"

"Jill, I suggest that when the time comes, you get a good lawyer, even for the separation. From what I know about Derek, he will want to fight you every step of the way. I hope I'm wrong. Remember, people can change when they go through this. I thought my divorce from Dan would be amicable. But it wasn't. Remember?"

"Yes, I do."

"Jill, we had no kids, so I thought it would be easy. But I was wrong. He didn't want to give up control of the business or compensate me for my time and energy managing it with him."

"Yes, this does sound familiar," I agree.

"Then, the medical debt. We had so much debt from James' heart transplant. Add in his funeral costs, and it was awful. An emotional roller coaster. There I was, mourning my only child's death, and Dan was opening credit cards with my name instead of dealing with the medical debt head-on. He transferred the debt to my credit cards, which I had to pay."

"How awful, Amelia. I'm sorry you had to go through that."

"Indeed, divorce can be ugly. No way around it."

"Thank you, Amelia, for sharing your experience with me. It is preparing me for the worst. In a way, this is a good thing because I can ready myself for whatever lies ahead.

"All this talk is making me sleepy.

"Yet a few pages await me to finish reading them. What do you think if we call it a night?"

"Oh, Jill. Absolutely. I had a long day and have a date with my bed. Goodnight. I hope the last chapter is worth staying up for."

"Okay, goodnight."

I force my droopy eyes to read until the end.

Finally, I close the book and turn the light off.

Whew. Glad it is over.

Strained from reading, I shut my eyes and reflect on Amelia, her divorce, and the book.

Sleep comes fast.

AGITA & A NAP
DAY 10

I wake up extra early, write for about an hour in my journal, and drift back to sleep. Finally, after speaking with my kids at ten o'clock, I kick myself out of bed.

A molasses and apple cider vinegar drink follows me to the sunbeam waiting outside on the patio. This morning, it is sunbathing only – no reading or writing.

Just thoughts.

Thirty minutes later, I make a breakfast shake and return to my sunbeam. For another half hour, introspections consume my mind. Beads of sweat run down my forehead and drip onto my chest.

That's my signal.

Too much sun. Time to go inside and cool off.

Just as I slip through the sliding doors, the phone rings. It is Derek. He wants to chat, which is odd. To my surprise, our conversation is halfway enjoyable. We talk about our children and the weather. As innocuous as that sounds, I still get agitated when I speak with him.

"Hi, Jill. I called to see how the trip is going."

"Namaste. It's going great. I'm sunbathing, swimming, and doing a lot of reflecting. Plus, I'm having quality *girl time* with Amelia. She has Bunco tonight, so I'm looking forward to alone time."

"What is Bunco?" Derek asks.

"It's a dice game. As people play, they rotate from one game table to another. So, eventually, you get to meet everyone. It's a great excuse to socialize. Don't you think?"

"Sure, Jill. Whatever you say. That is nice. I'm glad you are connecting with Amelia. I know how much she means to you."

"We went to dinner on Monday. On Friday, I'm heading down to Thousand Oaks to visit Lata. How about you?"

"I am not going to lie. I need you to understand the consequences of your so-called 'visit.' It has been hectic, but I have everything under control, as usual. Of course, I do. I am the boss."

"Of course you are, Derek."

Derek's tone shifts: "We are doing quite well without you. In fact, we don't need you at all. The kids and I played a marathon of Pachisi last night – Zola won. No surprise. The twins were holding their own; they played well.

"We will be going camping at Boulder Beach Campground this weekend.

"The children are thrilled– even Zola.

"I am looking forward to it."

"Thank you for sharing this, Derek. I'm glad you are doing so well without me. On the other hand, I didn't like the barb."

"Jill, you are being way too sensitive as usual. Get a grip. The world does not revolve around you."

"I know, Derek. I'm glad you'll be having a camping adventure this weekend. I'm sure the kids will love it."

"Jill, seriously, I hope you find what you are looking for. You do need help. But we do miss you, honey. I can't wait for you to come home. I have to go pick up the twins now. Ciao."

"Thanks – bye." I blurt out.

After hanging up, I feel confused and bewildered.

Here, I am thinking about separation, and he misses me.

Derek tries to be cordial, as if he is impersonating someone else. It's so out of character; yet, he can be such a smooth talker. But, deep down, it feels like manipulation. On the other hand, he sounded nice. Part of me wants to feel hopeful. The other part of me isn't so sure.

Hearing my belly rumble, I put the task of sorting out my emotions on the shelf. The refrigerator contains the delicious leftovers from the other night.

It is a noodle dish with an incredible peanut sauce.

Sixty seconds later, the microwave beeps.

The first bite is warm with a delectable balance of sweet, sour, and saltiness. I taste peanuts, red pepper, honey, and sesame. Delicious! I don't want to think about some of the ingredients, like salt, sugar, or artificial coloring.

Finishing my meal makes me tired.

I lie on the living room couch, thinking about Derek. He has a knack for being charming and then, in the blink of an eye, ruining the moment with some snide remark.

Over the years, there have been many examples of mixed messages from him. Recalling them is draining. As they swirl around in my head, my eyelids grow heavy. The next thing I know, I'm waking up from an unexpected nap.

It will be a late night for Amelia, so, I walk around the corner to the pizza shop and order a pizza with veggies. Teetering and tottering, I carry the large white pizza box back to the chalet, heading straight to Amelia's movie theatre. At least that is what she calls it.

The opening scene plays.

Anne Hathaway slides down a pole, grabs her lunch, and proceeds to scooter to high school. I recognize the movie. It is *The Princess Diaries*. It is about an awkward, nerdy teenager named Mia. Unbeknownst to her, she is the granddaughter of a queen who lives in some obscure country on the other side of the world. It is one of my favorite movies, so I am delighted to be entertained.

Midway through the movie, I place it on *pause* and phone my kids for our routine goodnights. Returning to the film, I savor the happy ending. Thirty seconds later, Amelia walks through the front door.

"How was Bunco?" I ask.

"It was great, but a bummer as well. I didn't win any rounds. So, it was a little disappointing. But that's alright. There is always next time."

"I'm sorry I missed you this morning – I got up early, wrote a bit, and then fell back asleep. How was work today, Amelia?"

"Work. I'm so excited. We are embarking on a major expansion. Since the business is doing so well, we need to add more rooms for guests and corporate events. We are also considering adding an indoor water park to attract more families. What do you think?"

"An indoor water park sounds fun," I speculate. "As long as there are separate sections for different levels of swimmers. Otherwise, it might be disastrous."

[239]

"Good thought. I'm so bushed – plus, I had too much wine tonight. Goodnight," Amelia slurs as she stumbles up the stairs to her room.

I raise my voice a bit so she can hear me, "Goodnight, Amelia. Sleep well. Drink some water, perhaps?"

With a chuckle, I head to bed myself.

I think about how comfy and spacious the bed is.

How great it feels to be alone and free.

Free from worry about the kids.

Free from worry about what mood Derek will be in.

There is a sense of openness and spaciousness in Napa. This morning, the sky is a mixture of beautiful blues with fluffy white-grayish clouds. They drift yet seem to stand still at the same time. The grass is a luscious green. Between the sprinklers and God's glistening rains, the grass gets all the water it needs. It emits a velvety glow as if it is a magic carpet. It makes me want to climb aboard and ride.

Napa is a quiet, peaceful place.

Above me, on certain days, depending on the air traffic pattern, airplanes hum as they fly up into the sky.

Higher and higher they go.

Disappearing into the endless blue space.

Once they pass, the birds resume their singing.

*****

That same outdoor serenity spills into Amelia's lovely home. The view. The décor. The love in the air. An abode to unwind in after a long day at work.

Amelia's master bedroom is on the second floor. It has an adjoining master bath overlooking the Napa Valley

[241]

vineyards. The guest bedroom is on the first floor, to the left of the front door. A large guest bathroom is in the left corner of the suite. A jetted tub beneath a window affords a scenic valley view. Adjacent to it is a glorious outside patio.

Today, the plan is to stay on the patio.

I want time to simply be me and, in the process, try to understand and appreciate myself again. For a long time, I have been living in a foreign land, pretending to be someone else.

Thoughts of my younger sister, Polly, enter my mind. We didn't get along too well growing up. As adults, we are closer and accept each other for who we are – warts and all.

Polly has a natural gift for knowing when someone's plate is full. During the past few years, she has been incredibly supportive. I am so grateful.

Her husband, Bill, is a gem, too.

He invited me to the County Health Fair. While there, I gave mini-massages to anyone who wanted one. I had a blast. It took my mind off my problems for two glorious days.

*****

There is leftover pizza and a beer in the refrigerator. I grab them and return to the patio, settling into the chaise lounge.

Derek's sexuality is the topic of the hour.

[242]

Questions lurk.

When I am in the heat of desire, Derek shows no interest in my advances.

Why is this?

It makes me feel self-conscious and unattractive.

What is wrong with me?

My body? My scent? My personality?

Self-doubt is so common it doesn't surprise me that I question what is wrong with me first.

My femininity. My womanhood.

Again, it is perplexing.

If it isn't me, what is wrong with Derek?

Why is he so disinterested in being intimate?

Is Derek even capable of losing himself in the spontaneity of a passionate moment?

*****

A stoic, no-nonsense, independent type of guy, Derek stands six foot four inches in his stocking feet. He barely walks through the hallway into the kitchen without having to duck his head. His brown hair contrasts with his fierce, bright blue contact lenses.

One time, in a conversation with Derek's brother, Willem, he told me Derek had teamed up with one of his high school buddies who lived down the street. They formed the Las Vegas Horse & Carriage Service. On their own the two lads had built the carriage to hook up to the horses.

The velvety carpeted carriage displayed oversized fluffy cushions. They charged $150 per thirty-minute ride and did this part-time during their years in high school. It was a popular excursion for newlyweds and other couples seeking a romantic outing.

In confidence, Willem told me that couples riding in the horse carriage would have their hands all over each other. However, Derek wasn't like that. When he was out with girls, he kept his hands to himself. Willem had the impression Derek struggled with his sexual identity. It seemed to Willem that Derek's lack of sexual interest and desire bothered him.

Other boys boasted about their romantic conquests.

Not Derek.

He would change the subject.

He didn't want to talk about it. Then or now.

*****

After the sunbeam bids me farewell, I check my email. Time to get back in touch with reality for a while. It's not long before my stomach tells me it is time to make dinner.

Pancakes and an omelet sound good.

I'll add vegan cheese, sausage, and bacon, too.

[244]

At six o'clock, I grab a bottle of champagne from the fridge to make a batch of mimosas.

"Do I smell bacon?" Amelia asks as she returns from working all day.

"Sure is. How does breakfast sound for dinner?"

"Sounds great, Jill. I'm so hungry I could eat a horse."

"No horses here – just pigs, chicken, and turkeys," I giggle.

*****

Sitting at the table and sipping our mimosas, we chit-chat about our day.

"I can't wait to dig in after a long day at work. What were you up to, Jill?"

"It was a lazy day for me. The patio called my name, and I spent most of this sunny day reminiscing about Polly and Derek. How was your day, Vice President Amelia?"

"Well, I'm dealing with a human resources situation right now with my assistant."

"Sounds intriguing. Tell me more."

"My assistant, Matt, is having issues at home. I have to figure out how to have him work from home more often. He has a daughter with autism, who is low-functioning and requires a lot of care. Her name is Sadie. I empathize with his situation and hope to resolve it quickly."

"Sounds complicated, Amelia."

"I'm sure I'll be able to sort it all out. The tricky part is finding someone to handle Matt's 'on-call' schedule... without it being me."

"Amelia, I have an idea. Remember when I managed the Rediscover Research Weekend? You know – the dude ranch thing? Each senior and middle manager had to sign up for a four-hour 'on-call' time slot. In case of emergencies. Do you think something like that might work for you?"

"I'll have to think about that. A variation of what you described might actually work. Thanks, Jill."

I feel my lip curl, and my eyebrows raise to query, "So, my dear Amelia, if I have such good ideas, why can't I get a job? I've sent out hundreds of resumes and only had three interviews."

"It is pretty competitive out there right now, Jill. You know, you have been out of the full-time job market for nearly ten years, right?"

"Well, it's actually thirteen years now."

"You come across just a little short in the self-confidence department. It probably stems from the situation you are in right now. Give it some time, and something will open up for you. Don't get discouraged. You got this!"

"You are right. I'm a basket case. I can't pretend to pull my act together with this mental block I seem to have. I have unique talents to bring to the table. But Derek makes me feel so inadequate."

I need to work on this.

"It is no surprise Derek belittles you based on what you told me. He is dealing with his own demons. Like you said, he grew up with this, so it is the only way he knows how to be. I'm sorry he makes you feel like crap about yourself. You care so much about your family. He is not helping the situation."

"You're right. I'm sure releasing the Derek put-downs from my mind will help. Being here and away from home is slowly shifting my perspective. But something else has been gnawing at me."

"What is it?"

Red Flag #5

"Something I've been contemplating all day. Do you think Derek is gay? I know you said earlier you thought he might be having an affair, but what if that affair is with another guy?"

"An interesting question, Jill. I'll have to think about it. Is it possible that he would hide such a thing?"

"I really don't know. But if Derek is gay, that would explain a lot. It would be a relief if he was, so I wouldn't have to blame myself anymore."

"Why would you blame yourself?"

"If he isn't gay, then something is wrong with me. If he is gay, then that is another story."

"Is that what you think? I can't imagine finding out my partner is gay."

"Derek's sexuality has been bugging me for a long time. His not wanting to be intimate is very confusing."

"Yeah, I guess that would be a red flag."

"Funny, you should mention red flags. I've spent time trying to identify all the red flags I neglected to see since I met Derek."

"Don't beat yourself up, Jill. What it is – it is. You can't change the stripes on a zebra."

"I know, but I've spent years trying! There's no denying it. Do you know what I mean? Gay, straight. Fat, skinny. Hair, no hair. You just never know."

"You're right, Jill. You never do know what lurks inside someone."

"So true, Amelia. In the end, people are mysteries, aren't they?

"Yes, they are," she agreed.

"God created us in his image – and what a mystery that is! Life itself is a mystery if you ask me."

"It sure is, Jill. You think you are heading in one direction, and then all of a sudden, something comes out of nowhere, and you are going in a completely different direction. It makes me think of James. One minute, I'm a mom, and the next minute, my son is in heaven."

"Life does have a way of taking all types of turns. Like my marriage. You think someone is going to love you forever. Then, one day, you are in a therapy session, and your husband tells you he doesn't love you anymore!"

"Jill, I know this is a rough patch you are going through, but I promise it will get better. Eventually. Look at me. I'm finally on my own. Building a career I love. Involved in a church family I adore. Life is finally getting better for me. Sure, I still grieve every time I see a baby. But I have faith, and my faith says, 'Carry on.' And so, I do.

"Speaking of carrying on, I'm fading fast, Jilly and need to power through a report for tomorrow's meeting.

"Can we continue this talk tomorrow?"

"Of course. Go, finish your report. Make it outstanding."

"Not sure how outstanding it will be after the mimosas, but I'll try my best, you silly goose. See you in the morning."

[249]

"Indeed, Amelia. Thanks for sharing your thoughts with me. I didn't mean for it to get so serious. Goodnight, my friend."

"Goodnight, Jill."

People. Life. Mysteries.

I'll have to think about that.

DIMITRI & THE DEVIL
DAY 11 ~ EVENING

I pack my bag for the trip to Thousand Oaks, call my kids, and snuggle under the covers. Before I drift off to sleep, the bizarre Pastor Juan encounter from over twenty years ago comes to mind.

*****

I was sixteen and dating Dimitri, my high school sweetheart, who happened to be a Russian immigrant. I met Pastor Juan at Peace River Church and asked him about pre-marital relations.

"Hello? Is anyone here?" I called out, walking onto the red carpet of the church lobby.

"Yes."

I heard a voice from down the hall.

"I'm in my office. Come on down," the voice directed.

On the way, the chrome spout of the white porcelain water fountain sparkled. I took a sip from it on my way to the office.

"Hello there, you must be Jill."

"Yes. Thank you for agreeing to meet with me."

"Certainly," Pastor Juan responded.

[251]

With his hand, Pastor Juan signaled me to sit in the chair across from his desk.

"My heart is heavy, Pastor. I am seeing a nice young man. His name is Dimitri. I love him so."

"I see," noted Pastor Juan. "Is he a Christian?"

"Yes. Dimitri is Russian Orthodox. He recently played the part of Joseph in the Christmas Play at his church," I bragged.

*****

Dimitri.

I have so many happy memories.

He was a sophomore.

I was a junior.

Because he believed in me, I was more confident about myself.

The captain of the tennis team.

And the chess club.

Impressive, to say the least.

He was also smart.

Extraordinarily so.

Like Valedictorian smart.

It was love at first sight and, over time, I fell more deeply in love with him. We were *so right* for each other. We loved tennis, and we each possessed a deep faith in God.

[252]

"Jill, you are too smart to be in the dumb classes. Why are you in them?" he would ask.

I'd remind him, "Dimitri, my parents have told me time and time again there is no money for college. So, what is the point?"

One day, he took my hand and said, "I'm taking you to my guidance counselor who will help you get into college. No, if, ands, or buts."

Yes, Dimitri cared about me and he didn't want me to settle for mediocrity.

*****

Pastor Juan, recently returning from a five-year mission trip in El Salvador, continued our conversation.

"Jill, you said on the phone the other day you wanted to ask me a question. Go ahead. Ask."

"Well, Pastor, I love Dimitri and want to make love to him. What do you think?" I asked brazenly.

Pastor Juan tilted his head, took a deep breath, and chose his words carefully, "Jill, Christians don't have pre-marital sex. It is clear. Those who do are sinning against themselves and against God. It seems to me, young lady, you are sinful and a loose cannon for even thinking these things. You are playing with the devil. Now, go home and pray for

[253]

forgiveness. I'll see you in church on Sunday," Pastor Juan scolded.

Ah, I don't think so.

He stood up and barked, "Goodbye, Jill."

I stormed out of his office, saying, "Whatever."

*****

Pastor Juan called me "sinful" and a "loose cannon" during this bizarre meeting. All because I had the hots for Dimitri.

NOT cool.

He also said that a young girl should never be alone with a young boy.

Group dates only.

That didn't sound like a good idea to me.

His recent mission trip had kept him out of touch with current American culture.

For goodness' sake, I wanted to make love to Dimitri. A minister I hardly knew was chastising me? He didn't seem very "Christian" to me. This Christian "authority" had made me feel like trash, which led me to question both my faith and the Church. What had I done that was "sinful?" To me, love was not "sinful." Love was…well…simply love.

Besides, it was my body.

My heart. Not the pastor's.

*****

In hindsight, that episode shifted my faith and belief system, creating tons of questions about my integrity, value system, and physical urges. Why had God made me this way?

*****

Dimitri and I dated for six years and then broke up when he decided to date Miss New Mexico. That's when my heart broke into a million pieces.

He married Miss New Mexico right out of college and divorced her a few years later.

It seemed like a lifetime ago.

We should have married each other instead.

*****

Reflecting now, I see Pastor Juan, a powerful male, exerting control and doing psychological damage to a young, vulnerable girl.

The girl had questions.

She needed her voice heard.

Not called names.

With this memory fresh in my mind, I drift off to sleep.

BEWARE OF ARNOLD
DAY 12

I wake up with an urge to find a specific journal entry I had written to God a few years after Zola's birth and before my pregnancy with Nisha. Flipping through the pink journal, I find it marked with a bookmark.

Dear Holy One,

I am so sorry for the way my marriage is right now. Only you know that the less time Derek and I spend with each other, the better. I have needs and desires. Derek does not know how to satisfy them.

Most nights, I fall asleep sad, yearning for a long cuddle, a caress – or anything sexual. What I have now makes me feel anything but sexual. Is it asking too much to want someone to smother me with love and laughter?

Oh, how I miss the urge to be spontaneous. Living with such a hard shell of a husband that nothing can penetrate is very difficult. But I know you can change hard shells. Please soften his.

I'm tired and I don't know how much longer I can do this. Oh Lord, grant me peace.

Amen

*****

Before I leave for Thousand Oaks, I take a moment to reflect on my trip so far.

Napa.

Such a beautiful place to seek clarity. But what do I see? It's not beautiful. I see another red flag.

Red Flag #6

It was early on in our relationship. Derek and I agreed to keep a regular date night schedule. Yet, said plan went out the window when I told him I was pregnant. Feeling unwanted and undesirable was not a great way to start a pregnancy. Having our mutually agreed upon plan ignored or thrown out the window was a warning sign I didn't see.

What other plans would fall through after we have agreed to handle a situation in a certain way?

*****

My attention shifts to my trip to visit Lata. She is fifteen years my senior. It will be a five-to-six-hour drive to Thousand Oaks. I go through my checklist, making sure I have everything I'll need for the next few days, and add one suitcase to my usual items.

I grab a protein bar, pour coffee into a travel mug, and leave Amelia's gated property to turn onto the main road.

The day's pace and rhythms of peace and quiet morph into whizzing sounds of cars and trucks.

I take *"I-80"* west to *"5,"* heading south to Westlake Village where Lata lives.

[258]

Driving alone in the car opens my mind to new anticipations and possibilities.

Finally, I can take a breath.

There is no judgment here – no wonder I love Napa so much. Instead of feeling defeated and missing the mark, there is joy. Something I haven't felt in a long time. The lens is clear. I see my authentic self.

In this moment, I realize I have freedom…power…and control. I'm not used to feeling this way.

Enjoying this adventure and anticipating what will unfold, I spend the rest of the drive gazing through the front window on the road ahead, while glancing intermittently in the rear-view mirror.

Pondering.

Wondering.

Wishing.

Hoping.

I round the corner and see the gatehouse in the distance. Easing off the gas pedal and gradually tapping the brakes, I bring the car to a stop at the gate.

"Your name, please?" the security officer asks.

"Jill Mandela. Namaste."

"Who are you visiting?" asks the guard.

"I'm here to see my cousin Lata Shaw.

"Her address is 2967 Bayshore Drive."

"Driver's license, please."

"Sure, here you go," handing him my license.

"Ah, yes, we are expecting you." The guard peers at his computer screen, "Here is your pass. Please display it on your dashboard for the duration of your stay. Have a good day, Miss Jill."

After driving a quarter mile down the road, I arrive safely at Lata's.

Her sea-green home, a three-bedroom, ranch-style house, sits on a cul-de-sac with a circular driveway. It is charming.

*****

Thousand Oaks, California

My mind is racing. I haven't seen my cousin in a few years. I hope she won't talk my ear off. I feel joyful, but I am tired from the drive. I've been running around, and it is finally catching up with me. Okay, Jill. Take a breath. You can do this.

I climb out of the car and hear a faint clank. Clank!

Lata opens the door with a seashell wreath hanging from it and greets me with open arms. As I reach the end of the front walk, I hug and kiss her cheek.

"Glad you are here, Cousin Jilly," Lata smiles.

"Me, too," I giggle.

[260]

"Let's get you settled," she says.

"Sounds good. It has been a long day."

*****

Through the front door and to the left, the guest room boasts a light blue hue, which is warm and soothing. The sea-shelled cotton quilt can reverse to a blue, green, and sandy golden striped pattern. It has pretty scalloped edging and is the crown jewel tying the entire room together.

The spacious kitchen has a pass-through into the great room. A casual living room is on the left, and a more formal dining area is on the right. The open-concept space feels light and airy.

*****

Shortly after my arrival, Lata's dog, Arnold, jumps up on the ledge where he barks.

Arnold scares me.

Lata tells me that Arnold is all bark and no bite.

But it doesn't help.

His barking reminds me of the time when a German shepherd bit me on the leg as a kid. It brings back bad memories. I know this response is irrational, but I can't control how my body reacts.

Luckily, Arnold hides most of the evening. When he does appear, I do my best to ignore him. I settle down a bit.

[261]

"Dinner is ready," Lata announces.

"I almost forgot. I'll go grab the bottle of white wine from the car I picked up on my way in," I say, opening the front door.

We sit down to a lovely dinner of fish masala.

A cream-colored tablecloth adorns the table with hardback placemats of Rembrandt prints. We chat about the weather and catch up on family news.

After a long day's drive my bones ache, so I excuse myself to crash on the bed.

When I call Derek for the day's update, he comes across as gentler than usual. He asks how the drive was and how my cousin is. It is a quick call because I can hardly keep my eyes open.

Drifting off to sleep, the somewhat warm, fuzzy conversation with Derek plays in my head.

MUZZLE IT, WON'T YOU?
DAY 13

I slept well that night after the long drive the day before. Waking up at eight o'clock this morning felt great. I phone the kids and remember to tell Rebecca to "break a leg" at the *Sound of Music* auditions scheduled to begin at nine this morning. Derek's schedule is tight, with Rebecca's audition and the drive to the campground.

Relax, Jill. He'll handle it just fine.

I shower and dress, then greet Lata in the kitchen.

"Top of the morning to you, Lata."

"Namaste, dear cousin. Help yourself to coffee and whatever else you need. I'm opening the store today, and I'll return afterward. See you later! Have a good time with Ryo. He should be here shortly."

Ryo, Lata's youngest son in his late twenties, is coming over.

When he arrives, I greet him at the door with a hug. He is a handsome young man with beautiful bronze skin. He is a manager at a local bar and grill. The same place where he used to juggle his studies as a bartender.

"So, Ryo. Tell me about yourself. What have you been up to?" I ask.

"The bar keeps me busy. In my free time, I surf. I'm happy. I met a new lady. We both love to surf and play video games. Mom set us up with new boards – it's been fun."

"Fantastic. It's nice to have a friend who you can share life with. As long as you are kind to each other," I say.

After Ryo departs to run errands, Lata returns home.

It is now mid-afternoon.

Together, Lata and I decide to tool around the lakeside. We visit a lighthouse where I buy a few postcards for my scrapbook.

Since Lata has to close up the surf and skate shop she manages, she drops me off at her place at five-thirty. This gives her enough time to close the register and lock the door at six.

In the meantime, I start dinner.

*****

As I cook, I recall Lata's own struggles.

Lata's ex-husband was a drug addict.

Not the kind who does it on purpose. The kind who starts relying on pain medication to manage a bad back.

That kind.

He spent five years in and out of drug rehabilitation centers. Which left her with three small children to raise by herself.

Lata moved after her three kids graduated from high school. Luckily for her, she moved next to a surf and skate shop owner. He offered her a job as a sales associate, and two years later, she became the manager. This was a testament to her resilience and hard work.

Over the years, Lata proved to be a resourceful woman. We kept in touch with each other, mainly through our mothers. At the time, we were wrapped up in our own lives, with her raising her family while I was finishing school.

Time has flown by.

Now, I'm the one raising a family.

Then, five years ago, when she moved to California, we began emailing each other. This strengthened our cousins' bond.

Lata understood and comforted me with her kindness and wisdom. She was the first relative I confided in about Derek because she understood how a troubled marriage can impact a family.

I looked up to Lata.

I admired her resilience.

She was after all, the first divorced person I knew. And I remember hearing from my mom how she struggled through her rough patch.

*****

While I wait for the rice to cook, I retrieve my laptop. I'm not sure what has come over me. But I feel compelled to research the impact divorce has on the finances of single parents. I poke around the internet and read this quote from startgrants.com.

> Housing or living space is arguably one of the biggest expenses faced by many women after their divorce. Typically, they go out of their home and they have to find a new place to live. If you were a housewife facing divorce, this can lead to financial disaster.
>
> *– Munir Ardi*

This quote made me think back on the early years of my marriage, when I wanted to leave Derek. But I didn't. Why? I asked myself that question a million times. I knew it would take money that I didn't have to make a move like that. Since my parents weren't in a financial position to help me, I had nowhere to turn. So, I didn't leave Derek. I stayed and carried on.

Lata's ex-husband had left her high and dry.

But it could have been so much worse.

Since she had a good job at the time, she was able to support herself and her kids. Plus, her parents helped her. They had become her rock, her village. She couldn't have done it without them.

*****

I put my laptop away and get back to making dinner.

A short while later, Lata walks in the side door as dinner sizzles in the pan.

"What smells so good, Jilly?" she asks.

"Salmon with roasted garlic. Is the shop all closed up for the day?"

"Yes. All closed up. The register and receipts matched perfectly."

"Glad to hear that. Can you set the table?"

We chat as I spoon the rice and the peas onto two plates. The conversation flows naturally, as one might suspect, with someone you have known all your life. We continue to gab at the table; she doesn't miss a beat.

"Chase and Ariel are my assistant managers at the Pro Shop," says Lata. "They are twins and cute, too. They go to college part-time. Chase is majoring in hospitality. Ariel is majoring in business. They love to skateboard, and they compete at the national level. That's why I have two other assistant managers, Zuma and Monty.

"Zuma is a single mom, and Monty is a retired accountant. Monty has four grandchildren, who visit from time to time. They are young. All are under ten since they are in summer camp."

As Lata goes on about people I don't know, I count under my breath: *one, two, three, four.* Keeping my impatience in check, I try to listen.

Meanwhile, Lata continues, "He fell off the ladder in the Post Office, and he hurt his back."

"Who, Lata?" I jump in.

"My ex, of course. That's when he started taking painkillers, which led to addiction. And drinking…"

Changing the subject, I asked, "So, Lata, who cared for the kids when they were little?"

"My mom and dad stepped up to help me. I got the kids ready for school, dropped them off, and went to work. My parents picked them up, brought them back home, and gave them snacks. You know, they didn't do all that much. Yet it made all the difference.

"Tomorrow, we'll go to the lake and have lunch with Ryo…"

Lata babbles on until I can no longer keep my eyes open.

*****

Lata is undeniably a talker. It runs in the family. My other relatives (okay, sometimes me, too) talk excessively. I admit it. I have learned to check and filter myself as much as possible because my mouth can run loose, too! Isn't that part of personal growth?

*****

Whispering "goodnight" to Lata, I tip-toe down the hall to the guest room. I wiggle under the soft sheets, thinking about excessive talking.

Once, my brother Jack talked non-stop for hours until I finally turned to him and snapped, "Would you please shut up?"

Hmm.

I'm glad he still talks to me.

Dozing off and on, I try to stay awake.

I can still picture that moment with Jack as we ride together from Seattle to the Los Angeles Airport.

It seems like yesterday. Yet it was decades ago.

Be that as it may, let me tell you, no one – I mean *no one* can hold a candle to Lata when it comes to talking a blue streak.

Now I know where the phrase *"talking your ears off"* comes from. With Lata, it was nearly impossible to get a word in edgewise.

EGG ROLLS & PIZZA
DAY 14

It's five in the morning. I can't get back to sleep. Finally dozing, I awake to my phone ringing at eight o'clock. It is Rebecca. I'm not surprised to hear from her, knowing the play director would be emailing the cast member hopefuls at eight this morning. Of course, it is one minute after eight.

I see Rebecca's cell number pop up on my phone. There is static on the line and I can hardly make out what she is saying.

"Hello? Is anyone there?" I ask.

"Mom, Mom. Are you there?"

"Yes, Pookie. We have a bad connection."

"I know. I'm in my tent in the woods."

"Oh, okay. I guess you opened your email?"

"Yes, Mom."

"Well, did you get the part?"

"*The hills are alive*–Yes, I got the part," Rebecca says in an over-the-top sing-song voice.

"I'm *so* proud of you! I can't wait to hear all about it. But right now, I have to run, honey; Lata is making breakfast. Have a great day, Pookie. Send a hug to everybody."

*****

Hearing Rebecca's voice makes me smile as I muddle into the kitchen, smelling the coffee. Joining Lata, I pour myself a cup, too.

There's not much time for chit-chat because we are trying to get out the door and make it to church on time. We leave a few minutes later and arrive for the ten-thirty service.

Lata and I sit in a back row seat. Several people recognize her and wave. I wave back, too. The service is slightly contemporary, with a praise band. The minister is female. The sermon is on the *Letter of James* in the New Testament. One of my favorites.

Walking back to the parking lot an hour later, I shake my head in amazement.

Faith versus works. What does that mean to me?

It was a well-executed sermon.

From the second chapter of James.

Good food for thought.

"I enjoyed the sermon, Lata. People have been debating faith versus works forever. Right?"

"Pastor Katie is sharp as a tack. She went to Cliftonian Seminary and did her undergraduate degree at West Belle. She is well-bred, Jill."

"Back to the faith vs. work issue. Lata, let me tell you a story about Kara, who lived down the street from me. We were both ten. It was the summer before fifth grade. My parents forbade me to befriend Kara. Why? Because she didn't attend the right church. Can you believe that? My parents would say, 'If anyone thinks they can earn their salvation they would be wrong!'

"You know, like trying to be good.

"Or by confessing sins to a priest.

"Or giving money to the church.

"Today's sermon reinforces that salvation is a gift through grace. It is freely available to anyone who accepts it. If you accept this gift, you will want to choose to do good deeds because of it. Pastor Katie hit the nail on the head. Lata, you were right, Pastor Katie is one smart cookie!"

"I can't believe your parents wouldn't let you be friends with someone who practiced another faith? I find it disturbing. I thought they were so welcoming."

"All I can say, Lata, is they had a bizarre theology not necessarily taught by the church I grew up in. I finally realized this when my friends' played cards and went to

[273]

dances while those things were off-limits to me. That's when it pretty much slapped me in the face. My parents' "rules" were THEIR rules, not the church's rules!"

*****

After lunch, we slip into bathing suits to swim at Westlake. Honestly, I had pictured a serene lake – who knew it would turn out to be The Westlake Village Community Pool. Sure, there's a small lake nearby, but as we look around, the vibrant crystal-clear pool takes center stage.

The sun warms my skin.

The gentle breeze softly hits my face.

We claim two lounge chairs – one in the sun and the other in the shade.

In the distance, the waterfall gurgles as the lazy river carries our tubes around and around.

Two hours fly by as we float the afternoon away.

We head to our next adventure once we peel off our wet suits. Meandering through The Lakes at Westlake. One would think this place would be a nature preserve or something outdoorsy. Nope. It's a shopping haven boasting chic boutique shops full of unexpected treasures.

A charming place to explore before dinner.

Keeping with the earlier plan, we meet Ryo at California Pizza Kitchen. Exotic items such as pineapple egg rolls and

[274]

Thai chicken pizza call from the menu. Lata and Ryo share a pepperoni pizza. I indulge in Avocado Club Egg Rolls, which have a creamy, crunchy texture and come with a light onion-garlic flavored sauce. The mixture of flavors and textures dance on my tongue.

Our conversation flows effortlessly as we touch upon various subjects of mutual interest, from good seafood restaurants to surfing and skating.

Since it's a work night for Ryo and Lata, we toast ourselves with refreshing mojitos. Then, we share a piece of decadent key lime pie, the perfect ending to a sweet day in paradise.

"Check, please," I say, grabbing the tab. I am immensely grateful for this time spent with my family, especially Lata, who has known me since birth. Derek generously gave me money, asking me to treat Lata, and I'm more than happy to oblige.

*****

After our full day of activity, I sit down and call Derek. His phone goes straight to voicemail. I imagine they're returning from their camping trip, and I can't wait to hear all about it.

Settling into bed, I can't help but reflect on the past three days with Lata. There's so much I've experienced and felt.

[275]

Her ability to juggle the roles of hostess, innkeeper, chauffeur, cook, and tour guide truly warms my heart. I feel incredibly fortunate to have such a fabulous cousin in my life.

I can't help but see her as another angel!

Lata sharing her struggles as a single mom and Ryo's face lighting up talking about his girlfriend are memories in the making. Knowing we have a family that provides unwavering support brings me joy.

Catching up with them did my heart good; I will cherish this time for years. The deep love and connection I share with Lata have made this time together profoundly meaningful.

As I drift off to sleep, I reflect on Lata's compassion, God's love for us, and the sweetness of the family bonds that tie us together.

A DRIVE ON THE BEACH
DAY 15

Chipper? Yes!

Giddy, too. I'm not quite sure why. Perhaps it's the anticipation of my morning check-in call. Derek picks up the phone. His tone is upbeat, if not exuberant.

Who is this man?

Derek briefs me about the camping weekend. He tells me about how they all worked together in setting up the camp. How helpful the big kids were. He mentioned that Dustin was an added bonus to the trip. He went on and on.

He hasn't sounded this happy since his last hunting trip.

Then, he passes the phone to Zola. As I hear her familiar voice on the other end of the line, a burst of brightness bubbles inside me. Today, Zola is a delight. Her enthusiasm is contagious as she talks my ear off about the past few days.

"Zo, I really want to hear more about your weekend, but it's a long drive back to Amelia's, and I want to stop at the mall to buy something special for Dad. Can we talk later?"

"Oh, okay, Mom. I think that's a great idea. Good luck with that. I know he is hard to buy for."

"Right, you are, Pookie. One more thing, Zo, I plan to stop at Pepperdine University because it's not too far from where I am. I haven't seen the campus since I was your age."

"Mom, you went to Pepperdine?"

"No, it was one of the schools I applied to, but I decided not to go there."

"Why, Mom?"

"Well, that is a good question. I think it had a lot to do with the Pacific Ocean."

"Huh? I don't get it."

"I remember thinking how beautiful the campus was. I wondered how I would study with the ocean literally steps away. Plus, I'd have to buy a plane ticket each time I wanted to come home."

"Oh, gotcha. Gotta go, Mom. Bye."

"Bye, honey."

A warm fuzzy feeling lingers from the phone call that makes me smile. With the call behind me, I focus on what lies ahead.

But first, coffee.

I begin the checklist. Lata, already at work, gave me precise instructions. With Arnold napping in his cozy bed, the house is silent. The sink is spotless, the dishwasher full, and the counters sparkle. Everything is in its place.

The front door closes with a thud and locks after a tug. I search for the brown rock next to the palm tree. There, I find the secret place to hide the key.

Finally, the moment I've been waiting for. With the car packed and the key safely hidden, I am ready to hit the road.

Sitting in the car, I text Lata: "All good. Key safe. Heading Out. Tx a bunch. ♥"

*****

I am free! Free for my adventure to begin.

With the open road ahead, no one in this car can tell me I can't stop here or there – I can stop anywhere I want. Wow!

Which reminds me of another red flag I must have ignored.

Red Flag #7

Derek is inflexible. Again, it was his way or the highway. He wouldn't deviate from the set plan when we were in the car traveling to spend time with family or friends or running errands. There was no stopping between points A and B unless it was pre-arranged.

No last-minute stops.

Period.

Like the time Nisha vomited in the car.

"Dad, I'm not feeling good. Can you stop the car?"

[279]

"Nisha, how many times do I have to tell you. We are on a schedule. We don't have time to stop. You will be fine."

"Derek, I think you should pull over," I said.

"No, Jill, Nisha will get over it. You'll see. Give her a piece of gum, will you?"

"Sure, Derek. I'm on it," I say as I retrieve a piece of gum from my purse.

I reach my arm around to the back of the car, "Here you go, Pookie."

Nisha took the gum and put it in her mouth.

Within ten seconds....

"Dad, I think I'm gonna be sick."

"Stop whining, Nish. Suck it up. Give the gum some time to work."

"Dad, Daaad...uh-h-h."

Well, that car ride didn't end too well.

The funny part was when Derek did finally pull the car over, he was so embarrassed he cleaned up the mess.

*****

The trip from Thousand Oaks to Pepperdine will take twenty-five minutes, leaving plenty of time to reflect on my earlier phone call with Derek and Zola. Something was a bit off, but I can't put my finger on what it is. My emotions start swirling, and the collywobbles do somersaults in my stomach. On the surface, the earlier phone call with Derek and Zola seemed cheery and exciting. Yet, underneath I felt a layer of angst that was troubling.

As I thought about Derek's comments about the camping trip, I was genuinely happy that he enjoyed spending time with the kids. He went on and on about it. Ordinarily, it would have made me furious. This time, the implication of him being the fun dad and me the horrible mother didn't bother me. What did bother me was Zola and her new boyfriend, Dustin. Zola was thrilled she could bring Dustin along.

I was not.

Suddenly, a shiver runs down my spine.

Zola!

I start to panic.

Then, it clicks.

I recall the abuse from my childhood – it comes flooding back. It was a feeling of being helpless and trapped, mixed with a strange sense of belonging and craving attention.

O God, keep my child safe!

I can't help but think every person of the opposite sex will harm Zola. I know this is irrational. Yet, the feeling consumes me.

I sure hope Derek protected her.

Wait. Take. A. Breath, Jill. Zola is fine.

*****

The past can't shackle me forever. Can it? No, it can't.

Little by little, I am recognizing the pattern of my old wounds. I'm proud of myself for being able to sit with my emotions before I let them get the best of me.

So, I will reshape my thinking:

Yes, Zola spent the weekend with her boyfriend. But Derek was there. I'm sure he would not have allowed Dustin to be alone with her.

Breathe, Jill. Breathe.

I realize that my fear is an understandable response. It's okay to panic. I just need to –

Relax, Jill.

I pause, sit with my emotions, and then switch to a more hopeful mindset. I take a deep breath and choose to be confident of Derek's parental instincts.

*****

Now, onto my other kids.

Nisha made a new friend, Sara.

And the twins, well, they had plenty of open space to let loose.

Nisha and the twins inflated their air beds while Zola, Dustin, and Derek set up the tents. Hearing that everyone

[282]

pitched in and worked together was heartwarming. I imagine they kept themselves busy, swimming and kayaking while camping all weekend long.

I loved hearing how the kids were just being kids.

Then, Derek told me how Zola and Dustin watched the younger kids while he practiced his shooting skills at a nearby range. Zola even played soccer with the twins. She had fun! Which was a small miracle because she hates soccer.

My little girl is growing up.

Zola went on to share how fun it was to entertain the younger ones and keep them out of mischief. (God help us!)

Everyone came back in one piece.

And that was good news to me.

*****

Malibu, California

Pepperdine's campus is like a fine white wine. Notes of citrus, tropical fruits, honey, and flowers dance through the air. They blend into the backdrop of a breathtaking coastline. In the distance, an endless sea of sapphirine stretches north to south. The view brings me back to the giddiness I felt earlier this morning.

Summer classes are in session, and the campus is quiet. A few students sit nearby under a patio umbrella. I nod a hello to them.

They smile and nod back.

Nice and friendly, I like that.

A young woman in a linen dress, walks across the dining area and introduces herself to me.

"Hi, I'm Tanvi, the Dean of Career Development. May I join you?"

"Absolutely! I'm Jill."

"What brings you here today, Jill?"

"It's a funny story, really. I applied to go to college here years ago. But when I came to visit, the campus was so gorgeous, I thought I'd have trouble focusing on academics. I lived in Nevada at the time and the ocean captivated me. I still live there. I was visiting my cousin not far from here, so I'm just passing through."

"Well, you picked a great spot, Jill. You have the best view of the ocean right where you're sitting. It's a great place to have coffee."

"Yes, it sure is. And the view is stunning!"

"Do you have kids?" Tanvi asks.

"Yes, I do. Four. Zola, my oldest, is a sophomore in high school, then Nisha, and my twins Kobe and Rebecca."

"Sounds like a lovely family. What is Zola interested in?"

"She loves science and dance."

"Has she taken her PSATs yet?

"No, she'll take them in the fall."

"I see. Well, we have a top-notch School of Science. We offer the usual courses, as well as environmental science, data science, and forensic science. Our newest program is in artificial intelligence and will offer an "Ethics in AI" course. Since you mentioned that Zola likes dance, she might like our "Dance in Flight" extracurricular activity. The dance troop has performed yearly to a sold-out audience since 1993!"

"Miss Tanvi, I'm sure Zola would want to hear more about your dance program. It sounds amazing. Do you have a business card?"

She hands me her card, which I put in my purse.

"Do you have children, Miss Tanvi?"

"Yes, I have two little ones. But I think about their futures all the time. I wonder if they will go to college? If so, what type of college? And what they will study?"

"I ask myself the same questions! Maybe it's a mom thing?"

"I think you're right, Jill."

[285]

Tanvi gets up from the table, shakes my hand, and says, "I'd like to stay and chat, but I have a meeting shortly. I enjoyed talking with you."

"Me, too. Enjoy the rest of your day, and I hope your meeting goes smoothly."

*****

I walk out to a comfortable spot on the patio with a second cup of coffee. Staring off into the distance, I reflect on my chat with Tanvi a few minutes ago. It's like she turned a light bulb on in my head.

College is right around the corner for Zola, and today's conversation has suddenly got me thinking about it. Like Tanvi, I wonder where my kids will land after high school. Will they go to college? Graduate school? Law school? Medical school?

These questions fill my mind, and I can't help but feel a mix of excitement and a tinge of anxiety about their future. Applying to colleges and figuring out how to pay for it all those years ago was an overwhelming experience for me.

But what did I expect? I didn't have a fairy godmother.

If I wanted something, I had to earn it. Like the bike when I was twelve. Or working all those jobs to pay for college.

Then, I had to sell my gold Dodge Charger to pay tuition for my junior year of college.

That hurt.

Derek didn't understand what I went through. But, like me, he wanted our children to have the experience of going to college that he didn't have. He felt he had grown up too fast.

Which was true.

I love this campus! I could drink coffee here every day with this spectacular view of the Pacific Ocean.

*****

What lies beyond the iridescent water in front of me? It is truly a mystery. It's like the game of Clue. Who killed Mr. Green in the Dining Room with the scalpel? But in this scenario, which kid will go to what college and study what major? I am curious to find out.

Derek and I have talked about college ever since the kids were born. So, unlike me, our kids know they can go on to college and will have our full support whatever they decide.

I was clueless about such matters when I was Zola's age. I can't believe she is sixteen already!

It seems like yesterday I was changing her diaper. I remember the first time she said, "Mama," and when she took her first steps.

Where has the time gone?

And, before I know it, she'll be off to college.

Time does not stand still.

But does it have to fly by so quickly? The world has changed so much over the years. Every facet of the work world has changed.

When the time comes, I hope my kids get into whatever college they want and transition smoothly. I don't want them to worry about having to work while studying. I want their focus to be on their studies and having a social life. A social life that I didn't have. When it comes down to it, isn't a better life all we want for our kids? I sure think so.

No matter what path they choose, I will be their biggest advocate. I can't wait to see where life takes them.

*****

All this thinking about college reminds me of my college years.

Starting with high school.

Back then, no one other than Dimitri had encouraged me to consider college. Heck, I didn't even think I was going to college until late in my junior year. That's when I finally decided to apply.

But it was late in the game, and I had to catch up. I had to take three more classes before I could even apply to college, which I eventually did. To three different schools.

Looking back, it would have been so different if my parents had encouraged me.

What would that have looked like?

One thing was for sure: I would have been preparing for college much earlier than I did. As it turned out, I piled on part-time work to save up money for college. Lord knows I wasn't getting any tuition money from my parents.

At my retail job, I had a coworker named Guy with curly hair. He was a really nice guy. I can still see him as if it were yesterday: lanky, blue shirt, black tie, and khaki pants. The type of guy shy girls like me admire from afar. I wish I had kept in touch with him. A safe friend would have come in handy over the years.

*****

Exiting the campus, I pull over and snap a selfie in front of the "Pepperdine University" sign.

Point. Click. Shoot.

I want to commemorate my visit.

Into the car I climb back in.

On my way to the outlet mall, I phone my brother Jack to ask if I should do anything else before returning to Napa. He suggests driving *on* the beach in Oceano.

Now, that ought to be interesting.

*****

[289]

Pismo Beach, California

But first, I stop at the outlet mall, hoping to find something to bring home to Derek. He is not the easiest person to find a gift for.

Recognizing some familiar stores, I roam through the maze. Along the way, I see a shoe store, a candle shop, and a famous lingerie sign. I stop at the store directory to find a store that carries hunting gear.

The directory lists a Hunt Bear shop in the blue corridor on the map. It is just around the corner from where I am. Most people would call this luck. Not me. I call it a *"Godcident."*

I'll likely find something here. And I do, as I spot a pair of Hunt Bear thin wool half-gloves. Perfect.

*****

Back on the road, there is a sign marked Ventura. Then, Montecito. Traveling north on Route 101, or as Californians say, *"101,"* I follow signs to Pismo Beach.

The sun is beginning to set. The sky paints a breathtaking watercolor skyscape. Waves of foam hit the sandy shore on the beach. My eyes are drawn to the sunset. The blue-green ocean competes with vibrant streaks of orange, red, and pink. Like a blank canvas unveiling a masterpiece.

There is nothing quite like it.

[290]

Since time is short, I park as close as I can to the water. My collywobbles start to speak to me.

What if a wave comes and pulls me into the ocean? Or what if it swamps the car?

Relax Jill. It will be okay.

I choose to ignore the collywobbles.

With a hint of hesitation, I kick off my shoes and frolic in the water. Its coolness against my skin invigorates me. The salt air fills my lungs. I take a deep breath in and appreciate God's awesomeness.

As the tide rises, a surge of panic grips me. I'm afraid it will sweep my car into the ocean. That sounds ludicrous, but I run to it, hop inside, and dry my feet with a towel (Lord knows I can't stand sand between my toes!) With a sigh of relief, I drive my car safely off the beach.

*****

Napa Valley, California

By the time I get back to Amelia's, it's dark. I settle in quickly and join her to watch *Dancing with the Stars*, a show we both enjoy.

"I could use a stiff drink. How about you, Amelia?"

"I'll pass, I'm enjoying my tea," she says.

"Ah, that sounds good, too. I'll stick to scotch.

"Enjoy it. You deserve it after a long drive. Now, kick off your shoes and finish watching the show with me, Jilly the Wanderer."

Sipping the scotch, I zone out, watching the dancing couples. Sleepiness starts to set in.

After chugging the last three gulps of my drink, the credits roll on the screen. It is time to say, "Goodnight, Amelia." And so I do.

*****

A reflection from the patio light catches my eyes. A heavenly being who appears to be smiling enters through the window.

"Huh? Who's there?"

The silhouette approaches, hovering above the bed. I'm not sure whether I should be glad or scared! But then love radiates from this Spirit as she gazes into my eyes.

"Speak Spirit, I'm listening," I say.

This is what she tells me:

Fear not, Jill! God hears your prayers, sees your angst, and knows you love your children. Give them to God. Your Divine Creator will take care of them – I promise. God also knows how much you have loved Derek over the years and how you have tried to make your marriage work. It will be okay. Derek needs to find himself. Don't worry about him. God loves you. And God loves him as well. Keep your eyes on heaven, and remember to follow your heart.

I whisper, "Thank you, Angel!" and fall asleep while thinking…

Keep your eyes on heaven,
and remember to follow your heart.

A DIP IN RAGS
DAY 16

Sacramento, California

Sacramento – here I come!

The sun is high in the sky, shedding its rays on earth. A few sprawling clouds are off to one side. It's going to be a great day. I can feel it in my bones.

The love of relatives fills the air. I couldn't have asked for a better visit with Lata. Except, of course, for Arnold.

Now, it's now time to visit my cousins on my paternal side. They live an hour northeast of Napa. I can't wait to catch up with them. After a quick check-in at home, I dress and pull together a few items for my next adventure.

*****

The rich, bold scent of coffee greets me as I amble into the kitchen.

"Good morning, Amelia. How did you sleep?"

"I slept well, and you?"

"I slept like a baby. I had the strangest experience, though. Do you have a few minutes?"

"Sure, what's up?"

"Please don't think I'm crazy – but do you believe in angels?"

"Of course I do. Angels are everywhere."

"How can you be so sure?"

"Well, it is something you feel. If you believe in God, you have to believe in angels. God sends them to tell you important messages."

"I'm glad you say that because I heard an angel last night. While lying in bed, an angel told me to give my children to God and not to worry."

"Well, you best not worry, my dear Jill. It looks like God has you covered. When you have the Creator of the Universe on your side, nothing, I mean nothing else, matters."

"I appreciate you, Amelia. Thank you for your insight."

I shift from a serious side to a more humorous one, chuckling, "It's your lucky day. You'll get rid of me for another couple of days."

"Where are you going now?" Amelia asks as she pours me a second cup of coffee.

"I'll be heading to Sacramento shortly to visit cousins on my dad's side. I'll stay with Sophie, my dad's niece, and her husband, Pavan. While I'm there, I'll visit her two sons. Manny and his wife, Bonnie. And Tarus, who is married to Priscilla.

"I'm looking forward to seeing Priscilla because I haven't met her yet. They married a few years ago. They all live within walking distance, so it'll be great to go back and forth between them."

"Well, it sounds like you will have some quality family time. Drive safe. Try to have some fun – will ya?" Amelia wisecracks.

"I'll try. Have a great day at work."

At the front door, I run my checklist in my head, turn, and say, "Bye."

*****

Today, my adventure begins by selecting unique gifts for the kids. They will be expecting something; after all, they are kids. Finding the perfect souvenirs is on the agenda.

"*I-80*" takes me into Fair Oaks, twenty minutes outside Sacramento. I exit the interstate to find the dance shop just off Sunrise Boulevard. There, I pick up a black bodysuit for Zola.

She loves anything black – such a teenager.

I see an art gallery just a short distance from the dance shop. I pull into a parking space. A small art kit for Rebecca catches my eye.

She'll love it. I'm sure.

[297]

Back on *"I-80,"* the *Garmin* leads me to the nearest *Target,* where I find the sporting goods department.

A pair of neon green goggles shout Nisha's name, and I place them into my red plastic basket.

I hope the green will match her new swimsuit.

A pair of soccer socks in the next aisle has Kobe's name written all over them.

Kobe loves socks. And loves soccer.

Win/win for me.

I smile. I'm so happy I skip back to the car.

*****

I swing onto *"I-80."*

It is a beautiful sunny day with a gentle breeze through the car's opened moon roof.

The sun beats down on my arm, resting on the driver's door. Near my final destination, the car sails south on the light-traffic highway. The sign on the right side of the road reads, "Sacramento – Exit 2 miles."

The *Beach Boys* come on the radio, and I crank up the volume.

As *California Girls* blares out the window, my mood soars like an eagle. There I am, bouncing up and down like a teenager as I bop to the music. My rearview mirror reflects a wild-looking middle-aged woman.

Who is she, I ask?

I pull off the exit and into a parking lot, where I see a bunch of balloons. Close by, a clown makes balloon animals. A DJ plays pop music. The smell of hot dogs cooking comes from the truck parked in the lot. On it, a sign reads, "Happy 10th Anniversary."

At the grocery store, I pick up fresh pastries for Sophie. They smell so good. On my way back to the car, the clown hands me a balloon angel and says, "Here, Jill. This one is on me."

How did he know my name?

Funny, he knew my name, right?

"Thank you, Mr. Clown," I reply with a sheepish giggle.

God works in mysterious ways and has a sense of humor, too.

*****

The plan is to stay with Sophie and her husband Pavan. I'll spend more quality time with her two sons, who are closer to me in age. These odd age gaps stem from my dad's birth order. He was the youngest of seven children.

Sophie and Pavan have three kids: Kumar, Tarus, and Manny. Manny and Tarus live nearby, and Kumar lives in Colorado. Manny is a year younger, and Tarus is three years older.

We often reminisce about our wild adventures from years ago. As teenagers, we would go off, ride horses, and attempt to ride jet skis. We usually got into trouble, too. Our shenanigans have kept us bonded all these years, so we stay in touch.

*****

I pull into Sophie's driveway.

Manny and Tarus arrive shortly after, and we all catch up. I give them the short version of my Napa trip and update them on my troubles. Sophie and Pavan listen as I tell my story. Time flies by. Sophie checks her watch and excuses both herself and Pavan to run errands in Lemon Hill.

Tarus returns to his home about a hundred yards down the street. I promise to stop by to visit him next.

Then, Manny and I jump in the pool.

The inground pool is kidney-shaped, with a jacuzzi off to one side. It's royal blue color contrasts the aquamarine water. A mermaid floats on top. Another "*Godcident!*"

I remember my Art History professor. He was an odd duck. A short guy with curly hair. He spent one whole class lecturing about mermaids and what they symbolize: A balance between heart and mind.

This mermaid is trying to tell me something.

I know it.

It's not just a raft with cup holders.

It has a message for me. The message is to fight for my self-identity.

My spontaneity.

My individuality.

My sacredness.

I feel a sense of peace wash over me as we dip into the ninety-two-degree pool, where we discuss marriage in more detail.

"Manny, what is the magic between you and Bonnie?"

"I don't think it's magic, Jill. It is respect. My dad was all about that. Bonnie and I respect each other as we try to parent our boys. Why do you ask?"

"I'm having a hard time accepting Derek's lack of respect for me and our children. I see so much conflict in him. My guess is it comes from childhood wounds. He doesn't confide in me. He never has."

Whoa. Did I just say that? It sounds so weird saying it out loud. Kinda like a two-by-four hitting me over the head.

"I think you are on to something, Jill. At least it's something to think about. For some reason, this reminds me of what your father said to me years ago. He said, 'Best deeds are like dirty rags.' Do you have any idea what he meant by that, Jill?"

[301]

"No, I have no idea. It seems to be such an obscure statement – my guess is that it's something biblical. Maybe from a passage from the prophet Isaiah in the Old Testament. Later, I'll investigate this further over a glass of wine and let you know if I can figure out what it means."

*****

Manny gets out of the pool, leaving me to ponder what my father meant – and why he is remembering this now.

I have no idea…Or maybe I do.

The verse is speaking to me about my marriage.

Even with the best of intentions on our part, our marriage may amount to nothing more than a filthy rag.

Am I trapped in a damned if you do, damned if you don't, type of situation?

Will my choices lead to withered lives and damaged relationships? Like dried-up leaves?

I have a choice to make.

*****

Yes, dried-up leaves – a fire hazard.

The conflicts between Derek and me can burst into flames at the drop of a hat for the most ridiculous reasons. When the fire extinguishes the smoke still lingers. It permeates the air, from the crawl space in the attic to each room in our home. It leaves the whole family gasping for air.

[302]

It has taken me a long time to reach this point. I can no longer go on this way. My dad's stern voice still reverberates in my memory, "*Peace at all costs.*" And I've been repeating this mantra for decades.

Peace at all costs?

I don't think so. Not today. Enough is enough.

My peace meter has reached its capacity. My father was wrong. Dead wrong.

It's time for the "happy family" charade to end. I will no longer expose my children to the arguing and tension. By stepping away from the turmoil, I will create space for peace. Yes, it will be painful. But I will do whatever it takes.

Bam.

The weight of this decision hits me like a ton of bricks.

Why? Because I see that "ties that bind" have disintegrated beyond repair. So, I ask myself, am I sure I want to do this? ...Yes. Removing myself from the situation is the only way. I need fresh air to breathe. As do my kids.

I feel a heavy burden lift from my soul.

Thank you, God.

Like the symbol of the mermaid floating in the pool, aligning my heart with my mind will guides me to peace.

I have made up my mind.

MY DECISION STANDS FIRM!

Hallelujah!

Last night's Angel visit foreshadowed this. I see that now. It marked a turning point.

A moment of realization.

A leap of faith.

Her appearance was a sign from heaven above: *"All will be well."* What was it that she told me?

"God knows how much you have loved Derek over the years and how you have tried to make your marriage work. It will be okay."

The doctrine that "divorce is a sin" was drilled into me a million times during my childhood. But that was then. This is now. It's time to let it go.

I know that once I set this in motion, THERE WILL BE NO TURNING BACK.

But then I hear the Angel's final words echo within me:

"Keep your eyes on heaven and remember to follow your heart."

Yes. That's what I must do.

Shortly after Manny climbs out of the pool, I do, too. I dry off and change into fresh clothes. Manny accompanies me as we stroll to Tarus' house on the next block.

Terracotta roof shingles bake in the sun.

Vibrant Gerbera daisies line the front garden.

Ding dong.

Wide yellow double doors squeak open to reveal a sparse yet spacious foyer.

Tarus, in his wheelchair, greets us with a smile.

Decades ago, a bizarre alligator accident during spring break in Florida left him with amputated legs.

His right arm dangles from the chair, damaged by the horrific event.

Tarus is now almost fifty.

"Took you guys long enough to get here," he quips.

"Sorry, bro. Lost track of time at Mom's pool," Manny replies. "Listen, I have a few things to do back at the ranch, so I will leave you two alone. You guys have a lot to catch up on."

"Bye, Manny. I'll see you later at dinner. Thanks for walking me over," I say.

"No problem. Have fun," Manny replies before leaving.

"Later, Bro," Tarus adds.

"Well, Jilly, what are your first impressions of my home?"

"So far, so good. I admired your home as we walked up to the front door. Your chartreuse Gerbera daisies are to die for. I love the clay roof, too."

"I'll give you one guess how the daisies got there," he jokes.

"Ha, Ha! Priscilla?"

"Right, you are Jilly. She sure has brightened up the place. You are going to love her. You'll be able to meet her after dinner," Tarus says, beaming ear to ear.

"I look forward to that, Tarus. How are the two of you?"

"It's going great. I'm grateful for Priscilla. Her veterinarian training, from Lithuania, gives her the expertise to deal with me. That's no easy task!"

"I bet it isn't. I'm glad you found her. She sounds like a Godsend."

"That she is, Jilly. If it weren't for her, I'm not sure I'd be here today. I'm sorry to hear your marriage is in trouble. I sure hope you can glue it back together."

Tarus is the kind of guy who sees the glass half full. He is upbeat and positive. But I know he will understand the life-altering decision I just made. A few hours fly by like they were minutes. Until, suddenly, it's time for dinner.

*****

[306]

We meet Sophie and Pavan for dinner at the Bombay Craft House. My entrée choice is Tandoori Salmon roasted in a Tandoor – a clay oven – with a side salad, no dressing, and bottled water. The rest of the crew orders authentic chicken and lamb dishes.

On the way back from the restaurant, we swing by Tarus' house to meet Priscilla before we go to Manny's. She couldn't join us earlier because of an upcoming exam she's studying for. She works as a paralegal now at a nearby law firm by day and attends law school at night.

Priscilla, a short, pixie-haired lady, greets us at the door. "Nice to meet you!"

We exchange pleasantries, and then Priscilla graciously offers us beverages and sandwiches.

Manny and I opt for coffee since we had dinner a short while ago. But when Pricilla mentions homemade yogurt, I can't resist asking for a taste. She also surprises me with sugar-boiled watermelon rinds – which I had not heard of before.

Wow. Delicious!

Who would have thought you could boil them?

Priscilla's resume is impressive. She is a soon-to-be lawyer working as a paralegal. She was a veterinarian before immigrating to the United States. Her work ethic and stick-to-itiveness add to her charm.

Since Priscilla needs to finish studying, our chit-chat is short. I say goodbye and head over to Manny's house.

*****

A few blocks from Tarus' home lives Manny, his wife Bonnie, a chiropractor, and their two sons, Manuel and Benny.

And a cat named Penny.

Manny and I arrive at the front door. He heads inside, while I excuse myself to make a phone call. It will be a late night. Standing on the cement path leading up to the green stained-glass front door, I call home.

Afterward, entering their sandy-colored stucco home, Bonnie greets me and offers me a cup of tea. She tells me Manny is putting the boys to bed.

"I'll pass on the tea, but can you tweak my neck? I've been driving so much; a little relief would be nice."

"Sure." Bonnie smiles, her eyes light up, and she points toward the kitchen counter. "Go ahead and sit in this chair."

"Okay." I sit obediently.

"Take a deep breath," Bonnie instructs.

[308]

She does her one, two, three magic with her arms around my head and neck – Yank. And presto! The tightness in my neck – vanishes.

Manny joins us, and we share a glass of *Altamura Cabernet Sauvignon* with cheese, crackers, and coffee. Conversation and laughter permeate the air.

The wine has a hint of anise.

It creates a unique pairing to the Gouda cheese served in a wedge within its natural red wax casing.

Transitioning from family stories and moving to Sacramento from Boulder City, we visit more emotionally charged topics like church, spirituality, and raising children.

The night flies by, and Manny drives me back to Sophie's home at eleven o'clock.

In the car, tears well up in my eyes. I turn to him, "Manny, can I get your perspective on something? Derek told me I don't know how good I have it. Manny, I'm telling you, I don't have it so good."

Manny's eyes reflect acceptance and compassion. I continue, "In fact, it's terrible. It is a destructive marriage in more ways than one. I have one question for you.

"Am I just like Derek?" I pause momentarily, tilt my head, and lean toward Manny, "Am I walking out on him like he walked out of that parenting workshop years ago?"

"Jill, you are not like Derek. You have been through a lot. Remember, marriage should be a place of safety and respect. If you don't feel safe, then I am 100% behind whatever you decide to do," he replies.

"Thank you, Manny." A tear trickles down the side of my face. "This means the world to me, as do you. Goodnight."

Quietly opening the front door, I navigate through the darkness.

Following the nightlight, I find my way to the guest room and change into pajamas. The late-night cup of coffee finally kicks in, and sleep eludes me. I pour myself a glass of *Canyon Road Sauvignon Blanc* and open my Bible.

All my efforts to save my marriage feel futile. It's as if everything is going up in smoke, like the dirty rag in scripture.

All of us have become like one who is unclean, and all our righteous acts are like filthy rags; we all shrivel up like a leaf, and like the wind our sins sweep us away.
                                                        – Isaiah 64:6

Feeling helpless, I decide to catch a few winks.

Sleeping isn't easy with multiple clocks ticking on the wall.

Tick tock, tick tock, all night long.

A WINK AT THE LAKE
DAY 17

Pavan asks me to join him in his morning Jacuzzi ritual. I better shake off the crankiness and replace it with a smile, especially after not sleeping well. After all, it's going to be a full day of activities.

"Jill, I'm delighted you can join me," Pavan beams as I enter the bubbly water.

The coolness of the air contrasts with the hot tub.

"Ah, this feels good, Pavan. Thank you for inviting me."

Pavan continues, "Sophie is not a fan of the Jacuzzi. So, it's nice to have company. How is your trip going so far?"

"So far, so good. I have had so much time to think about my life, as well as what comes next. My marriage is blowing up in my face, and I am finding it difficult to come to terms with that."

"Jill, I hear you. What I can say is I've learned a thing or two about relationships over the years. Let me tell you, respect and honor are the foundation of a strong marriage. Without them, cracks start to form. Marriage is tricky. It is so important to be with a loving and kind partner. You don't have a marriage if you don't respect each other. Sophie and me, we're married for over fifty-two years now. It hasn't been all roses. But one thing is for sure, I love her. And she loves me. Jill, you need to do what is right for you and your kids. Having them grow up with Derek disrespecting you is not good."

"Those are wise words, Pavan. I will mull them over."

We climb out of the water and into the delectable ninety-degree swimming pool. Funny to think ninety degrees is refreshing. The pool feels like a cool summer breeze. The soft gurgling of the pool pump and a slight hint of chlorine fill the air. Next up: Pavan and I play a mean pool paddle ball game – until the restroom calls.

*****

Mornings are tough.

I plan my day around my overactive bladder. For instance, I reduce liquids when traveling, shopping, or going anywhere I may need access to a bathroom. These unwelcome interruptions impact my life.

Why is my body working against me?

*****

"Manny will be here in twenty minutes to pick you up," Sophie shouts out from the kitchen. "Let's try to sort out one branch of our family tree, starting with my sister, brothers, and parents."

[312]

"Okay, sure thing, Sophie."

Before long, Manny arrives.

Minutes later, I find myself in the pool again.

This time, I spill my heart, tears, complaints, and disappointments to my cousin. It amazes me how precious it is to share my woes with family members who listen and care so much.

*****

After changing into dry clothes, we visit Tarus.

Despite his amputated legs and limited mobility, Tarus can get around quite well in his custom-built, motorized wheelchair. Yet there is so much he can't do for himself.

I am in awe of the strength, courage, and perseverance he summons.

Each day.

Every day.

If I had been in his place, could I have done so?

I shake my head. I don't want to think about it.

But I can't help it.

Tarus is so resilient. Right after his accident, it was hard for him to adjust to his new limitations.

"Jill, remember the early years, how much I struggled?" Tarus asks, his voice strains with a mix of sorrow and strength.

[313]

"Yes, I do. How did you get through those dark days?" I ask.

"First, it was all about loss. The loss of my leg. The loss of my mobility. The loss of my independence." Tarus pauses.

"It almost sounds like death. Is that what you are saying, Tarus?"

"Yes, like death. Death of a life I used to have. I had to learn some things all over again. Like personal hygiene. Or dressing. Or taking a shower. Everyday things. Then, I had to face another reality. The reality of losing important people in my life."

"Oh, now that you mention it, this sounds familiar. Lopa, right?" My voice softens as I recall her name.

"Yes, that was the girl I was going to marry until the accident. She deserted me, and I never saw her again."

"I'm so sorry you had to go through that."

"Losing limbs is devastating, Jill. There is no denying the pain is physical and emotional. Throw rejection and abandonment into the picture, and you have one hot mess. It was tough to trust people afterward. That is when I realized how precious family is. My dad stepped up and told my brothers that family is the most important part of life, and they had to help me."

[314]

"Good thing you had Pavan as your dad."

"A rock he is. Absolutely. He is my family's 'general,' barking orders to rescue and tend to the wounded soldier. The troops fell in line and cared for me day after day. This act of compassion motivated me when I couldn't motivate myself. This army slayed my demons of grief, fear, and anger.

"A surge of determination overcame me. From then on, my perspective changed. After all, I was alive! So, I try to look at the bright side and push through the tough spots."

"I'll say! You certainly have a spirit of perseverance. Thank you for sharing with me, Tarus. I feel privileged to hear your story. So, what keeps you going every day now?"

"I think it is about choice, Jill. You can give in, or lean in, to your limitations and learn to overcome them. It's more than survival. It's about joy. It's about taking pleasure in the small things in life.

"Like the trees, the flowers, and the birds. Or steering my wheelchair through the door."

"I hear you, Tarus. I have tried to lean into my limitations by trying to fix my broken marriage. But only recently have I realized it takes two people to mend a relationship."

"Life is short, Jill. It doesn't take a rocket scientist to know when to jump ship. I have been ridiculously lucky with

Priscilla. She is another reason I keep going. She may help me with my physical limitations, but we share an emotional intimacy that is stronger than concrete."

"That makes sense." I continue, "A marriage built on sand will be swept away by an ocean. A marriage built on solid rock will endure the test of time. Mine is definitely not built on rock. Wow! I can't believe that came out of my mouth."

"It doesn't surprise me, Jill, you are a sweet, kind person who doesn't deserve this."

"You are so right. Thank you, Tarus, for inspiring me today. Now, tell me more about this entertainment world you live in."

*****

Tarus knows what teenagers like as far as movies go. Since Zola and Nisha are teenagers, I am all ears. Learning about current films intrigues me.

"Before you tell me about what you do, Tarus, I have to admit, I don't know much about movies. They were off-limits to us in our childhood. My dad thought it would promote bad behavior. Maybe start with how in the world do you manage a theatre and show movies from your wheelchair?"

"It's a fair question, Jill. The buildings must meet specific requirements with the American Disabilities Act (ADA).

They need to be wheelchair accessible. I had to put in extra ramps to make it easier to go back and forth between different rooms. My theatre is for much more than movies, Jill. We have areas for video games, skeeball, and hoops, too. Each one is handicap-friendly."

"It must be gratifying to see your facility being utilized by those who are physically limited."

"Yes, it really is. Fun fact: We were the first movie theatre in the United States to earn an honorable mention for being ADA-compliant."

"Congratulations! I bet you're proud."

"I am. I owe it to my parents. They are the ones who took me and my siblings to the movie theatre when we were kids," Tarus recalls. "The actors came to life. It felt as though they jumped off the screen and into my heart. Sounds sappy, right?"

"It sounds like a really nice memory, Tarus."

"All our movies are family-friendly, like *Teenage Mutant Ninja Turtles, Pokémon, Yu-Gi-Oh!, Lego, and Monster Trucks.* You get the idea."

"Yes, I do. Hmm. Monster trucks. Kobe loves trucks. So, we all went to a Monster Truck show not too long ago. It was pretty awesome."

Tarus' eyes light up with excitement. "This industry is a bit like the show you went to. These events are entertaining. Right? It is something to do together as a family. That is what we are aiming for here."

"It sounds fun."

"Well, Jill, you can't replicate this unique experience at home unless you are a millionaire. Ha-ha. The space bustles with energy, with friends and family members enjoying time together, which they can talk about for years to come. They can play video games, compete in skeeball, or watch a movie. There's lots to do here. It's gratifying to see our patrons having fun. Especially the parents."

"Yes, Tarus, I'm beginning to see the bigger picture, now."

"I hope you can bring your kids soon with Derek. It might help your relationship," Tarus offers. "Just a thought. …Bring Amelia, too."

"Amelia would love this place. I know I do, even if my dad calls places like this the work of the Devil. Tarus, maybe you could add the word 'Christian' to the business name? That way, my parents can be on board. Silly, isn't it?"

"Frankly, Jill, your parents are a bit odd."

"Oh, you think?"

Tarus chuckles.

[318]

I glance at my watch, noticing the time, as I move to close out the conversation.

"Time is flying, dear cousin. I better get going. Manny and the boys are picking me up in a few minutes to go kayaking. It ought to be fun.

"Thanks for the chat. I learned so much today."

*****

Rancho Murieta, CA

Patience.

Manny's two sons, Manuel, age ten, and Benny, eight, are waiting for our trip to the lake.

Having consumed only a protein bar earlier this morning, I throw a snack together to eat on the way.

The double cab pick-up truck jalopies down the highway and turns into the parking lot. I find myself bumping up and down on the seat.

Finally, the truck stops.

Relief.

My feet feel the warmth of the sandy dirt as I step out of the pick-up.

Lake Clementia, here we are – in the middle of nowhere.

I notice its natural beauty.

The air is humid and hazy, yet not too hot.

It's serene, like a sanctuary.

The noise of the kayaks being pulled out from the truck snaps me out of the peaceful moment.

I squint at Manuel and Benny with a grin. That's all it takes for them to sprint at full speed toward the lake.

Kerplunk! Kerplunk! Kerplunk!

They carry their kayaks and laugh as I run to keep up.

Crackle, crackle, the leaves crunch under our feet until they hit the soft, lumpy sand.

The glistening lake smiles as the sun peeks out of the clouds. It is one of the most tranquil lakes I have ever seen. The water is a tinge of malachite yet clear enough to see all the tiny fish swimming underneath.

Stress disappears as I paddle in unison with my cousins. A whiff of a fishy aroma enters my nose as the kayak glides on the water.

Exhilarating.

Refreshing.

We float, we stroke, we glide.

*****

Sacramento, California

Next, it is time to drive to Café Bernardo for a late lunch. Bonnie calls to tell us that her patient appointment has ended early.

[320]

"Why don't we all meet at the Café? I can join you shortly. Will that work, Jill?" Bonnie asks.

"Yes, what a great idea. See you soon."

The café is an open-air restaurant with a bar. It overlooks the Sacramento River and an active marina where small boats come and go – primarily sailboats and catamarans. Super-sized seagulls perch on the nearby pier. A blackbird is nesting atop a light fixture in the distance.

The salad intrigues me with its "Voted Best Salad in California" seal beside the menu item.

I'll be the judge of that.

"What's so funny?" Bonnie asks.

"I see the 'best salad' sticker on the menu. I love salads, so I'll see how good it is."

Bonnie also orders a salad and Manny chooses a burger. Manuel requests fish sticks, and Benny asks for chicken fingers with ranch dressing.

A salad of mixed greens, onions, peppers, cucumbers, and tomatoes arrives shortly at the table. The waitress gently sets the plate down.

Waiting for all the plates to be served, I pray a short prayer thanking God for this radiantly colored food in front of us.

I reach for my fork and take a bite.

[321]

It tastes so fresh, as if they were from a garden just around the corner.

Tangy, juicy, and crispy.

"Drum roll, please. This does win the 'best salad' award, in California or anywhere else, in case anyone needs to know."

The conversation shifts to the boys. We talk about the upcoming school year, details about taking the bus to school, and having lunch in the cafeteria.

Bonnie's phone alarm goes off, alerting all of us that time is slipping away. She has another appointment and needs to return to her office.

After saying our goodbyes, Manny drops me off at Sophie's, gives me a big hug, and wishes me luck.

"You are one strong woman, Jill," Manny affirms. "Keep your head up. Don't let Derek bully you again, promise?"

"Okay, sweet cousin, I promise. I also don't plan on shriveling up like that leaf, either. My rag will be as clean as snow!

"Thank you so much for these past few days. They've meant the world to me."

*****

Before heading back to Napa, Sophie asks if I want to shower, and which one would I like to use, "The pink one or the guest bathroom with the fancy multi-head shower?"

I choose the guest bathroom.

The high showerhead spews water, which I make sure, hits my shoulders and back so my hair doesn't get wet.

Soaping.

Shaving.

Soaping some more.

The lake.

Off my flesh and down the drain it goes.

I concentrate on the shower nozzles. The second shower jet targets my upper body, and the third hits my lower body.

Lovely.

A few minutes later, I turn off the water.

With my cousin sitting in the next room, a LONG hot shower isn't an option. But, under the circumstances, even a quick one is worth it. Having the time to stretch it out and to savor it is, well, secondary.

*****

I am nice and clean.

The shower energizes me, and now I am ready to get back on the road as I run the same checklist I did yesterday before I arrived.

[323]

I hit the road and begin the hour-plus drive back to my home base in Napa. It will be nice to catch up with Amelia and share a glass of wine.

The award-winning salad evaporates as the hunger pains slowly churn in my stomach. I grab my lunch bag with a wiggle-wiggle and a yank, and start nibbling on my leftovers. Life is too short to eat and then drive, when I can eat *and* drive at the same time.

Note to self: Avoid eating and driving when you have passengers. For that matter, maybe don't do it when other drivers are on the road, either. In any case, be extra careful.

*****

Napa Valley, California

On the drive home, Derek answers my call, and we converse congenially. There is a sense of confidence as I talk to Derek; the collywobbles have disappeared for now. He updates me on the children and their activities.

I mention the girls' day out tomorrow, including the golf lesson and the wine tasting. He warns me not to drink too much, asks me to send his best to Amelia, and to thank her for her hospitality.

Of course, I answer, "Yes." I decide to take his warning as a friendly gesture rather than a controlling remark.

Meanwhile, Amelia is finishing a report for work at the dining table as I place my grocery bag on the counter.

I roll my suitcase into the guest room and change into my jammies.

Returning to the kitchen, I pull out the wooden cutting board. On it go the grapes, crackers, and cheeses. Amelia joins me for a glass of wine, swirling it gently in her hand. We settle into the cozy living room, where the scent of the patchouli soy candle drifts through the air.

Amelia sips her wine, her expression inquisitive. "So, how was your day? You look like you had a lot of fun."

"Before I tell you, I want to express my deep gratitude. Not only for sharing your home with me but also for our years of friendship. You are my anchor, Amelia. You are family."

I pick up my wine glass and clink it against Amelia's.

"To you. To me. To friendship. To family."

"I consider you family, too, Jill. We have known each other a long time. Remember, as long as I have a place – you have a place, too."

My eyes tear up. "The first time I entered your home, I felt peaceful. Your home has been the sanctuary I needed to sort out my life. We have come a long way since Henderson."

"It really goes to show you, Jill, a true friend sticks with you through thick and thin. Now talk to me. I'm dying to hear about your visit to Sacramento."

*****

"It was amazing. I spent time with Pavan, the dad, and his sons Manny and Tarus. They welcomed me with open arms. They were each inspiring in their own way and facilitated my seeing things from a different perspective."

"That's great. What did they say?"

"Well, Pavan gave me some advice on marriage and respect. He said respect is the glue that holds a marriage together." I pause, then continue.

"He also told me how much he loves Sophie and how they have been together for over fifty years. Impressive, isn't it?"

"Very," Amelia agrees as she sips her wine. "Wow. Fifty years is a long time." Amelia raises her glass and says, "God bless them."

Raising my glass, I continue, "What amazed me most was Pavan. A man who is sincere about his love for Sophie and how proud he is to be her husband.

"It was an eye-opener for me. Mainly because I don't sense that in Derek at all. He does not care about me, let alone respect me."

"Jill, it seems to me Pavan is an unusually sagacious man."

"Amelia, did you learn a new word? What's this sagacious thing?"

"It is the perfect word for Pavan, Jill. It means wise."

"Indeed, he is, Amelia. The rest is a blur. Sophie's pool, Tarus' pool, kayaking at the lake. Lunch at a café on the water and dinner with the whole crew at an Indian restaurant." I chuckle, recalling the conversation with Tarus.

"I had a fascinating chat with Tarus about theatres that offer more than movies. It blew my mind that there are spaces in his theatre that have different purposes. Yet, all of them provide fun and entertainment. He said next time, you and I can come together. When we do, he'll give us a tour, and a game card to play all the skeeball we want."

"Really? That's so generous of him."

"I know, right? He is the real deal. His presence makes you feel like you are invincible."

"Well, cheers to that. Cheers to you, Jill. You are doing great."

"Cheers and thank you, Amelia. You are the best!"

The wine bottle empties as we pour our last two glasses.

More cheese.

More crackers.

[327]

More grapes.

More wine.

"So, Amelia, tell me about your day before I pass out and fall over."

"Not much to tell. I worked on a report all day."

"That surely doesn't sound like fun. Was it?"

"Nah, but it's okay. At least it is interesting, and I can dream about the new construction. Speaking of dreams, I will put the cheese away and head upstairs to bed. Nighty night, Jill. Sweet dreams."

"Sweet dreams to you, dear friend. Nighty night."

Pajamas on, teeth brushed, I slip into bed and smile. Content.

Life is so much better when you can share your day with someone who cares.

GIRLS' DAY OUT
DAY 18

Headaches. Ugh! I've been living with them all my life. This dull ache on the left side of my head is annoying. Yet, it is not painful enough to derail the visit to the Bentevino Winery in Livermore that Amelia and I have planned.

Aside from a few dinners, we have spent little time together. Between Amelia managing her business and my excursions, we haven't had enough fun.

There will be no trip cancellations today!

Sniffing breakfast cooking in the kitchen, I ask, "What smells so divine, Amelia?"

"I'm making vegan sausage and eggs for us," she replies, smiling.

"Well, Amelia, Vegan? I'm impressed! Is your beef sausage hiding under the table?"

"How did you know? You silly Jilly. Go ahead and sit down, and I'll serve you in a minute. Help yourself to …get ready for this…organic orange juice AND organic coffee. It's already on the table."

Our *girl's day outing* to the vineyard, about an hour and a half away, has begun.

We enjoy breakfast leisurely and yack about Amelia's work and church. Time is slipping by as we finish loading the dishwasher.

As Amelia grabs her car keys, I pour two coffees into to-go cups. Snatching my black bag by the front door, I head for the garage to find Amelia's car.

*****

Livermore, California

All around us, we see the sprawling vineyards stretching for miles and miles.

Amelia pulls into an empty space in the parking lot at Bentevino Vineyard.

The scent of grapes and oak wine barrels wafts through the air.

Wildflowers with tiny petals surround a tranquil pond as we walk to the golf course.

Indigo. White. Magenta. Saffron. Yellow. Ivory.

Since we are running late, we don't have a minute a spare to enjoy the scenery. We're due to meet Brad, the golf instructor, for our forty-five-minute lesson that starts in one minute. Ahead, golf carts line a path up a slight incline. A handsome man leans against the cart at the front of the line.

"Welcome, ladies. You must be Amelia and Jill, my eleven-thirty lesson," Brad confirms.

"Here we are!" I giggle. Pointing to Amelia, "She's the golfer. I'm her sidekick."

What a pleasant diversion.

Brad must be in his early thirties.

He wears a thin black half-zip pullover with khaki slacks. His slender build makes him a good candidate for a golf player.

Brad's eyebrows raise, "Where y'all from?"

Exchanging smirks with me, Amelia chortles, "We grew up next door to each other in Henderson, Nevada. How about you?"

"I'm from Friday Harbor, Washington."

*****

After our lesson, we walk to The Grill for lunch. I read the menu.

"Amelia, Bentevino Vineyards, founded in 1883, is the oldest family-owned vineyard in California. Wow. Did you know that?"

"No, I didn't know, but it doesn't surprise me. Napa Valley has been making wine for ages. Their wine consistently wins awards."

[331]

"Hey, Amelia, get this. The family is from France, and this place is full of French traditions and culture. Scan the room, Madam Cherie."

I point out the gorgeous French country décor all around.

The ambiance.

Soft instrumental music plays in the background.

Tall wooden chairs with wrought iron inlay line the bar area. We sit at a crisp white tableclothed table in front of a large window overlooking the vineyards. The window treatments are a medium blue fabric with a floral pattern gathered at each end of the cornice. The upholstered chairs boast a matching fabric.

Stunning.

*****

Amelia orders their signature 1883 burger, and I order their black bean burger for lunch.

Nadine, our server, returns fifteen minutes later with our meals.

Another twenty minutes go by as we savor our juicy burgers and sip the lemon-infused waters.

It's dessert time.

Nadine asks if we want their famous key lime pie with butter-graham cracker crust for dessert.

"What do you think? Shall we splurge? It sounds so good," I ask Amelia.

Amelia answers, "Yes, let's go for it."

We both respond to Nadine, "Yes. Two coffees, too, please."

A few minutes later, Nadine arrives with two pieces of decadent-looking key lime pie and two cups of black coffee.

"Here you go, ladies. Don't worry – these are zero calories," she giggles, setting the desserts down.

"Zero calories?" Amelia asks. "Well, then maybe we should order cake, too."

"Let's not get carried away, Madam Cherie." I pick up my fork and take a bite. It is light and fluffy, tart yet sweet, with each taste more heavenly than the last.

*****

With full tummies, we walk over to the wine-tasting room.

Here, the Estate and Single Vineyard Selections come in samplings called a flight.

Five tastings per flight.

We sit at a teak table under a beige canvas market umbrella on the terra cotta tile patio outside.

Surrounded by the aroma of blooming flowers, a gentle breeze flows through the air. With it, the scent of grapes from the grapevines lingers. The fields paint a lush carpet of green velvet with lighter green and red dots.

"I swear it feels as if I am in Italy," I remark as we wait for our server to deliver our flights. I remember our trip to Italy, two decades earlier.

"It sure does!" Amelia nods.

It is a gorgeous day, and the sun shines bright.

My wine flight arrives from the *Serenity, Harmony, Duetto, Sonata, and GSM Artist Series*.

Amelia's flight combines single vineyard and small-lot wines.

My "Italy" remark sparks a trip down memory lane as we reminisce on our travels there. And other parts of Europe, including skiing in the Alps.

"Jill, remember the ski trip to Switzerland? We were ready to conquer the mountain, weren't we?"

"Yes. I remember you skied circles around me. I remember feeling adventuresome yet nervous. The skis glided down the steep mountain, and I tried not to fall!"

"Jill, I remember you losing your balance, falling and dragging your ski because it didn't release. You cracked me up."

"Yes, Amelia, you saw me making a spectacle of myself, and you burst into laughter. When I came to a stop, snow

[334]

covered me from head to toe, remember? My ski finally released, slid down the mountain, hit a tree, and stood straight up. It was hilarious."

"Jill, you looked like this delicate swan instantly becoming clumsy and taking a dive into the water – except it was snow."

We both start to chuckle. Then laughing loudly, we lose it entirely. People nearby begin staring at us. But we don't care. I catch my breath as my soul fills with joy and delight.

Boy, I feel much lighter – laughter is good medicine.

Amelia takes a sip of her wine. "Jill, you have to try the Chardonnay. It's like sunshine in a glass," she exclaims, offering me a sip.

I raise an eyebrow, "Really? Let me have a taste." I take a small sip, allowing the wine to sit on my tongue.

The crisp, fruity notes tingle.

Swirling the wine in my mouth, it tastes like a sun-kissed orange.

I notice that the weather is becoming hazier and more humid. As the day passes, the wine flights eventually empty.

By mid-afternoon, the heat finally hits us. (The wine tasting did, too.) Agreeing that we are both getting too hot from the sun, we wrap it up.

[335]

Amelia reaches across the table and squeezes my hand. "You mean the world to me, Jill," she says warmly. "We'll get through this rough patch together."

"I look forward to sharing more times like this with you. We have so much fun together."

I lean in and tell Amelia, "I haven't had this much fun in a long time. Thank you."

Before Amelia becomes too woozy to drive, we head home. In the car, I reflect on our day together and how much it soothed my soul.

*****

Napa Valley, California

We intended to have dinner and a movie night with Amelia's girlfriends, but I can't muster the energy to go because my headache is worse.

Ironically, Amelia became more alert from driving and wanted to proceed with her dinner plans.

All I want to do is collapse, and with that, I crash onto the bed and sleep soundly for two hours.

Soon after I wake, I grab a snack and groggily phone home.

Gathering up a tiny splash of enthusiasm, I greet Derek.

"Namaste."

"Hi," he returns in a flat tone.

"I'll be coming home tomorrow. I'll call you when I land. Will that be okay?" I ask, hoping for some reassurance.

"Fine – sounds good. I'll hand the phone to Nisha. Kobe and Rebecca are asleep, and Zola is out with her friends."

Nisha answers the phone as if I had interrupted something important.

"Hello," she snarks. "What do YOU want?"

I take a deep breath and try to ignore her words which drip of sarcasm.

"Hi, Pookie. How was your day? I'll be coming home tomorrow."

"Fine. Gotta go. Bye," Nisha snarls.

"Bye, Pookie – love you."

Suddenly, I hear the dial tone. Then silence. The line is dead.

It's hard to imagine how my feelings can change so fast. One minute, I'm delighting in a flight of wine with my friend, and the next, my snarky kid is disrespectful.

It makes me feel sad with familiar collywobbles on top of it. My emotions are in a blender. My energy is zapped. I'm so sick of it. I turn on the television to escape.

My negative emotions slowly disappear as I glue my eyes to the screen, watching a royal wedding. This diversion allows my body and soul to realign with each other. Thirty minutes later, the credits roll and I decide to honor my body – and soul – by turning in early.

Drifting off to sleep, I think of royal weddings and happy marriages. I sure love a happy ending.

REFRESHED & EMPOWERED
DAY 19

Waking up refreshed, I have no headache whatsoever. At nine o'clock, I call home and talk to the kids over the speakerphone.

"I'll see you all later today. Mommy is flying home in an airplane in a few hours. I can't wait to see you. I love you guys very much. I've missed you. See you later today!"

Amelia leaves for work, and I spring into action.

Take the sheets off the bed – done.

Put the sheets in the washer – done.

Grab towels from the bathroom – done.

Throw them on the floor so I remember to wash them while the sheets are drying – done.

Whew.

I wipe down the counters in the bathroom, believing *good guests are tidy, and leave the space how they find it.*

While the sheets are in the washer, I vacuum the tile floor.

I pack and place my toiletries in the suitcase, zipping it up and putting it near the doorway.

Check that task off the list.

[339]

Beep!

I hear the washer signal, take the sheets out, put them in the dryer, and set the cycle to "delicates."

While the sheets are drying and the towels are washing, I sit in the living room, open my Bible to *Hebrews,* and start reading.

My mind and body slow down.

My eyes dart across the words. I have to re-read passages because they are rich and complex.

The opening verses are refreshing my mind about how God spoke through prophets in the past. Now, he speaks through his Son, Jesus. *(Hebrews 1:1-2)*

Then, there is a section about angels. Angels worship Jesus. My mind wanders to the angels who have shown up in my life so far.

God is trying to tell me something.

I need to breathe and tell God I am ready to listen.

God, quiet my mind so I can hear.

*****

I discern a gentle voice inside my soul.

I am here, Jill, right beside you. I will continue to hold your hand on your life journey. Remember the next few months will be extraordinarily challenging. Keep your faith, my daughter. All will be well. — The Holy Spirit

---

I see a soft smile and a sense of profound peace reflected in the mirror on the wall. A more confident woman is emerging from the ashes. This woman has a mountain of faith and is curious to discover what more God will reveal to her.

*****

Next, I read about the heavenly calling.

Heavenly calling? I'd like to know what that is all about.

It has to do with being called to Christ by God. It may be a predestination theology. Although it baffles me why God would select some people over others. It doesn't seem Christ-like.

God is supposed to love us all equally.

Isn't that what humanity is all about?

Or is it more about having a personal relationship with Jesus? After all, Jesus received a crown of glory through his death on the cross. I remember that from chapter two.

Personal relationships.

They sure can be tricky.

You have to be careful about what you say.

And how you say it.

Human relationships are exhausting.

But not with God. I know one hundred percent God will be there for me.

Why?

Because He lives inside of me.

Where I go, He goes.

I can't think of a time when God was not in my life. My parents' church minister baptized me when I was twelve. Yet I remember knowing as a little girl, way before the age of twelve, that God lived in my heart.

Memories of a large blue book come flooding back. It is a hard-bound book from my childhood with a little girl and a little boy on the cover. The title is *God Loves Me*, by Mary Alice Jones.

On the front, the little girl is holding a doll. One of the few books I had. The words *"Be not afraid,"* and *"God loves me"* sprinkled the pages.

God is more than a person, a spirit, or life itself. God lives in me. I can't imagine how a person can live life without God.

*****

I read 4:16, "Let us then approach God's throne of grace with confidence, so that we may receive mercy and find grace to help us in our time of need."

Wow.

I need to hear this.

I am beginning to fill my confidence bucket.

I want to receive mercy and find grace.

Yes. God has such a wonderful way of speaking directly to me. Thank you, God.

About forty minutes later, I jump as I hear the dryer beep, signaling the end of the cycle.

Chores – done.

The Book of Hebrews – done.

All while waiting for the towels to dry.

God's grace exhilarates and refreshes me to face whatever lies ahead. I bow my head and thank God for Amelia, all the angels in my life, and the message I received during my special Angel visit.

I will fear not.

Taking a deep breath and shifting my focus back to my afternoon tasks, I survey the space and re-check the bedroom and the living room.

Everything is in its place.

It's time to bid farewell to this sacred space.

Goodbye, guest room.

Goodbye, sunbeam.

Goodbye, Napa Valley.

Until we meet again.

*****

I climb into the rental car and shift into "Drive." I head south on Glory Court and make a right. Merging onto "*37*" east in Vallejo, I steer according to the directions of the Garmin toward Amelia's office.

Dropping off her keys, I hug her, whisper thanks, and say, "Cheers."

I walk away and turn back.

Taking Amelia's hands, I gaze straight into her eyes. They are tearing up. The right words escape me, so I squeeze her hands and mouth, "I love you."

Leaving is hard.

*****

San Francisco, California

Back in the rental car for the last time, my mind swirls with emotions.

Excited. Apprehensive. Anxious.

Focus on driving, Jill.

I follow signs marked "*I-80*" west and pick up "*101*" south – leading right to the airport.

Following signs for "Rental Returns," I pull into the line to check out. Leaning toward the passenger seat, I scoop up an empty water bottle, a tissue, and a gum wrapper and toss them in a nearby trash can.

I gather my stuff and once again do my checklist.

Suitcase? – Check.

Black carry-on case? – Check.

Cellphone? – Check.

Amelia's keys? – Returned.

Rental car keys? – Returned.

Walking and dragging my suitcase, I feel a bit "draggy" myself. Following the signs to "Security," I see a short line.

Grateful.

The security screening process is the final hurdle.

Off with the belt and shoes.

I walk through the device with no issues.

Hurdle cleared.

The loudspeaker announces, "Boarding call for Flight 348 to Las Vegas."

*****

Once again, doing a mental checklist, I gather my belongings and find my place in line with the other passengers. After boarding, head up high, the *28C* seat sign comes into focus. Finally, near it – a window one, I scoot in and take a deep breath, feeling like a sardine in a can.

It sure has been an awesome, life-changing trip.

Remember Jill, have faith, summon courage, and be strong. The rest will fall into place.

[345]

I'm anticipating the next few weeks and not looking forward to it.

Nope. Not one bit.

My black carry-on lies on the floor under the seat ahead. I glance up, and two angelic-looking young ladies sit next to me. Their smiles glow a mile long. Both wear a plain black skirt, a crisp white blouse, and a religious necklace. Each one holds a sacred text.

They are missionaries.

Of all the crazy things to happen – this is a "*Godcident*" for sure!

The girls introduce themselves as Sister Abby and Sister Kristina. They are on their way home from an eighteen-month missionary journey.

Within minutes, we slide easily into a dialogue about relationships and the meaning of love. The topic of family takes center stage. We talk about parents, children, boyfriends, and husbands.

We read passages from scripture about Abraham and Sara, Ruth, the Song of Solomon, and the Prodigal Son.

We giggle.

We cry.

And we share from the heart; despite me being old enough to be their mother, we bond like three sisters. It's as if we knew each other in another lifetime. Uncannily comfortable.

Our conversation revolves around topics that matter. Core values, if you will. Like respect. Kindness. Taking responsibility. Doing the right thing even when it feels wrong. We talk about good and evil and seem to settle somewhere in the middle. Like there is no right answer. We agree on human frailties because we all have them.

These matters of the heart resonate with me in such a way that they somehow reinforce my love for God and my decision to live in peace, no matter the cost.

Choosing her words carefully, Sister Kristina asks me why I had stayed in such a painful marriage for so long.

"That is a good question, Kristina. For one thing, my Christian upbringing preached divorce as a cardinal sin. For another, I'm afraid of Derek. His strength, temper, and iron grip on our finances prevented me from leaving. But I have decided to separate from him. It's long overdue."

For the first time, my words have a ring of certainty. Like I finally matter. And I'm not crazy. My life is falling into place right before my eyes.

My lengthy chats with Amelia.

The missionary visits.

My trip to see Lata.

My heartfelt talks with Pavan, Tarus, and Manny. Each interaction built upon the other. It all makes sense now.

*****

As the plane begins to descend, I turn to the Sisters and say, "You two are a breath of fresh air. Before you sat down, I was feeling anxious. You made me feel better. Thank you, Abby and Kristina. Now, I want to leave you with these thoughts: When looking for someone to settle down with, I urge you to be curious. Don't be afraid to ask questions. Think about emotional intimacy. And consider choosing a partner who wants to talk about the things that matter most."

Sister Abby replies, "We will pray for you, Jill, and Derek, too."

Sister Kristina says, "Remember, Jill, God loves you and so do we."

The plane lands, the lights go on, and the pilot announces clear skies. Excitement fills the air while passengers file out of the plane. At the end of the jet bridge, we hug and say our goodbyes.

*****

My journey to Napa over the last nineteen days is ending. Wrestling with my decision changed me in a way I can't quite put into words.

Yet I know it leaves me empowered.

[348]

I trust Yahweh will send me a new partner. A lover, a God-fearing man – who will love me as I deserve.

I sense optimism, for a change. And it feels so good.

After all, God wants the best for me. Of that, I am sure.

*****

Las Vegas, Nevada

Once I disembark the plane, I lean against the side of the wall in the corridor and text Derek.

"Off plane, c u at Level 2."

It is pretty straightforward. The departure curb on "Level 2," adjacent to the ticketing area, is where Derek will pick me up at Terminal 3. Switching the pick-up and drop-off points saves us a lot of waiting time in traffic.

We figured that out a long time ago.

I stand with my suitcase at the curb, peering down the three-lane road, watching for Derek. I feel more confident than I have felt in years.

Happy and cautiously optimistic.

A few minutes pass by, and Derek's van approaches. I wave, and he pulls up to the curb.

Opening the side door, I hoist my suitcase onto the floor behind the passenger seat. Then maneuver to sit in the front seat. I lean over and kiss Derek on the cheek.

"Thanks for picking me up."

"It's good to see you, Jill." Derek returns.

"It's good to be back home. I can't wait to see the kids. Is everyone okay?"

"Yes, the children are all fine. What were you expecting? I had everything under control. But they still missed you, although I don't know why."

With that, Derek receives a work phone call, leaving me to my thoughts, as his attention turns away.

Some things don't change.

My old self would have felt annoyed by his "I don't know why they would have missed you" comment, followed by his decision to take a phone call from work.

Yet, my new self feels a bit liberated. I have tried all I can to repair my marriage.

No more. I'm done.

*****

The kids are playing outside as the van pulls into the driveway. They stop dead in their tracks and dash toward us as soon as they see us. Their faces light up. Beaming ear to ear, I open my arms, and all four fly in to hug me. The love I feel energizes me after a long day.

Ah. It is so good to see my children.

*****

In the kitchen, Kobe volunteers for the Chef Assistant position. Together, we prepare Derek's favorite meal, butter

[350]

chicken, a South African dish. It is tender chicken pieces in tomato sauce to celebrate our reunion. Kobe brushes the garlic and butter onto the bread.

Malva pudding, our family's favorite dessert, completes the meal. A sweet pudding made with apricot jam.

Derek sure loves apricots.

Around the dining room table, I share stories with my kids from my Napa trip. I can imagine their visions – of me kayaking – dancing in their heads.

After dinner, I reach under the table for the gift bags and hand them out. I know Derek will love the gloves I picked out for him.

For me, it is a peace offering.

I hope he sees it that way as well.

I turn to Zola.

"You first, Zo. Go on." I encourage.

"Mom, I love the black bodysuit," Zola exclaims as she wildly pulls it out. "It's rad – you know how I love anything black. Thanks, Mom!"

"Okay, Nisha – you're next."

"Wow, green goggles!" Nisha grins happily, "I love having an extra pair of swim goggles. It's good to have a spare. Thanks, Mom."

"Rebecca, your turn."

[351]

"The art kit is cool. Thanks, Mom!" Rebecca says as she opens it.

"Kobe, go ahead, Pookie."

"Mom, how did you know I needed another pair of soccer socks? Thanks!" Kobe smiles and winks.

"Your turn, Derek. Go on."

"Fine, Jill. You know I do not like anything you like. What is this? Are these Hunt Bear gloves?" Derek asks. "How did you know I wanted these?"

"I saw how you admired them in the magazine right before I left for Napa."

"Thank you, Jill. These are great."

"Okay, kids, I want to talk to Dad. Go on upstairs and get ready for bed."

I remember my Angel, who appeared to me in Napa, reassuring me, saying, "...*It will be okay. Derek needs to find himself.*"

So, I take a breath and turn to Derek.

"Derek, I'd like to discuss separation at our next therapy session."

*****

After completing the going-to-bed routines, I pour a glass of wine and kneel in prayer.

I ask God to *"answer me speedily,"* walk beside me, and direct my path. *(Psalm 143:7-9)*

To love and cherish me.

To deliver us from our demons.

And to give me the courage to bring peace to myself and my family.

Answer me speedily, O LORD; My spirit fails! Do not hide Your face from me, lest I be like those who go down into the pit. Cause me to hear Your lovingkindness in the morning, For in You do I trust; Cause me to know the way in which I should walk, For I lift up my soul to You. Deliver me, O LORD, from my enemies; In You I take shelter. – Psalm 143:7-9(NKJV)

For reflections on relationships, visit:
iandthoureflections.com

EPILOGUE

Nineteen days in Napa solidified my decision to separate from Derek. This trip gave me the space I needed to see the truth. Sometimes, a marriage can't be fixed, no matter how much you want to "live happily ever after."

Napa wasn't just about saving my marriage - it was about saving myself. The early chapters of my life had wounded me in such a way that I required empathy.

Someone to walk the path of life with me.

To make me feel safe.

Heard.

And valued.

Derek wasn't that guy.

This realization liberated me from the burden of a failed marriage. I was finally at peace, knowing I had done everything possible to repair it.

I thought the Napa trip would convince Derek of my value as a mother and wife. Instead of seeing me as "*a pathetic brick,*" I had hoped Derek would fly out to Napa, pledge his love, and ask my forgiveness.

[354]

That is not what happened.

Sometimes, marriages break.

It isn't necessarily anyone's fault.

My childhood experiences influenced and distorted my expectations and views of marriage. I believed it was supposed to be a refuge, a happy place filled with unlimited intimacy. A place where two people could simply be themselves – warts and all. A place where two people could raise their children together as partners, with a united front.

*****

I still believe these things.

With all my heart.

Which will make our separation, when it happens, all the more difficult.

But that will be a road to drive down another day.

*****

My Napa trip allowed me to confront the haunting ghosts of my past. I knew there was still one more weight I needed to lift if I truly wanted to move forward.

Nelson.

I needed to have closure.

So, I called him.

We talked about the cycle of domestic violence and abuse. After asking Nelson multiple times, he finally

[355]

admitted he, too, experienced childhood molestation. He apologized.

The apology helped. It was a moment of closure, a step toward healing. At least I could have compassion, which felt good to me. Our talk broke an unexpected curse I had lived with for decades. This enabled me to move forward.

With confidence.

A fresh start - none too soon.

Like the first breath of a new life.

ACKNOWLEDGMENTS

Thank you to Hank Zona, for his wine expertise. His website is: www.thegrapesunwrapped.com.

Thank you to Maya, Concierge at Wente Vineyards who was kind to supply me with details of the flights of wine from their Wine Tasting Room.

MAIN CHARACTERS IN ALPHABETICAL ORDER

Amelia – Jill's longtime friend, former next-door neighbor.

Derek – Jill's husband who is an electrician, father of four.

Dr. Jack – Marriage counselor early on.

Dr. Kate – Marriage counselor prior to separation.

Dr. Victoria – Jill's psychotherapist prior to separation.

Lata – Jill's cousin.

Kobe – Jill's youngest son (twin to Rebecca).

Jill – Married to Derek, former special events director, licensed massage therapist, mother of four.

Nelson – Family friend who sexually molested Jill in her youth .

Nisha – Jill's second daughter.

Pastor Don – Pastor of Community Church where Jill. Led weekly Bible study.

Pastor Juan – Pastor of Peace River Church where Jill grew up.

Pavan – Jill's cousin, married to Sophie.

Rebecca – Jill's youngest daughter (twin to Kobe).

Sophie – Jill's cousin, married to Pavan.

Zola – Jill's oldest daughter.

If you are a fan of Dr. Joshua Coleman, you may like:

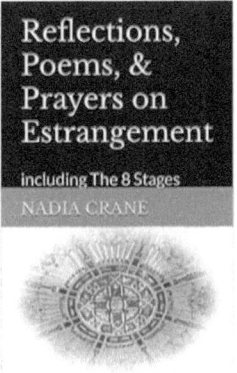

Available on Amazon.com

If you enjoyed this book,
please rate and write a brief review on Amazon.
Every review makes it easier for others to find.

You may also want to watch out for a new upcoming
devotional series on human relationships, *Sacred Traits.*
The first one in the series will drop early 2025.

Connect with Nadia Crane – Author
On Facebook